THE SHAPE OF MY HEART

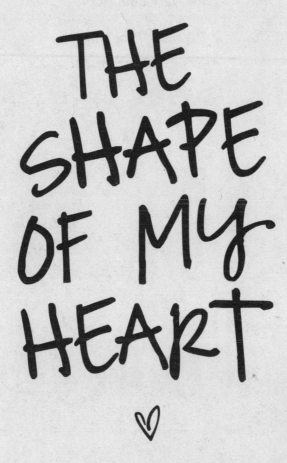

**Also available from
Ann Aguirre
and Harlequin HQN**

I Want It That Way

As Long As You Love Me

THE SHAPE OF MY HEART

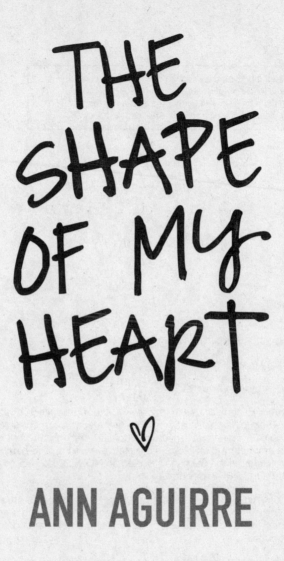

ANN AGUIRRE

HARLEQUIN® HQN™

Recycling programs
for this product may
not exist in your area.

ISBN-13: 978-0-373-77985-7

The Shape of My Heart

Printed in U.S.A.

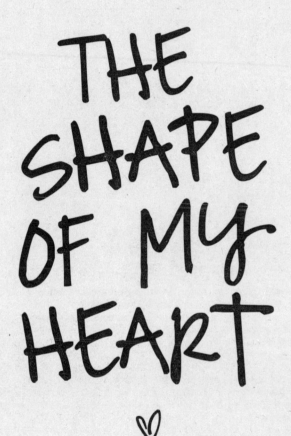

THE SHAPE OF MY HEART

♡

CHAPTER ONE

If my life were a romantic comedy, I wouldn't be the star.

I'd be the witty, wise-cracking friend, telling the Reese Witherspoon character to follow her heart, and I'd be played by America Ferrera, Hollywood's idea of an ugly duckling. But not conforming to societal beauty standards didn't cause me any angst; I wasn't harboring a secret desire to take off my glasses and flip my hair, so my secret love interest would realize I was beautiful all along. In my view, my looks supplied simplicity. Anyone who got with me wanted the *real* me, no question. Romance ranked dead last on my to-do list at the moment, however.

"You're too picky," Max said.

He was curled up on my bedroom floor, skimming emails on his tablet. With her boyfriend's help, our soon-to-be-ex-roommate, Nadia, was currently carting the last of her belongings downstairs, and the other half of my room was conspicuously empty. I scowled and threw a common cold plushie at his head. He batted it away with impressive reflexes, still scrolling. Since he'd posted flyers around campus, along with his email, Max was handling first contact on the apartment.

"Swap with me. You and Angus can share the master bedroom and then you can put whoever you want next door."

As expected, he passed with an as-if gesture. "We'll keep looking. How about this one? 'Hey, my name is Kara. I'm a physical education major, I work part-time at Kelvin's and I'm a sophomore. I saw your flyer, and I'd love to meet you guys. My apartment fell through when the landlord sold the place out from under us and now I'm scrambling.' She seems fine. All the words are even spelled correctly."

I pretended to mull it over. "Basic language skills *are* important to me. Put her on the call-back list."

"You make it sound like we're casting a movie."

"This is way more critical," I reminded him. "This person will be living in my room, potentially watching me sleep."

"I wish you'd let me help," Nadia said, coming in to grab the last of her boxes.

Ty, her tall ginger boyfriend, plucked a carton from her arms. His four-year-old son was running around the living room, bothering Angus, who didn't seem to mind. I waved at both of them but didn't get up. Truthfully, I was more than a little *verklempt* over her leaving, even if she was only going downstairs. In the six months since I'd moved in, we'd become good friends. When I moved in, I'd taken over Lauren's half of the room; she had been Nadia's best friend from high school, so it wouldn't have been surprising if Nadia had resented me. Instead she did her best to make me feel at home. And it wasn't like she hadn't given us notice that she'd be moving in with Ty. I just hadn't acted on it because I'd secretly hoped their cohabitation wouldn't pan out, like maybe she'd realize what a huge step it was to take on someone else's kid.

"It's fine," I said. "I'm the one who procrastinated."

Max nodded. "If I hadn't made flyers, Kaufman here would still be waiting for the perfect roommate to drop out of the sky."

"It could work. A skydiving roomie would be pretty sweet."

Ty grinned. "I'd be worried about the rent."

"The man makes a good point." Max waved as they left, taking the rest of Nadia's worldly belongings. "Here's another possible. 'Saw your ad. About me: Carmen, drama major, junior. I have no annoying habits and an aversion to being homeless. Email me back!'"

"How am I supposed to choose—"

"She attached a picture." Max handed me the tablet. "I'm inclined to say yes."

When I saw it, I knew why. Carmen had long silky black hair, golden skin, big brown eyes and an amazing body. While I'd definitely bang her, I didn't want her living in my room. The possibility for problems boggled the mind.

Shaking my head, I passed the iPad back. "No way."

"Why not? She's perfect!"

"She sent a wet T-shirt contest photo, dude. To random strangers. Does that speak highly of her common sense?"

He sighed. "Not really."

"I don't want to come home to someone shooting amateur porn in my room."

"Are you sure? I'm positive that would look great on a résumé."

"You're such a weirdo."

"Guilty." Max glanced toward the doorway, where Angus had propped himself like a fashion model.

In different ways, my two roommates were both hot as hell. Blond-haired, green-eyed Angus radiated the moneyed *GQ* vibe; he was always put together, clean-shaven, well-dressed and delicious-smelling. Max, on the other hand, was a dimpled and scruffy, tattooed, motorcycle-riding hooligan. Right then I had the bad boy *and* the dream boy in my bedroom, pretty much winning the whole hot-guy lottery, but neither was interested in me. Angus had a boyfriend, and Max always had women blowing up his cell phone. But it wasn't like I was pining; I hadn't been in a relationship since Amy, and I wasn't looking, either. Still, for pure eye candy, it didn't suck to be me.

"House meeting," Angus said, sauntering over to flop across the foot of my bed. "Any progress on the roommate issue?"

Hunching my shoulders, I wrapped my arms around another plushie microbe, an adorable ovum this time. "I'm working on it."

"It's true. She's rejected four possibles since I came in."

I cut Max a look. "You're not helping."

"But I've been reading emails to you for the past ten minutes."

Ignoring that, I nudged Angus's thigh with my foot. "Do you know anyone who's looking? Preferably not a random stranger."

"Actually, that's part of the reason why I'm in here."

When I bounced, his head jogged on my mattress. "Spill it."

"I've been in pre-med with Kia since freshman year. She mentioned she wants to break up with her boyfriend, but she's been putting it off because it'll mean moving out. I didn't say anything because I wanted to talk to you guys first. But—"

"Is she nice?" I cut in at the same time Max asked, "Is she hot?"

Angus smirked. "Yes and yes. I think she'd make you both happy."

Then he got out his phone, flipping through the gallery until he found a selfie of him with a pretty African-American girl. She had a great smile, bright and friendly, dark skin and short, natural hair. Sometimes the faces people made in photos gave me a vibe about them, and she seemed like she'd be fun.

I took his cell, brought up her contact info and said, "Call her."

"You mean I made flyers for nothing?" Max grumbled, but I could tell he was glad to have it settled. Maybe.

He got off the floor and wormed his way between Angus and me. Three people on a twin, probably not what the manufacturer intended. "If you break my bed—"

"Shh. It's ringing." Angus frowned at us like we were delinquent children. "Kia? It's me. Do you have a minute?" That sounded like code for *Can you talk freely?*

The volume was loud enough for me to hear her reply. "Yeah, I can email you the notes."

"I get it. Call me back when you can."

"Whoa," Max said. "Sounds like the boyfriend's a controlling asshole."

Angus nodded. "I've been telling her to get out for three months."

"Is he abusive?" The answer wouldn't change my mind about rooming with her, but we might need to amp up security around here.

"Depends on your definition. In my view, he's overly invested in where she goes and who she talks to. And he disapproves of me. A lot."

"Homophobe?" I asked.

"Young Republican, so…probably? He wears a lot of sweater vests, comes from a conservative political family in the Bible Belt."

"Ah. He's lousy with privilege," Max guessed.

Angus's phone buzzed then and he grabbed it on the first ring, putting it on speaker. "Kia?"

"What's up?"

"Is Duncan giving you a hard time today?"

"Always." She sounded tired.

No wonder. Between the last year of pre-med and a demanding boyfriend, she must be sick of the drama. But we needed to speak up before she said something she'd hate revealing to strangers. "Hey, this is Courtney, one of Angus's roommates."

"And I'm Max, the other one."

"Are we on a conference call?" She sounded amused more than annoyed, so that was a decent start.

"I talked to them and if you really want to dump the D-bag, you can move in here. Courtney would be sharing with you. Want to come over, see if it's a good fit?"

"Yes, please." Her response was heartfelt.

An hour later, Kia was on our couch, after a quick tour

of the apartment and my half-empty room. She was taller than me, thinner, too, no surprise there, but nowhere near as imposing as Nadia. From listening to her conversation with Angus, I already knew I wanted this to happen. If it didn't work out and we had to call in Physical Education Kelly, I'd be bummed.

"I feel like I need to be up-front about this," I said.

Max elbowed me. He thought I was going to tell her that I was bi, but there was no reason to lead with that. Frowning at him, I went on, "I'm a touch OC and I might alphabetize your books and/or CDs if you decide to move in."

She laughed. "Girl, have at it. That's not my thing, I don't have time to obsess. But it won't bother me if you organize. Just don't move stuff so I can't find it."

"Don't worry, you won't come home to find all your makeup sorted by brand."

"Hey, I'd much rather be sharing with somebody who cleans. My boyfriend doesn't."

"You mean your ex?" Angus asked hopefully.

"Give me a few days. Is next weekend soon enough?" Kia pushed to her feet with an inquiring look.

"Yep, it's great." I fought the urge to hug her, mostly because it was settled.

"Let's swap numbers." Angus forwarded her info before she finished speaking and I sent a test text. Her phone pinged again, suggesting Max had done the same.

Kia grinned. "I guess I don't have to worry about being welcome. Wish me luck."

"Dump him." That was my best encouraging tone.

Max walked her to the door. "Agreed. Dump the crap out of him."

Once the door closed behind her, I grabbed Angus's hands and whirled him around in a circle. "She's perfect. Seriously, thank you. You don't know how relieved I am."

"Save the victory dance until she moves in. You never know, Duncan could talk her into giving him a second chance. She's been on the verge of leaving him for like a year."

I sighed as the satisfaction drained away. "Now you tell me."

"You worry too much. If need be, we'll split the rent three ways until we find the right person. I can manage a month of that, and I know Angus can." Max slung an arm over my shoulder and hauled me to the sofa. "Come on, let's shoot stuff."

Angus ruffled my hair and I pretended to swat him. "Hey. Hands off the purple."

"Can't help it, it's all adorable and spiky."

My mother called my current look a "punk" phase, and she expressed a devout wish for me to get over it every time I saw her. She hoped I'd trade Doc Martens and cargo pants for dresses that sparkled, grow my hair out and get a nose job. That would never, ever happen. Which bummed my mother out; she'd rather I marry a nice Jewish doctor than become one. Of course, that wasn't on the table, either. Since I didn't know exactly what I wanted to do, I was studying business, though friends who'd already graduated were telling me I needed to specialize or there was no way in hell I'd find a job.

But the idea of wiping my originality like a dry-erase board for a corporate gig bummed me out. I liked my piercings—at last count I had eight: eyebrow, nose, three in my left ear, two in my right, plus the belly-button ring; I couldn't remember if my mother had ever seen the latter. Maybe I'd use the money my granddad left me to start my own company, though at this point, I had no idea what product or service I'd offer.

Max bumped me with his shoulder. "Are you playing or not?"

"I'm in." Picking up the controller, I joined him onscreen, though it pissed me off that in most of these shooters, I always had to play a dude.

"Have fun. I'm out with Del tonight." The brightness in Angus's voice told me things were going well, so I just waved as he left, focused on not shooting Max in the back.

We played for an hour before I got hungry. I pushed Pause on the controller and ambled to the kitchen. Max came up behind me, resting his head on my shoulder as I peered into the fridge. Max was exceptionally hands-on with his friends; maybe he didn't get hugged enough as a kid or something. When I'd first moved in, I thought he was hitting on me, but he thumped and patted Angus about as much, so I went with it.

"Cook something," he pleaded.

I jabbed him in the gut with my elbow. "Get off me and maybe I will. How do patty melts sound?"

"Like manna from heaven. I speak for all starving college students everywhere when I say, words cannot do justice to your munificence."

Snickering, I put the ground beef in the microwave. "Calm down, I already agreed to make the food. No need for sweet talk."

"But it's fun. Your nose wrinkles when you laugh at me."

I fought the urge to cover said nose. Some girls could do adorable bunny wriggles, but mine was too long—beakish, according to an ex who'd had enough of my shit. As personal problems went, however, it wasn't exactly original. There were tons of other Jewish girls in the same situation; I wasn't special. In fact, I probably wasn't even the only princess rebelling with piercings and alt-hair. So I made a face instead of revealing that he'd made me feel self-conscious for a few seconds. On two occasions, Max and I had made out. Both times, we were messed up emotionally and it was good that we'd confined the rebound sex to kissing. Otherwise it might be tough to fry meat while he talked about the work he was doing on his motorcycle.

"Wait, I thought you were done?"

He sighed at me. "The mechanical overhaul is done, but now I'm working on cosmetic restoration. I can't stop until it's finished."

"The fate of the world hangs in the balance?" I teased, shaping the thawed meat into patties. Next I sliced up some onions to caramelize.

"I promised somebody, that's all." His expression was strange and serious, unlike the guy I'd known for three years.

But Max was…odd. Like, he gave the impression he was all jokes, all about the party, but then he flipped a switch and revealed a glimpse of the real person underneath. In all honesty, I was much more interested in that guy—the serious, smart, intense one. Most people had no idea he was a mechanical engineering major, which required knowledge of physics, thermodynamics, kinematics, structural analysis and electricity. And hell, I only knew that because I looked it up on Wikipedia after finding out what he was studying.

"That sounds like a story," I said quietly.

He held my gaze for two beats, then looked away. "I guess it is."

Message received.

I finished our food and we ate in front of the TV, then went back to killing things in the game. But by nine, I was bored. I put down the controller, stretching my stiff muscles in an exaggerated arch of my back. "Okay, I'm done."

"Don't go," he said.

"Huh?" Startled, I swung back toward the couch, catching a bleak, sad look in his dark, dark eyes.

It was like realizing a friend had been hiding raw slashes under their sleeves all this time. His thick lashes swept down, covering the expression, but it was too late. *I can't unsee it.* My chest felt tight with indecision. If I made a joke, he'd take his cue from me, and it would be like this never happened. Maybe that would be for the best.

"I don't want to play anymore," I answered.

"We could go for a ride."

To me, it seemed like Max didn't want to be alone tonight. He rode his bike when he was running from something, but he'd never invited me along. There was no excuse to refuse since classes hadn't started up again. I made a snap decision.

"Okay, let me get a jacket." My pants and concert T-shirt were fine, so I added boots and a hoodie with a skull on the back.

"That was fast." He jiggled his keys with one hand and grabbed me with the other, yanking me out of the apartment and down the stairs. As we approached his bike, he asked, "Have you ever ridden one of these before?"

"What do you think?" I was curious what he'd say.

"Probably...yes."

"You are correct, sir. Don't worry, it's not my first time."

"If you knew how happy it makes me to hear that." He flashed a flirty grin over one shoulder, but I identified it as bullshit.

The wounded eyes? Those were real. Not this. So I put on the helmet and wrapped my arms around his waist, content to be the warm body on the back of his bike. I didn't need to be beautiful to be a friend when he needed one.

Just for a few seconds, he set his hands over mine, where they rested on his abs. "Hold on tight. I'm about to show you something amazing."

CHAPTER TWO

"Where the hell are we going?" I yelled.

Max didn't answer, but he turned off the highway, so the going got much rougher, and I tightened my arms around his waist. We bounced along for another mile, following the natural curve of the road. Before I saw the rapids, I heard the rush of the river, audible as the motorcycle dropped to lower idle. He parked the bike and I swung off, unnerved by the complete darkness. Without speaking, he led me through a tangle of branches.

"If you want to freak me out, it's working."

"Trust me." His fingers folded around mine, and I clutched tight.

ΔOut here there was only the fast-moving water, the wind through the leaves and the chirp of insects. When we emerged from the trees, my breath caught. The sky opened up before me in an endless stream of stars with the river cascading below, tumbling over the rocks in a burst of white foam. Moonlight shimmered on the water, a fairy trail luring men to their doom, if you believed in old legends.

"Wow. How did you find this place?"

"I drive around at night…a lot." He wore a contemplative look as he added, "'It is Earth's eye—looking into which the beholder measures the depth of his own nature.'"

"Did you seriously just quote Thoreau?" I didn't mean to sound so surprised since I knew as well as anyone that Max was smarter than he let on.

"Are you judging a book by its cover?"

"Sorry, reflex. Please continue astounding me with your big brain."

"No, now you went and made me self-conscious. But just look… It's amazing, right?"

I nodded. "Just like you promised."

"Come out, just a little farther." He led me onto a rise overlooking the river. "I sleep out here sometimes."

"Nadia's convinced you're hooking up or crashing at the garage when you don't come home." It was weird saying that to a guy, like we were family or something, but sometimes it actually felt as if we were.

"The garage office reeks of oil and sweaty ass."

"I can see why you'd prefer it here, though I'd probably wet my pants the first time an owl hooted. Is that a thing?"

"Yes, there are owls here, city girl."

"Hey, I was born in Chicago, and my mother is opposed to camping on principle. 'Our people have wandered the wilderness long enough and from now on, we sleep in warm beds.'"

"She sounds opinionated."

"You have no idea."

"Sit down. Unless you're scared."

"No, I'm okay." Though I wasn't quite sure why he'd brought me out here, I couldn't deny that it was beautiful. I plopped down beside him, crossing my legs in a crooked Lotus pose.

Max let out a shaky breath, staring out at the river. He was careful not to look at me. "I got a call from my dad today."

From what I knew of Max—not a whole lot, granted, as he didn't talk much about his past—that was a huge deal. In the three years we'd been hanging out, he'd never mentioned his family. "Yeah?"

"My grandfather died." His tone gave me no clue how to react, and the shadows were too deep for me to read his expression.

"Okay, so is this a 'wow, I'm so sorry' moment, or more 'thank God the old bastard's finally gone'? Give me something here, Max."

He sat in silence for a few moments. "Little from column A, little from column B. See, I come from a long line of violent assholes. Good drinkers, too, proud, easily offended, even though none of us have ever amounted to shit."

"Looks to me like that streak ends with you." I put my hand on his where it rested on his knee, and he leaned toward me. Not going for a kiss but to rest his head on my shoulder.

"You always know what to say." His voice was softer, warmed by my smooth talk.

"So what're you doing about the funeral? Do you want me to help you pick out a floral arrangement or something?"

"No, that's the thing. I brought you out here, hoping

the incredible scenery would make you willing to do me a favor."

"What's that?" He had no pets and no classes yet that I could audit for him and take notes. So I was drawing a blank as to what Max could possibly need from *me*.

"I was hoping you'd come home with me. To Providence."

"What? Why?" Those were the first of many questions to sputter out of me.

"I haven't been back since I went away to school, and I can't be alone with my dad, not even for a minute. It... won't be good."

I submerged the impulse to ask, *Isn't there anyone else?* Because I knew the answer already, and I wouldn't force-feed him that vulnerability on top of the shit sandwich life had already forced him to sample. But I couldn't just pack a bag and ride off without some basic fact-finding. "How long will we be gone?"

"It's a twelve-hour drive, but we'll take regular breaks since you aren't used to a long haul on the bike. I'm guessing five days, including travel."

"Wait, we're taking the motorcycle all the way to Rhode Island?"

As he turned his head, the moon popped out from behind a cloud, illuminating his smile. "You said *we*. So I guess so."

"If I'm crazy enough to do this, you owe me some insider info on why."

"Why?"

"You know what I'm asking. Why can't you be polite long enough to put your grandfather in the ground? Or whatever you *shegetz* boys do." I spoke the last sentence in a teasing tone.

Max got out his phone and turned it on, bright enough to startle me, then he pushed back the tumble of black hair, revealing a thin white scar. The screen flickered off, leaving me with the impression of his tan skin, dark eyes and the mark in sharp contrast. "I got that from my dad when I was eleven. Beer bottle. He chucked it, I didn't duck in time."

"Damn."

"It's not the only childhood souvenir." He shrugged like it didn't matter. "But that's not why I can't forgive him."

"What happened?"

"Right now, I need an answer. Will you come?"

Angus and I didn't have jobs, unlike Max and Nadia. Even if they disapproved of me, my parents still sent a regular allowance and paid my tuition. So there was no reason I couldn't go to Providence with him; I just wasn't sure it was a good idea. Some intuitive part of my brain sensed that it would change everything.

"Okay," I said.

"Thanks so much, Kaufman. You have no idea how much this means to me."

"Because you don't want to miss the services?"

Max shook his head. "My brother will be there."

Before I could ask, he pushed to his feet, dusted off his ass and offered his hand. I took it and let him tow me upright. We retraced our steps back to the bike as I pondered how bad this was likely to be. My family might not be perfect, but nothing like this; it was only a matter of me refusing to conform to expectations, and my mother's weapon of choice was guilt. He swung onto the motorcycle and I got on after him, troubled for reasons I couldn't articulate.

The ride back to the apartment felt faster, probably because I knew where we were going. Angus still wasn't home, so I just nodded a good-night to Max and headed to my huge, half-empty room. He surprised me by following, pausing in the doorway as if waiting for an invite.

"You can come in," I said.

"I wasn't sure. But I just wanted to tell you to be ready by seven."

"Oh, my God. It's already midnight. Go to bed, Max." After setting my alarm, I got ready, packed a backpack and followed my own advice.

In the morning, Max tapped on my door as I was lacing up my boots. I'd packed a black dress and some flats, along with clean panties and a few spare T-shirts. The cargo pants would have to last until we got back. Fortunately, riding on the back of his bike wouldn't even faze my hair, no need for curling iron or straightener. That made it easier to travel light.

"Ready?" he asked as I stepped out.

"Yeah. Let's go."

"Thanks."

"You said that last night."

"I want to be sure it comes across. There's no way I could go back by myself."

A small, curious part of me noticed that he didn't say *home* but it seemed like the wrong time to dig into his motivations. Pausing in the kitchen, I rearranged the fridge magnets to read: Gone. Back Later. I'd text Angus at a more respectable hour and explain the situation, assuming this wasn't top secret for reasons unknown to me.

"We can't do this in one day," Max said as he stuffed our bags in the top box. "Or you'll be too sore to move afterward."

"Promises, promises." It was the sort of joke I always made, expecting him to goof back with me.

Max paused, frowning. "I don't think that's hot. Or funny."

"Huh?"

"Fucking a woman so hard it hurts her. The idea makes me sick, actually." That was more sincerity than I generally got from Max in a week, but it was too early for me to parse.

"There's a difference between being pleasantly tender, the result of good, rough sex, and crawling away from the bedroom all bruised and bloody."

"I know, sorry. That's just…one of my hot buttons."

Pausing, I wondered about that story, but it wasn't the time to ask. "No problem. Shall we roll out?"

The weather was perfect for taking to the open road, sunny sky in summer blue, not a cloud in sight. After two hours on the bike, I understood what he meant, though. It wasn't like riding in a car; my arms were tired from holding on to him and my ass was numb, both from the pavement and the vibrations. Just past ten in the morning, he pulled off at a rest plaza in Ohio. The place was huge, almost like an auto-mall, plenty of parking, three fast food places, picnic tables, a strip of green for pets. I stumbled as I swung my leg over, and it hurt when I straightened my back; I had been leaning forward, pressed against Max for too long.

"Sorry. I should've stopped sooner. You hungry?"

"Yeah. I didn't have anything before we took off."

"Me, either."

"I need the bathroom first, so I'll meet you in the food court."

I used the facilities, washed my hands and stopped, drawn by my reflection. Mirrors were too honest, showing me a woman with a sharp nose and deep-set eyes. I used the purple hair to distract from my face, like a male bird strutting his colorful plumage. My body wasn't bad, though I carried extra weight in trunk and saddlebag. I'd long since come to terms with the fact that I didn't attract looks from across a crowded room. In fact, I was pretty used to being the grenade a wingman would fall on in order to give his buddy a shot at my hot friend.

But on a global scale, problems like that were minuscule, and I was smiling when I found Max waiting with my favorite breakfast sandwich. Pretending to check it over, I sat down across the table from him. "Hmm. Bacon. Egg. Cheese. This passes inspection."

"Glad to hear it. I didn't know if you wanted coffee or juice so I got both."

"Then I'll drink both. How're you holding up?"

"You make me sound decrepit. We haven't been riding that long."

Dropping my voice, I leaned forward, as if I was about to whisper a dirty secret. Max met me halfway. "I meant emotionally."

"Oh. Then I'm wrecked." The flat tone belied the truth I glimpsed in his eyes. "I don't even know if my brother will talk to me."

"What happened?"

"You want my sad life story in a travel plaza?"

Put that way, it sounded wrong, but I couldn't deny my curiosity. So I ate my breakfast sandwich and followed him back outside, where I stretched for, like, five minutes. Max did the same, then we continued the trip. Though he was considerate and stopped every two hours so I could move around, by the time we hit the middle of Pennsylvania I was ready to call it quits. I'd have paid big money for a hot tub, but we stopped at an interstate motel, no Jacuzzis to be had, and I'd rather eat a bug than risk a yeast infection by soaking in a strange bathtub.

Max offered to spring for my room, but it seemed stupid for him to pay double. "Just get one with two beds. It's not a big deal."

"Thanks. I'm doing this on a shoestring budget."

I could've told him that I had plenty of money and a decent limit on my plastic, but I suspected he'd be offended. It was a point of pride for Max to pay my way since he'd asked me along for reasons I didn't entirely understand. Arms crossed, I waited by the motorcycle while he went into the office, and when he came out, he had the room keys.

"Come on, we're around back."

Climbing on the bike made me wince, so I could only imagine how I'd feel tomorrow. *Worth it for a friend*, I told myself. Max parked and handed me the keycards.

"Go on up, I'll bring dinner. Are you in the mood for anything in particular?"

I shook my head. "Get my backpack? I'll shower while you're gone."

"Good idea."

"Some women might find that offensive, Cooper."

"You know what I mean."

Grinning, I took my bag and jogged stiffly up the rusted external steps. This place was a step down from a Red Roof Inn, and the room was about as depressing as I expected: dated decor in overly bright hues with hutch, tiny dining set and grubby, striped arm chair. But at least there was a coffeepot and a relatively new TV. Usually the smell gave away the worst places, and this only gave off a musty scent, like a room that had been closed up too long. The windows didn't open so I turned on the air conditioner, which banged to the point that I imagined tiny gnomes inside the radiator with wee hammers. The added ventilation helped, though, and I got my pajamas, then went into the bathroom.

Water pressure was decent, and I took my time scrubbing off the road dust. By the time I came out, drying my hair on a scratchy towel, Max had pizza and beer waiting at the chipped table. He'd seen my pj's countless times before, so he didn't blink as I came over to get a slice of extra cheese, extra mushrooms and peppers.

"No meat?" I asked.

"Seems safer this way since we're traveling tomorrow."

I grinned. "Your forethought is both impressive and disturbing."

The pizza wasn't bad for a random dive, certainly not the worst, though it didn't compare to the deep-dish Chicago-style I'd grown up on. After dinner, I propped up on my bed and checked my phone for the first time all day. I had a text from Angus and two from my mother. Angus had just replied with Finally eloped with Max, huh? Name your firstborn after me. Boy, girl or other, doesn't matter. Make good choices! Sighing, I read the maternal messages next.

Ma, text one: Why aren't you picking up?

Ma, text two: Where are you? I tried the house phone. Are you avoiding me?

Yes. That's the only *reason I wouldn't answer.*

She hadn't wanted me to move out of the dorms until I told her my roommate was into illegal drugs. Then she'd supported the apartment idea wholeheartedly. Since she regarded spontaneity as her nemesis, she'd be pissed about this trip. I could hear her already: *Vacations should be planned, Courtney. You can't just take off this way.*

I typed back, I'm hanging out with a friend. What's up? That was sort of true, right?

"Everything okay?"

"Hmm?"

"You look pissed."

"It's just my mother, trying to track my movements. I'm surprised she hasn't chipped me like a Chihuahua. Though if she *has*, you'll probably be arrested for kidnapping." I smirked, rubbing the back of my neck as if searching for parental hardware.

He paused with a slice halfway to his mouth. "You know, that sounds like it sucks, but I also wonder what it would be like to have a parent so…invested."

"Your mother's not around?"

"She died when I was five, having my brother. Amniotic fluid embolism. I was fourteen before I even knew what that meant."

I still don't. Mentally I made a note to look it up on Google ASAP. "So your brother's sixteen? What's his name?"

Max nodded. "Michael, but everyone calls him Mickey.

Or…they did. I haven't seen him since my dad kicked me out."

"Wait, what?" I figured he'd just put up with a shitty home life until he got accepted at Mount Albion, and then he was all *Sayonara, suckers*.

"Yeah. I've been on my own since I was sixteen."

"Did things get worse with your dad?" I asked.

"You could say that," Max said quietly. "That was when I put my brother in a wheelchair for life."

CHAPTER THREE

So many questions ricocheted around my brain, but Max's shoulders were pulled up almost to his ears, his chin nearly on the table. Without looking at me, he shredded the napkin in his hands into four pieces and then in half again. The waning sunshine streaming in the smeared window behind him haloed his dark hair, so that the highlights shone blue instead of tawny or copper.

"You don't have to tell me a bedtime story," I said gently.

"No, you need to know. So you understand what's going on and why it's so tense when we get there."

"Okay. If you're sure."

"I'll set the stage." His tone was brittle, uneven, and the bits of paper in his hands kept getting smaller. "I was sixteen, just got my license. My dad was drinking, acting like a fuckhead. Business as usual. When he started in on Mickey, I grabbed the keys. Figured I'd get us both out of there for a while. I don't know if you've noticed, but taking off is kind of my specialty."

"Between your bike, the garage office and the place you showed me by the river, I've picked up on the pattern, yeah."

"I thought I was doing the smart thing, you know? But I was driving too fast and some asshole blew the stoplight. T-boned us. Mickey got the worst of it…weeks in the hospital without knowing if he'd make it. Then, once he stabilized, we found out he'd never walk again." He curled a fist and slammed it onto the table, making the pizza box dance. "Ironic, huh? I was worried that my dad would hurt Mickey but I'm the one who—"

"Not true," I cut in. "That's a textbook accident. Don't tell me you blame yourself."

"It's impossible to do anything else. No, wipe that look off your face, Kaufman. I didn't open up to make you feel sorry for me. I just want you to know the deal going in. I mean, my dad's the biggest asshole I ever met and *he* hates me, too."

"What about Mickey?"

"We weren't talking much when I left. Every day I think, what if I'd put up with my old man's shit for five minutes more? What if I'd picked a fight with him instead of grabbing those keys? I—" His voice broke on a shuddering inhalation.

Until this moment I hadn't realized how much weight Max carried on a daily basis or how good a job he did hiding it. I came out of my chair and rounded the little table before I consciously decided to make a move. Standing beside him, I hovered, unsure what to do. He answered the question by wrapping both arms around my waist and pulling me onto his lap. Unsettled—unnerved, even—I let him press his face into my shoulder, resting a hand on his head.

His breath warmed the skin of my throat, rousing an inappropriate shiver. *Now is* not *the time.* It wasn't like I'd never noticed his hotness; he specialized in a scruffy, soulful appeal that women of all ages seemed unable to resist. But it was so much better for him to call me Kaufman and confide in me instead of flirting. At the moment, Max needed a friend. I stroked his back for like five minutes before he raised his gaze to meet mine.

"Sorry. The closer we get to Rhode Island, the worse I feel."

"It's understandable. You have to be worried about how your brother will react when you see him." The rest of his family sounded like jackwagons. Though he'd only told me about his dad, if he had any decent aunts, uncles or cousins, they would've stepped up when his old man went upside his head with a bottle. A scar like that would take eight or ten stitches, minimum. I imagined Max as a scared kid with blood gushing from his scalp, and all of my protective instincts roared to life. People had been calling me a bitch since I was fifteen, and I was ready to wade in against Max's family. Yeah, the funeral might be tense and shitty, but if his family said one fucking word—

"You're looking especially fierce." Max was smiling slightly, his head cocked in apparent fascination.

It was interesting that my expression could distract him. "Just contemplating all the ways I can kick ass and take names." With a last twirl of fingers in his hair, I slid off his lap. "Your leg must be asleep, huh?"

Max was on the lean side, and I suspected I weighed

as much as he did, possibly more. In his case, the weight
was also stretched along eight additional inches. But he just
shrugged and shook his head. If I wasn't mistaken, a touch
of color also burned high on his cheekbones. *Wow, never
thought I'd see him blush.*

Clearing my throat, I moved away, taking my half-eaten
slice of pizza to the bed I'd dumped my backpack on. I
bounced onto it, completely casual, as if we hadn't just been
sharing deep emotional stuff. Max silently threw away the
napkin he'd shredded and went into the bathroom. The
shower switched on, resulting in an awesome banging of
pipes. I pictured them breaking through the wall and flooding the floor. By the time he came back barefoot, wearing
a ratty T-shirt and sweats, I had the TV on, watching a bad
action movie.

"Oh, this. I've seen it eight times." His offhand tone told
me we were good.

"Then line it up for number nine."

"Hey, Kaufman..."

"Yeah?"

"Thanks."

"Stop. Your boundless gratitude is freaking me out."

"Okay. I don't want to make you uncomfortable. So obviously I'll proposition you instead, get us back on familiar footing."

I grinned, wadding up a piece of paper from the pad next
to me and chucking it at him. "I'm not making out with
you."

"Does that mean sex *without* kissing is off the table?"

"Definitely. So far off, it's out the door, chained up in
the backyard."

He let out a mock-wistful sigh. "Poor coitus. What did it ever do to you?"

"It was the best of sex, it was the worst of sex…"

Max laughed, and it felt fairly glorious to bring him to this point so soon, relatively speaking, after he'd told me about the accident. "Are you butchering Dickens in a sub-textual pun or am I reaching?"

"That depends," I said.

"On what?"

"If you thought it was funny."

"Definitely." He shot me the lazy grin that crinkled his eyes and displayed a dimple.

Okay, stop being adorable, Max. It's bothersome.

"Then it was definitely on purpose. But why do you recognize a misquote of *A Tale of Two Cities*, science-engineering person?"

"I read."

"Dickens? Really? I disbelieve." I pretended to roll some dice. "Natural twenty! Now tell me the truth or I'll resort to drastic measures."

"Okay, Dickens was compulsory. It's not on my summer fun list."

"And what is?" I couldn't remember if I'd ever seen him with a book, but he did fiddle with phone and tablet a lot, so he might be reading that way. "Fictionwise, I mean."

"Oh, and here I planned to share all the freaky places I did it in August."

"Max." I infused his name with a warning tone, so that I sounded uncannily like the rabbi's wife, back when I still went to synagogue.

"Fine. My favorite genre is horror, but I also like sci-fi,

fresh and edgy stuff, not boring white guys saving the universe and banging space hotties."

Surprise popped up like a weasel. Great, now I had that
kids' song stuck in my head. "Wait. You read mostly genre
fiction? Max Cooper. You're a secret geek."

"Don't tell anyone, 'kay? Not that they'd believe you."
He flipped up his shirt to reveal tasty abs. Not mega ripped
but taut and fine with delicious V-lines revealed by loose
sweats. "I mean, just look at this package."

Fortunately, my brain had never let me down, no matter
how much sexy, muscled, yummy tan bod was on display.
"If you have to ask a girl to inspect your package, you work
for UPS or you're trying too hard, bro."

He smirked. "I don't like how you call yourself a girl.
It's demeaning."

"Hey, *I'm* allowed to say it. Dudes aren't."

"I'll bear that in mind."

We stopped talking after that, but the silence didn't thrum
with badness. Max seemed as okay as he could be, considering he was on his way to bury his grandfather and see his
brother for the first time in five years. And that didn't take
into account his asshole dad or the extended family, who
might make his life hell for the next two days. Though we
had another long day of riding ahead of us, I was looking
forward to sitting behind him on the bike more than our
arrival. The shit might really hit the fan then.

Before ten, I passed out on top of the covers and didn't
know anything until a pained sound roused me, however
many hours later. Shoving up on an elbow, I glanced around
in confusion. *This isn't my room, that isn't Nadia… What—oh.*

Max. He writhed in the bed next to mine, an arm lashing at the mattress, and he was bathed in sweat.

That's definitely a bad dream.

This was so far outside my jurisdiction—then again, maybe not. He'd invited me along, knowing we'd be in close quarters for the duration of the trip. So possibly he'd foreseen this development and didn't entirely mind? Whatever. When he snarled an unintelligible curse, I rolled out of bed and crossed to his, perching on the edge.

"Max. Wake up. You're bothering me." That was the first thing that popped into my head, but it didn't rouse him.

"No," he whispered. "No, no, *no.*"

The pure anguish in his voice told me he was reliving the accident. There was no way to know if talking about it summoned the dream or if this happened fairly often. For as much as we hung out at home, I'd never slept in the same room with him. Sucking in a breath, I rested my hand on his head, brushing the damp strands away from his brow. With the light from the sign outside illuminating his face, I saw a tear trickle from the corner of his eye, something I never imagined, ever.

Fuck me. Max cries in his sleep.

My heart twisted in my chest, and I couldn't stop myself from leaning down, touching my forehead to his. That was enough to rouse him, thank God. He blinked up at me blearily, his hands unclenching. "You okay?"

"Bad dream. Scoot over." Since he wasn't even fully awake, he mumbled as he did. I fell asleep with my back against his.

Hours later, I stirred in increments, then snapped alert when I realized Max was spooning me. His arm was strong and warm across my waist, hips snug against my ass, and I felt each slow breath into my hair. *Well, crap. No good deed, and so on.* It seemed unlikely that I could get away without disturbing him. The bedside clock read 5:45 a.m., so it was still mostly dark. As I shifted, he tightened his hold and nuzzled my neck. Obviously, it felt incredible, but it *had* been eight months. These days it didn't take much to turn me on. But I wasn't a shy virgin trembling with fear that he'd ravish me. So I lifted his arm and crawled out of bed. Max was rubbing his eyes when I went to the bathroom to brush my teeth and get dressed.

"Okay, did I imagine—"

"Nothing happened." I wasn't about to tell him that he was crying in his sleep so I figured I better go on the offensive. "My bed had janky springs, that's all."

"Uh-huh. Anyone ever tell you your hair smells like lemons?"

"That's the top-notch motel shampoo."

"Couldn't resist me, huh? This always happens, sooner or later. Should we just do it already, defuse the sexual tension?"

"As if. You were on my side of the bed. There are Russian hitmen who would pay big money to spoon this." I slapped my ass with a teasing grin and yanked the covers off him. "Come on, get up."

He immediately grabbed a pillow, going for basic crotch camo. "Are you kidding?"

"Oh. You already are. I'll take that as a compliment."

"I have to pee," he mumbled.

"Take your time. If you need me to step out, so you can—"

"So help me, Kaufman, if you don't stop talking, *right now*, I'll make you."

Smirking, I did a taunting little dance, hip swivel and half turn. "Sure you will. What, you gonna kiss me? Now, that's original. Besides, I'm *way* too good at it, remember? Pretty soon you'll be dry humping me and then come all over yourself. Let's not go down that road."

He scrubbed a palm across his face. "It's too early for this."

"Exactly my point."

Max slammed the bathroom door after stomping past me. He was in there long enough with the water running for me to consider teasing him, but honestly, what a guy did in the shower stall of a crappy motel bathroom was between him and the tiny soap. So I didn't say anything as we packed up and headed out to the bike. But I was thinking about it, wondering a little, when I swung on behind him and nestled close.

I could get used to this.

Of course, introducing my mother to Max might trigger the coronary she was always threatening to have, whenever I did something worthy of parental disapproval. Which was pretty much my entire life to date. She claimed she was in danger of a stroke when I came out as bisexual. In fact, my dad argued with me on the subject; he said that wasn't even a thing and that I probably just wasn't ready to admit I was gay yet—not that he *wanted* me to. So if I could just go quietly back into the closet and confine my sexual identity questions to watching interesting internet porn, that would be great. He didn't say that, of course, but over the years, I'd gotten great at reading between the lines. Conversations with my family were pretty much always frustrating for various reasons.

"You good to go?" Max asked, starting the engine.

"Yep, let's do this."

Like the previous day, we rode in two-hour increments, stopping to rest so my muscles didn't lock up. Max grew progressively tenser the closer we got to Rhode Island, and when we crossed the state line, his back felt like a brick beneath my cheek. Since I could only touch his abs, it seemed weird to rub his belly as if he was a spaniel and I was trying to make his back leg kick. As we rolled into Providence, he pulled into a gas station parking lot. The area didn't look awesome, but I didn't protest. I figured he needed a minute. Max disappeared inside for over ten minutes, and when he came out, he had on dress slacks, a wrinkled button-up and the ugliest tie I'd ever seen in my life.

"The wake's already started," he said.

"Then I should go change." I hadn't realized we were going straight to the funeral home.

Without another word, I took my backpack and did my best to look respectable in my black dress and ballet flats. Short of dyeing my hair and removing all my piercings, I figured I'd done the best I could, then I had to get back on the bike in a skirt. I hadn't thought of that when I was packing. There was no way to ride sidesaddle, so I tucked the fabric.

Max took off, gunning the throttle, and I could practically sense his tension. Fifteen minutes later, we stopped outside a run-down-looking funeral parlor called Cavanaugh and Sons. The building had clearly seen better days, pitted with wind and rain, and grass grew up through cracks in the sidewalk. Most of the businesses nearby had bars across the windows; the rest were vacant buildings.

"It's worse than I remembered," he said, pulling off his helmet.

Max took a couple of deep breaths, and I put my hand over his heart, feeling the way it raced at the idea of facing his family. As I stared up at him, his gaze locked on my face. I metered my breathing to his, willing him to calm down. *You can't start this way. It'll go up in flames sooner rather than later.*

"Whatever happens in there, I'm on your side. You know that, right?"

"My dad would punch me in the face for bringing you to fight my battles."

"He sounds like a catch. Has he remarried? I'm thinking I might have a shot."

"Don't even joke," he snapped.

"Sorry. The more nervous I get, the closer I come to doing standup. You should've been at my bat mitzvah."

"Did you wear a frilly dress?"

"And combat boots."

Smiling, Max pulled my hand off his chest and pressed it to his cheek for one beat, two. "You make me feel like this might be okay. Somehow. Come on. Let's go meet the family."

CHAPTER FOUR

Inside, the funeral home was cramped.

We stepped first into a small foyer with worn red carpeting, dusty silk floral arrangements set on tables to either side. I fought a sneeze as Max took my hand and led me into the chapel. A few white folding chairs were set up, but not too many, as most people were standing around in clusters, wearing their Sunday best and talking in low voices. Before, I'd only attended Jewish services, so this should be interesting from a cultural perspective.

There was a clear pathway with a runner leading up to the casket, arrayed with pictures, flowers and mementos to one side. Wearing a determined look, Max pulled me along, not stopping until we reached the coffin with the old man inside. From the look of him, he'd definitely lived a full life, complete with alcohol abuse, judging by the veins in his nose, poorly covered by the morbid makeup artist who worked for Cavanaugh and Sons. There were also plenty of wrinkles and liver spots. Reflexively, I took a step back, ostensibly to give Max room, but really I was getting away from the weirdness of staring at a dead person I'd never met.

Granting him some privacy, I turned away, taking stock of the crowd. There were middle-aged women in polyester dresses, bored men talking sports in low tones. Nobody seemed particularly broken up; I didn't see an elderly woman weeping like a bereaved widow. But across the room, I spotted a young man in a wheelchair, and he looked uncannily like Max, except for the upper-body strength. Max was lean, and he definitely wouldn't win at a gun show. This guy might compete in the Paralympics or something.

I put a hand on Max's shoulder. "I think your brother's watching us."

He whirled, scanning the room with hungry, worried eyes. Then his gaze locked onto Mickey—I was *that* sure of his identity—and the guy wheeled toward us. "It's been a long time."

"Yeah. How've you been?" From the flash in Max's dark eyes, he thought it was a stupid fucking thing to say, and he was already kicking himself, but it wasn't like these occasions came with a manual.

Before Mickey could answer, a man shouldered through the crowd toward us. He was maybe an inch shorter than Max with hard eyes and cuts on his jaw that suggested he'd shaved with an unsteady hand. I might be jumping to conclusions, but they looked like the result of sobering up suddenly, after a long bender. I put his age around fifty, so he might be Max's dad.

"Can't believe you showed. I bet your uncle Lou ten bucks you wouldn't have the balls."

"Enough, Pop." Mickey confirmed my speculation with two words. "This isn't the time or the place."

A blonde woman joined the group then, wearing a worried look. "Is that you, Max?"

"Hey, Aunt Carol. Thanks for the email." He leaned in to kiss her cheek.

She didn't seem like a horrible person at first glance, so I wondered why she hadn't protected Max back in the day. I noticed nobody was hugging him, though, or touching him at all. I finally understood why he was so tactile; it was reactionary, like bingeing on chocolate after a strict diet.

Clearing my throat, I offered my hand for her to shake. "I'm Courtney."

His dad skimmed me up and down, then his lip curled. "She must have money. I guess you're not a total idiot. Cash lasts way longer than a pretty face, and all cats feel the same in the dark, am I right?"

Wow. That wasn't the first time I'd heard that verdict, but it was the bluntest anyone had come across with it. Max lunged at his dad, and his aunt caught his shoulder. His jaw clenched as he shook her off. But I squeezed his hand, silently telling him to relax. *It's so not worth it.*

Carol smiled at me. "You're Max's…"

"Friend," I supplied.

From her expression, that wasn't the answer she expected. "Nice to meet you. I was surprised when Max said he'd try to make it. He didn't tell me he was bringing company."

"We're not staying with you," Max said. "So don't worry about it."

"Too good for your family." His dad snorted.

Max cut him a *WTF* look and I understood why. From

his father's tone, he made it sound like it was Max's choice, not involuntary exile. Before the tension could get worse, though, Mickey shook my hand with a friendly smile. This kid had incredible eyes, two or three shades lighter than Max's, and flecked with gold. He must already be breaking hearts.

"With all this bickering, I don't see an intro anytime in our future. I'm Michael."

Ah. So he's grown out of the nickname. Truthfully, he didn't look much like a Mickey, though I was definitely Disney-biased. I figured he'd been closer as a kid.

"I've heard a lot about you." Only a slight exaggeration. But from his expression, he was glad to hear it, so I smiled and pretended I knew some cute childhood stories instead of only having learned of his existence the day before.

Thanks, Max.

"All good, right?" Michael had dimples, too, plus a faint cleft in his chin. I had the urge to ruffle his hair, but he'd probably take it the wrong way.

"Stop flirting," Max said, folding his arms with a mock-stern look.

"Him or me?" I teased.

"Both of you. It's disturbing, Kaufman. I told you it's never happening between us, and I won't let you seduce my brother for revenge."

"So much for my nefarious plans."

Michael glanced between us, a strange expression dawning. "Don't take this the wrong way, but I remember you as...angrier."

That sparked a tentative smile from Max, like he was expecting a gong to clang and for his brother to melt into a dog-headed demon or something. "You want to see the bike?"

"No way, you still have it?"

"Yeah, I've nearly got it done."

"You promised me a ride, asshole." Michael didn't seem to notice the way Max flinched, but I did. His fingers tightened on mine. "Can we check it out now?" He was already wheeling toward the exit, leading the way.

I didn't know much about motorcycles, but the brothers seemed to be bonding. So I let go of Max. When he followed Michael without looking back, I decided it was the right move. That left me standing awkwardly with his father and Aunt Carol. Offering a tentative smile, I tried to come up with an innocuous topic for small talk.

But Mr. Cooper beat me to the punch. "Whatever promises the kid made to get you here, I guarantee they're bullshit. You're better off getting on a bus. Want a ride?"

"*Excuse* me?"

"I'm just offering to help you out, girlie."

Oh, no, you did not.

My fingers balled up into a fist, but before I could make good on my urge to introduce it to his nose, Carol caught my arm. "Let me get you some coffee. I think there are some cookies, too. Cavanaugh and Sons don't offer much of a spread."

"Like I'd pay top dollar to put that old bastard in the ground."

Since that was pretty much exactly what Max thought about the asshole in front of me—the live one—I stared over my shoulder as the older woman led me away. "Sorry. You must think we're awful."

A polite response to that failed me, so I took the Styrofoam cup full of bitter-smelling coffee and added powdery packets of fake creamer and yellow envelopes of sweetener until I could pretend it was a milkshake. Most people were surprised that I didn't just shoot up triple espressos because I exuded that vibe, but in fact, I didn't like hot drinks—with the exception of Angus's mulled wine. But normally, even on a cold day I'd rather have a chilled beverage.

Carol wasn't kidding when she said the pickings were slim. This looked like the employee break room with a few sad round tables, covered in napkins and newspapers, along with scattered cookie crumbs. This reminded me that I hadn't eaten since noon, and it was nosing toward seven. Silently I nibbled a stale snickerdoodle and pondered the life choices that ended with me in this current situation.

"So how do you know Max?" she asked.

Since I'd almost forgotten she was there, I came back with the absurd and defensive, "How do *you* know Max?"

Mentally I banged my head on the nearest wall when her pleasant face clouded over in confusion. "Um. Well, we've never actually met before, to be honest. I married his dad's younger brother two years ago. I didn't realize there was such...drama in the family, so I emailed him an announcement about the wedding."

Oh, she's an aunt by marriage.

"And he wrote back?"

"Yeah. I've been updating him about Michael, mostly."

"That was nice of you."

"It's the least I can do. I'll never understand the dynamics here. Sometimes it's like stepping through a minefield."

"Yeah, I can already tell Mr. Cooper's a character."

"Who, Charlie? It's okay, honey. You can say it. He's a jackass. Don't get him started on his addiction, by the way. He'll talk your ear off about his stupid chips." I must've looked blank because she added, "He joined AA a few months back, after his dad got really sick. So he's got sobriety tokens now, three months' worth. Luckily Jim doesn't have the same problems as his brother or his dad, may he rest in peace."

"Jim would be your husband?" I guessed.

"Right, you don't know anyone. Let me help." She took my arm and hauled me back to the chapel, where she kept me pinned to her side naming strangers.

Yeah, there's no way in hell I'm remember any of that.

It was nearly eight when Max and Michael came back in, so they must've had a good talk. I'd rarely seen Max smiling so wide, and pleasure washed over me at playing any role in this reunion. There weren't many people left, just close family, by this point.

Mr. Cooper scowled when he saw his sons together. "Okay, closing time. You don't have to go home, but you can't stay here."

That sounded more like last call at a bar than a suitable farewell at a viewing, a wake or whatever Christians called this deal. I much preferred Jewish services. But the stragglers cleared out in response to Mr. Cooper's impatient gestures, leaving a middle-aged man who looked a bit like Max with an arm around Carol—that had to be Jim—me, Max, Michael and their dad.

There was a lot of awkward staring until I said, "Can we get some dinner?"

Mr. Cooper snorted. "Better feed her. Asses like that don't grow themselves."

Max had been spoiling to punch his father all night, and while I shared the impulse, I wasn't ruining this service or going to jail. "Wow. Well, thanks for noticing...but it's slightly inappropriate. Try to stare at butts closer to your own age. Max, you hungry?"

"I could eat," he said, seeming surprised.

"Where are you headed?" Michael glanced between us, obviously angling for an invite. I could read the subtext, if Max was too pissed at his dad to catch on.

"I'm not sure. What's good around here?"

"The diner over on North Broadway isn't bad. It's cheap and tasty. I don't eat there often when I'm in training, though."

"You look like an athlete," I admitted.

"Is it the chair that gave me away?" He had a sporty, streamlined model.

"Frankly, it's your whole upper body." Which, from Max's death glare, might've been a weird thing to say, but his little brother was *fit*.

"What did I say about the flirting? He's still in high school, for shit's sake. You're gonna end up in a mugshot."

Michael laughed. "Stand down, bro. I'll let you know if I feel sexually threatened."

"You want to take point, show us how to find the eats?" I suspected he must have a ride.

In reply, Michael jingled his keys. "No problem. Follow me."

Somehow I mustered the last echo of a good upbringing and said good-night to Mr. Cooper without a sneer. I put some more warmth into it when I spoke to Jim and Carol, then we rolled out. Max was quiet as we got on the motorcycle. I didn't try to talk to him; there would likely be a lengthy deconstruction in the room after we ate. The snarl of the engine drowned out my growling stomach, at least.

The diner was small, a hole-in-the-wall place on the corner of Broadway and a cross street whose name I couldn't read. On the bike, we didn't have to worry about parking, though. Michael stashed his retrofitted Scion down the block; I watched as he rolled down the rear ramp and closed things up. Max moved like he'd go help out but I grabbed his arm.

"This is his life, you know? I'm sure he hangs out with his friends."

"Yeah. I just… I can't square it in my head. Last time I saw him, he was hooked up to tubes, frail as hell. Now he's—"

"Fine."

"You're such a perv, Kaufman."

I punched him in the arm. "Not what I meant and you know it. Did you seriously think he'd be sitting in bed, pale and sad for, like, five years?" At the flicker of his eyes, I raised my brows. "God, you mentally had him dying in a Victorian tuberculosis ward, didn't you? You watch *Tombstone* too much, I've always said that. And Doc Holliday looks nothing like Val Kilmer."

"What're you guys talking about?" Michael asked.

"Westerns," I answered before Max could get awkward. "What's your favorite?"

Max kept quiet as we found a table and moved a chair so Michael could wheel up. The resulting conversation carried us past ordering, and Max eased up once we switched to ac-

THE SHAPE OF MY HEART

tion flicks, something he had a lot to say about. He and Michael discussed the underappreciated genius of John Woo, then moved to the interesting stuff currently being filmed in Hong Kong. I added less than nothing to the convo, but since I had chicken tenders, I didn't mind. The fries were homemade, fresh cut, and the coleslaw was decent; I ate it so I could pretend the veg would counteract all the fried goodness. *In the immortal words of Max's dad—gotta feed dat ass.*

But midway through dinner, Michael said, "We should really talk about something Courtney cares about, too."

"Kaufman's fine. You are, right?" Max turned to me with a raised brow. He had nice ones, thick enough to make a statement, not wild enough to give him an evil-genius air.

"Yep. I could go for pie, though. Is it any good here?"

"Do you like pecan?" Michael asked.

"Do I like it? I almost married it. But my sweet pastry felt like I was getting all codependent, so we had this huge, messy breakup, and now I have sole custody of the tartlets. It's hard, man." Biting my knuckles, I dropped my eyes, pretending to wipe away the tears.

Max was used to my weirdness but Michael seemed startled for, like, ten seconds, then he cracked up. "Okay, no nut allergies, check. Try the pecan pie if it won't trigger a flashback."

It had been a while since I hung out with high school kids, basically since I *was* one, and I didn't remember guys being so mature and poised at sixteen. But that wasn't something I could comment on without it seeming strange and/or insulting. Max would also chide me for the third time about hitting on his brother, and that might open a hell mouth or something.

The waitress came over in response to Max's chin lift. One of these days, I had to learn that. To get a server's attention, I practically had to get out glowing batons and signal a plane.

"We'll have three pieces of pecan pie and the check."

"Any coffee?" she asked.

Before I could reply, Max said, "Nah. It's too late for me, the kid's too young and the lady doesn't like it."

I was kind of surprised he remembered, but Michael was glaring. He didn't speak until the girl moved off. "Too young, fuck you. Too young."

"So opposable thumbs are pretty cool," I said.

But things were melting down too fast for me to head them off. Max waded in with boots on, not that I knew why. "You're a kid, Mickey. It's nothing to be ashamed of."

"I can see why you'd think that, considering you haven't even *seen* me in five years. Guess what, I grew up while you were out." He took a deep, deep breath, brown eyes flashing. "Your phone doesn't work, Max? Dad said you had a reason for disappearing on us, and I've been waiting to hear it."

Part of me wanted to defend Max, but I bit my lip. *This isn't your fight, and you only know his side of the story.* Things probably looked much different to Michael.

Before Max could answer—tell his brother what he'd told me about being kicked out of the house—the waitress showed up with pie. By the time she walked off, Michael was seething too hard to listen.

He shoved away from the table and wheeled around with a dark stare. "Never mind, not in the mood for dessert. Nice meeting you, Courtney."

"That's crazy," I said, trying to lighten the atmosphere. "How is it humanly possible not to be in the mood for pie?"

Apparently that was the wrong thing to say. Because Max stood up and stalked out, stranding me in a strange diner in Providence.

CHAPTER FIVE

In reaction to my predicament, I ate one and a half pieces of pecan pie.

Michael was right; it was delicious. Then I asked the waitress to box up the rest. *I mean, how bad can the situation be if there's pie?* Once I had my leftovers in a sack, I paid the check and stepped onto the sidewalk. Part of me hoped I'd find Max pacing, maybe smoking a cigarette like he did when he was really upset or completely hammered, but the bike was gone.

By this point, it was half past nine. Swallowing hard, I went back inside. The waitress didn't look pleased to see me, but I rode it out. Local info could make all the difference.

"So I'm wondering if there's a decent motel within walking distance. I don't mind if it's crappy, just not a hellhole." I hoped she'd know what I meant.

"Oh." Her annoyance softened, leavened with sympathy. "Your boyfriend ditched you?"

It didn't seem worth it to clarify. "Yeah. There probably isn't a bus out tonight anyway."

I felt slightly bad for putting that on the table. If I left tomorrow, I'd fly back to Ann Arbor and ask if Nadia could pick me up. But the waitress wouldn't feel like helping me if she knew I wasn't as pathetic as I appeared. You'd have to be a complete sociopath to refuse to answer questions, given my apparent abandonment.

"You don't want to hang around the station that late, even if there is. If you can afford a room for the night, taking the bus during the day is a lot safer."

Since I had plenty of space on various cards and a fair amount of cash on me, plus my ATM card, this didn't present as much of a challenge as it might have for someone else. My style hid the fact that my family had plenty of money, though not like Angus, of course. Better for me to blend into the neighborhood anyway, especially at this hour.

"Okay, thanks." I smiled at her.

"There's a decent place four blocks away. I can draw a map if you want."

"No, that's fine. If you tell me what it's called, I can map it on my phone. Is it safe to walk in this neighborhood? I'm not from around here."

She nodded, naming the hotel. "Just keep your head down and stay alert. The first block is iffy, but there will be more people when you hit Little Italy."

After thanking her again, I memorized the route, then put away my phone. Even during the day, it wasn't a good idea to show you had no fucking clue where you were going. At night, it would be insane. Maybe I should just call a taxi but it seemed dumb as hell to wait twenty minutes for it when I could walk it in less than ten. The waitress was right about the first leg feeling sketchy, so I speed-walked. A few guys stared from their stoops as I jogged by, but nobody made a move.

More lights sprang up as I turned, and by the way the architecture changed, I could tell I'd found Little Italy. The buildings looked more European, painted in brighter hues. Checking the street sign, I saw I'd found De Pasquale Avenue, just as Google promised. I felt better here, as a number of restaurants were still open, mostly bistros and trattorias that reminded me of Rome. I found the hotel, no problem; it was a three-story building—canary yellow with white accents. The front rooms appeared to have balconies, and it didn't seem like a flophouse, even from the outside, though I could tell it wasn't posh.

My phone read 9:50 p.m. No messages from Max. Well, it wasn't the first time he'd taken off. But as I put my hands on the door, my cell rang.

"Where are you?" he demanded.

"I've been kidnapped by super generous criminals, who let me keep my personal electronics. It's too late. I'm a sex slave now, don't try to save me."

An older woman coming out of the restaurant next door aimed a shocked look at me. I beamed at her, waving like we were old friends. That made her quicken her step, lest she be forced to talk to me. She crossed the street to continue her journey.

"I'm sorry," he said. "Why didn't you wait for me?"

"Why didn't you tell me where you were going?"

He sighed. "Just tell me where you are, please. I admit it, I shouldn't have left. I was just trying to catch up with

Michael but I fucked up and he won't talk to me. I turned around when I realized how weird it was to chase him on the bike."

"You hurt his pride. And I didn't stay there because the diner was closing. I hate being the asshole who can't take a hint, even when they're cleaning up around you."

For a millisecond, I considered giving him a hard time, but it had been a shitty enough day, and it wasn't like anything horrible had happened to me. *I'm not a damsel in distress. I can handle my own business.*

"Kaufman."

"Fine." I gave him the address for Hotel Dolce Villa. "I'm getting a room. See you later."

Inside, the hotel was purple and white, surprisingly modern. No frills, but the lobby was clean, with an efficiently-designed counter and a vending machine against the wall. If the rooms were like this, clean and simple, then this would be nicer than the place we'd stayed in last night. Certainly the area was better than the interstate.

The receptionist looked slightly annoyed when I walked up. I tried a smile. "Sorry, I don't have a reservation, but I was wondering if you had anything available?"

"You're lucky," she muttered.

"Huh?"

"Check-in shuts down at 10:00 p.m. As it's nine fifty-seven and—" she checked the computer "—this guy's still not here, I'm making an executive decision and giving you the room."

Oh. That explains the irritation. She's about to shut down and go home. Some hotels had twenty-four-hour desk service, but apparently this wasn't one of them.

"That's awesome—thanks." I didn't feel like wandering Providence in hope of finding shelter, and after the tension at the funeral home and his argument with his brother, I imagined Max felt the same. "Is the hotel small?"

"Yeah, only fourteen suites. This is our last room. How many nights?"

The funeral was tomorrow, and there was no way we were heading out straight after. Max needed to make peace with Michael, if nothing else. *That's the whole reason we're here.*

I made an executive decision on my own. "Three. Can you put it on my card?"

"Sure. Are you alone?"

"No, a friend will be joining me shortly. He's parking the bike."

"We don't have a proper lot but he can stash a motorcycle out back."

I texted him that information. Ten minutes later, Max blew through the front door, weighed down by helmets and backpacks, wildly disheveled but hotter for it, somehow. It was frustrating to notice that about him. Pushing out of my chair, I waved at the receptionist and led the way to our suite without speaking. Our room was two flights up. I had a combination instead of a card, so I keyed in the code and let us in. Like the lobby, it was clean and modern, painted bright blue. White furniture and a tile floor made it seem like a small apartment, complete with separate bedroom and kitchenette. The room smelled overwhelmingly of plug-in air freshener, not the worst possibility.

Max glanced around in surprise. "Better than I expected."

"According to the brochure, the bed and pull-out couch have memory-foam mattresses."

"I'll take the sofa."

"Like I'd give you the bed after you ditched me."

He caught my shoulder as I brushed by. "Hey. I really am sorry. It was a dick move. If you want to punch me, go for it. Just...not the face, okay?"

I laughed and pulled away. "You're such an idiot."

"I'm trying to make it up to you."

"You know I'm not a dude, right? If I was upset, I wouldn't get over it by hitting you."

Max sighed. "Okay, tell me what to do."

"The apology was fine. But if you ever do anything like that again, I'm making a quilt out of your underwear."

"That's disturbing on so many levels." He paused a beat. "For instance, you can *sew*?"

"Don't judge. Junior year, I made my own prom dress."

"I don't know what's blowing my mind more, you being domestic or the fact that you went to prom. Do you have pictures?"

Normally I'd never go to the archives. *Eli's there. Eli.* These days I didn't talk to him in my head as much as I used to. Back in high school, I couldn't go a whole day without those fictional convos to get me through. Now I sometimes went as long as a week without asking his opinion. Which qualified me as beyond crazy. For Max, though, I plopped onto the love seat and connected to the free Wi-Fi on my phone. Then I flipped through the cloud gallery where I'd stored five years of precious memories. Pulling up my junior prom picture created an actual physical ache.

I'd worn a black taffeta strapless gown embroidered with silver skulls, fishnet stockings and black Converse, my hair done up in an Amy Winehouse–inspired masterpiece. My date stood only an inch taller, though I was in flats. I'd made his matching tie and cummerbund, too. I stared at his sweet, ridiculous face, so covered in freckles that I'd never finished counting them. I hadn't dated a blond guy since, but it was Eli's eyes I'd loved most, impossibly blue, and always trained on me, waiting for me to say something clever or make him laugh.

Max sat down beside me. "Wow, your hair was so long."

Cliché, but I'd hacked it all off after Eli died, donated it to Locks of Love. Even before he asked me out, I'd known that ending was a possibility...but I'd loved him anyway—with everything I had. Other people in our situation got miracles. Why not us? *Risk it all, right, Eli? Dance like nobody's watching.* I pushed out a breath, hating the tightness in my chest. So many years later, and it never got easier.

"Yeah."

Something about my tone must've tipped him off because his gaze snapped to my face. "Shit. Are you crying?"

"Maybe a little. I need to get to bed." I tried to stand up, but Max wouldn't let me.

His arm circled my shoulders, pulling me into his side. "Talk to me. If you shut me out, I'll feel like we're not actually friends. And then how I am supposed to feel about asking you to do *this* with me?"

That was fucking low, but I admired emotional sophistry. Wiping my eyes, I flipped to the next photo. "This was my high school boyfriend."

"It didn't work out?"

"He died."

"Fuck. I'm so sorry. I had no idea or I wouldn't have—"

"No, it's okay. I can't break down just because someone

asks to see an old prom picture." I swallowed hard, unable to breathe for a few seconds.

I had no idea why it was hitting me so hard tonight, but the hole was right there, bigger than ever. When he'd gone, Eli left a chasm in the middle of my heart, probably because we were best friends first. So I'd lost the love of my life and my closest friend on the same day. To this day, when I heard the flatline from a hospital TV show, my throat closed up. Too clearly I remembered how it felt to have his fingers cool in mine while the nurses tried to pull me away.

Gouging at my eyes with the heels of my hands, I thrust my phone at Max. "Here. Look at whatever you want."

"Are you serious?" He put it on the small table and drew me into his arms. "I don't care about the pictures. Right now I'm all about you."

His sweetness broke me down, and I cried into his shoulder. It had been years since I'd done this. Maybe it was the funeral? Max rubbed my back until I settled down. As I sat back, he swept the tears from my cheeks with his thumbs. His gaze was so dark, intent, that I had no idea what he was thinking.

He's thinking about kissing you, Eli said.

Oh, my God, shut up.

Seriously, it hasn't been that *long. You remember that look.*

But this is Max. He's just a friend.

Eli's laugh echoed in my head. *Yeah, well, so was I. Until I wasn't anymore.*

Unsettled, I pulled back. "Sorry. I think I'm just tired."

"Do you want to tell me what happened?"

Not really. But that was unfair, given how much he'd confided in me. And I'd told Nadia, so... I nodded. "It's not much of a story, but… I grew up with Eli. We played in sandboxes together, plotted world domination over juice boxes. When I grew boobs, he asked me out."

"What happened to him?"

"He was sick a lot," I said hoarsely. "Leukemia, multiple remissions. Our senior year, he wasn't strong enough for another round of chemo. He died of secondary complications when I was seventeen." That was such a clinical way to describe watching him getting weaker and weaker, until his face was all hospital pallor and electric blue eyes. At the end, his hands felt so frail in mine, bony fingers and parchment skin.

"I'm so sorry. I wouldn't have asked you to come with me if I'd known."

"Don't be stupid. Everyone's lost somebody. It's not like I'll never attend another funeral again because I went to Eli's. I'm happy you're letting me be there for you."

"Likewise," he whispered.

I let him tip my head against his shoulder. Max locked his arms around me, settling like he planned to sleep this way. For a minute, I considered it, but I'd be stupid to risk a crick in my neck when there was a bed in the next room. So I pushed against his chest.

"Not that this emotional catharsis wasn't completely awesome, but it's been a long day."

"Okay. G'night, then." Maybe it was my imagination but I thought I spied a flicker of…something as I pulled away. Disappointment?

No. What's wrong with you? Everything was weird in Providence without Angus and Nadia to make Max and me feel normal together. *Dammit, Eli. Now you've got me seeing stuff that isn't there.*

I picked up my backpack, and his faint sigh reached me as I got to the doorway. I couldn't deny the sense of unfinished business. "You want to sleep with me?"

Usually, at this point, Max would make a joke about how we were never, ever having sex. I didn't turn around.

"Would it be weird if I said yes?"

"It's fine, come on."

Like the night before, I used the bathroom first and got in bed before Max. This time, however, there was only one bed; as promised, the mattress was amazing. Since there was a club nearby, it was probably louder on the weekend, but tonight, the place was fine. I burrowed in and rolled over on my side so it didn't look like I was watching for Max. Tension crackled in my nerves, and it was an odd, anticipatory feeling.

Nobody's getting laid tonight, okay? That's not what this is about.

Eventually he came out and crawled in the other side. It had been a while since I'd slept with anyone, and if I leveled with myself, I missed it. Max edged toward me until our backs touched. The careful tenderness of it made me smile.

"That okay?"

"Yeah." I liked listening to him breathe in the dark. Such a small thing, but lovely.

"Can I ask you something? It's personal and might be stupid."

"Go for it. I'm sure I'll survive." It couldn't be worse than stuff my parents came up with.

"Have you always been bi? Or is that because...Eli..."

He fumbled the question, but I suspected I knew where he was trying to go.

I laughed softly. That was dumb, yes, but cute. "Yeah. It's not because he died and I'll never love another man, so therefore only women are left to me as romantic options."

"You must think I'm an idiot." The bed shifted, and I snuck a peek to catch him burying his face in his pillow as if in embarrassment.

"It's not the worst question I've been asked, trust me."

"Is it...superdifferent?" At the moment, Max might set the bedding on fire with hot awkwardness, but I could tell he was honestly curious, not perving on the idea of me with a girl.

"The energy's much different with a woman, yeah. But sex can be good or bad either way. I've been with women who expected me to do all the heavy lifting and men who didn't know where to touch. For me, it's all a head game anyway. My partner has to get me going intellectually before I want to fuck."

"You're definitely not shallow."

"I can't be," I said quietly. "I know what I bring to the table, and it's not a pretty face or a perfect body. Therefore, I value other assets and...I work with what I've got."

He was quiet for a few seconds. "I think maybe Eli was the luckiest guy in the world."

"Why?"

"Because you loved him."

CHAPTER SIX

Because you loved him.

As I put on the black dress again, I heard Max's whisper again in my head. Eli was silent. I toweled my hair since the dryer wasn't working, then I daubed on some make-up, subdued for the occasion. My hair looked strange, but I hadn't packed any product, so I smoothed it down as best I could and clipped the over-long bangs out of my face with a plain barrette.

Max rapped on the door. "You about ready?"

"Just need to brush my teeth. Give me a sec."

Hesitating afterward, I swung away from my reflection with a soft curse. I pulled a smile into place by the time I opened the door, so Max could shower. Doing him a favor, I hid the god-awful tie that looked like something my uncle Gilbert would wear and went into the other room to watch the small TV. Or pretend to, rather. The night before left me feeling strange and exposed. *Can't wait to get back to Michi-*

gan, back to normal. Where Max and I didn't act bizarre and emotional around each other.

I heard him bang out of the bathroom and rummage around the bedroom for a few minutes. He came to the doorway, dress shirt unbuttoned and untucked; I felt bad because I totally scoped out his chest and abs before I caught myself. The dark, trailing ink of an intriguing tattoo curled over his ribcage and under the white fabric. Surprise flared when I realized I wouldn't mind pulling his shirt all the way off and checking out his ink. *That's...inconvenient. Eyes up.* Raising my brows, I pretended I didn't know what his problem was.

"I can't find my tie."

"If you need one, we'll stop somewhere on the way, okay? I'll pick it out." That was meant as both a bribe and a distraction.

"Okay. I think I saw a menswear shop not too far from the funeral home."

Nodding, I grabbed my purse and followed him out of the small suite that belonged to us for the next couple of days. The bike was around back, so we went out that way, much less picturesque than the front, especially with the Dumpsters nearby, but since it hadn't been stolen, I counted that a win. On the way, we stopped for fast-food breakfast sandwiches and ate them next to the motorcycle, which he parked in a metered spot outside the clothing store. Silently I dropped in a quarter, taking in his tiredness and the shadows beneath his eyes. The cheap safety razor did a piss-poor job on his dark scruff, so his face was patchy, particularly on his chin.

"Can't take your eyes off me, huh? I get a lot of that."

"I'm sure you do." The circumstances made me gentle, but he surprised me by blushing.

"Okay, it freaks me out when you're nice to me."

"Can you put up with it for two more days?"

He smiled. "I'll manage."

Once we finished breakfast, I pushed into the cramped store to the jingle of customer-announcing bells. A gray-haired man came out of the backroom, wilting a little when he saw us. I guessed we didn't look like big spenders, and since Max only needed a tie, his radar was working fine. But he still smiled, which spoke well of his customer service skills.

"Anything I can help you find?"

I shook my head, leading the way over to a small table with ties laid out in a fan. "Are there any colors you hate passionately?"

"Lime green."

"I wouldn't do that to you anyway."

"How about this one?" Pulling a red, white, gray and black plaid one out of the pile, I held it up against his white shirt. Since he was wearing plain gray trousers, I thought it worked.

Max didn't look too sure. "Isn't it a little…"

"What?"

"Burberry. You know, designer-asshole-looking."

"This isn't the same pattern, but if you don't like it—"

"Do you?"

"What?"

"Like it."

I smirked up at him. "Well, the one you had on before was

a pimp-city special. The only way it could've been worse is if it had palm trees and glitter."

"Fine, I'll take this one. Obviously I have bad taste in dress clothes." From his sulky tone, he thought his old tie was awesome.

"Jackets are sixty percent off," the salesman tried. "With your build, I have plenty of blazers that would look great on you."

To my surprise, Max turned to me with a half frown. "Do you think I should I get one?"

"Do you trust me to dress you?"

"Yes," he said simply.

So I plucked a black blazer off the rack in his size, along with a thin cloud-gray sweater-vest. "Put it all on, including the tie."

He scowled, but he didn't protest, though I had to adjust the vest, unfastening the bottom button to show off his belt. Max fumbled at the tie until I took over, remembering with a knot in my throat how I used to do this for Eli, too. When Max shrugged into the jacket, the transformation amazed me.

"You're staring. Is it that bad?" Whirling, he studied himself in the mirror. "Holy shit."

"You look like you're about to have your picture shot for a men's magazine." No question, he had the lean build they preferred.

"I'd rather someone actually shot me." But as Max's dark gaze met mine in the mirror, a tiny smile curved his mouth. "Thanks. I want to look nice today. Prove everybody wrong."

"Both the blazer and vest are on sale," the salesman said. "The tie isn't."

"We'll take all three. Can you cut the tags off before he comes up with a reason why not? He'll wear the clothes out."

Max grumbled as he followed me to the register. While the guy rang things up, I sent him off on a fool's errand to look at handkerchiefs so I could ninja-pay. By the time he got back, I was already signing the receipt. His brows shot up.

"What the hell, Kaufman."

"There's no time to argue. The service starts in ten minutes."

As expected, that motivated him; he rushed out of the shop and was starting the bike by the time I hopped on behind him. Wrapping my arms about his waist, I settled in, leaning my cheek against his back. Though I'd never admit it, this was the best part of the trip. I loved holding on to him, his stomach hot and taut beneath my curled fingers. Just out of the shower, Max smelled soapy clean, overlaid by the new smell of his jacket.

The funeral home was only five minutes away, and he parked close to the building. I suspected I hadn't heard the last of this impulse-shopping spree, but Max had the sense to defer it. We slipped into the chapel as the minister walked slowly toward the podium at the front, pressing hands and smiling at familiar faces. I sat down in the back, expecting Max would join his family up front. Instead he nudged me to move over, granting him the chair on the aisle.

I wasn't sure what I expected, but the ceremony was sedate. The minister gave a touching talk about meeting in the next life; there were three musical interludes and a very old man went to the microphone on a walker to talk about Max's granddad. A few people sniffled but nobody cried. That seemed like the watermark of how nice you were in life. If people seemed okay with your passing, then you probably had some karmic restitution coming. Well, provided that the Hindus were right about reincarnation. *Eli was a good guy. He might be somebody's beloved new baby by now.* How I wished I believed that. Certainty would be comforting.

While I was thinking about how awesome it would be to come back as a house cat, the service ended. Everyone filed up to say farewell, but I hung back. Max nodded, probably not understanding my hesitance, but he was good at picking up cues. Michael was one of the first through the line, and I smiled when he rolled toward me.

"Hey. Sorry about last night. I was really rude."

"You and Max have some stuff to work out. I get it."

"We do. But you and I don't." Okay, I *definitely* wasn't imagining the flirty grin; I'd watched Max unleash it to devastating effect all through college. "You said you're not his girlfriend, right?"

"We're roommates, actually. You should come visit sometime." After I said it, I realized we were on the second floor, and Michael seemed fiercely independent.

"Are you from Michigan originally?"

"Chicago. It was quite a culture shock. I didn't even drive when I graduated." The L took me everywhere I wanted to go since I had no reason to venture into the 'burbs.

"And that was when?"

"Are you seriously asking how old I am?" Reluctant amusement sparked a smile, one that Michael returned with interest.

"I'm curious. Sue me."

"Twenty-one. If things go well, I'll graduate this year."

"Yet you don't sound excited."

"Eh, I'm a business major. It's not the employer catnip that it used to be, so I'm not looking forward to working at Starbucks. And, wow, you're good at this."

"What?" He opened his eyes, innocent, but I wasn't buying it.

"Charming information out of people."

"You think I'm charming?"

Max joined us in time to hear the question. "Are you hitting on my brother again?"

Smart not to call him "little." You're learning.

"I'm just laying the groundwork, so he'll remember me fondly when he's legal and I'm the antisocial cat lady living in your basement."

Michael answered before Max could. "I think you're shooting too low. You could totally swing ground-floor accommodations if you lean in."

Since I only knew about that book because of a sitcom and Google, I had to give him a fist bump for that one. "I'll try not to let you down."

"You want to ride with me to the cemetery? Dad's going with Uncle Lou." The offer included both of us, so I glanced at Max.

Ah, the mysterious uncle I didn't meet last night.

"Yeah. If you're sure it's okay." The hesitation in Max's tone broke my heart because I knew exactly how long he rolled around last night, memories chewing him up from the inside.

"I'd rather not go alone." Michael spun around and headed for the exit.

Up front, the casket was being removed out the side door, but we didn't stick around to watch it happen. Michael opened the rear doors and unfolded the ramp, then wheeled up to the driver's seat. Max and I hopped in, then pulled it up after us and closed up. I sat in back, leaving the front to the brothers. They talked quietly during the ride, and I tried not to eavesdrop.

Max, you should tell him.

The drive took almost forty minutes, and I texted with Nadia most of that time.

So Angus tells me you ran off with Max.

Yeah, we figured we'd get our first trial marriage out of the way early.

You realize I'm completely helpless without emoticons. You might be in Vegas right now!

I'll explain later. Everything's okay.

She texted me three more times but I ignored those. Max finally glanced over his shoulder. "Who's beeping you so hard, Kaufman?"

"Some things are just too private to share," I teased.

"Are you sexting?" He lunged for my phone.

To keep the joke going longer, I shoved it down the front of my dress and smirked at him, brows up. "How bad do you want to know?"

For two heartbeats, he considered going in. But then he mumbled something unintelligible and turned around.

Michael checked the rearview as I fished my cell out of my cleavage, then offered, "I could find out for you, bro."

Before things could get weird, I said, "I'm not sexting, it's Nadia. She just wanted to know what's going on with us."

"Ah. Tell her I said hey."

"Who's Nadia?" Michael asked.

I told him about her, along with Angus, a rambling mono-logue punctuated by occasional remarks from Max. By the time I finished, the convoy reached the cemetery, well out-side the city limits. The trees were probably gorgeous in fall, but it was pretty in late summer, too, green and well-kept. But it was hard to follow Max up the path, harder to see Michael struggle and know it would only piss him off if I offered to help. From this distance, I could see the tent, the coffin on burial scaffolding, a hole in the ground, the folding chairs set up on outdoor carpeting. They'd moved all the flowers from the funeral home, arrayed them around the coffin, so the breeze hit me in the face with the scent of sweet decay.

We were among the last to arrive, and this time Michael hung back with us. The funerary rites were mercifully brief; since the weather was muggy, hot and overcast, I'd have hated standing there for an hour. The wind died down, hinting at the prospect of a storm after nightfall. Maybe it would clear the air. One way or another we could use it.

They lowered the coffin and Carol tossed a flower into the grave. As people started to leave, I shifted, wondering if I should suggest…something. But really, Max needed to take the reins and sort out his family business without my intervention. So I kept quiet.

"What're you doing now?" he asked his brother.

"There's a potluck at the house," Michael said. "If you want to come."

His first reaction came in the form of leaping pleasure shining in his dark eyes, quickly dulled to uncertainty. "I don't know if—"

"It's not at Pop's, if that's what you're worried about. I've been living with Uncle Lou for the past four years." Though his tone was offhand, I sensed there was a boatload of a story behind that decision.

"Four years…" Max wore a stunned expression, so much that I put my hand on his arm, steadying him. "All this time, I thought I couldn't talk to you, see you. Not even to apologize."

"What?" Michael stared at him, equally flummoxed.

Tell him, I ordered with my eyes. In their shoes, I would've had this talk last night, but no, they only blabbed about the bike, apparently. This offer felt akin to falling on a grenade—I disliked their dad that much—but they needed some privacy.

"I'll get a ride with your uncle," I said. "Catch you later, Max."

Before he could argue, I hurried across the grass toward Mr. Cooper's retreating back. The man beside him must be Uncle Lou; he was both shorter and wider. I caught up with them, out of breath, and nearly tripped over a headstone. Uncle Lou had a kind, jowly face with deep-set eyes with pouches under them. His nose was bulbous, but I could practically taste the kindness in him. He was also older than I'd

THE SHAPE OF MY HEART

expected, probably Max and Michael's great-uncle. Which made the deceased granddad his brother.

"Can I beg a lift? Max and Michael need some time."

"Of course, sweetheart." Normally it pissed me off when men immediately defaulted to endearments; with Uncle Lou I didn't mind. I'd probably even eat a butterscotch if he fished one out of his pocket.

"You go to school with Maxie, do you?"

If anybody heard that nickname when he was a kid, ten to one they called him Maxipad.

I was basically ignoring Mr. Cooper at this point, and he seemed to be returning the favor, walking a bit ahead. So I yielded to the urge to brag about Max. "Yeah. He's doing really well in engineering, works part-time at a garage on weekends. It's amazing what he's achieved completely on his own."

Mr. Cooper's shoulders squared. *Yeah, I* hope *you're listening, asshole. Suck on that.*

"I'm so proud of him. Carol tells us what he emails to her, but he has the idea nobody in the family wants to hear from him because of what happened to Mickey. And the nonsense Charlie spouted right after the accident, of course." Uncle Lou sighed. "But I'm sure you know how stubborn Maxie can be. He gets an idea lodged in his head and nothing short of an earthquake can shake it out."

"He still blames himself," I ventured quietly.

"None of *us* do. I slammed into a parked car once because I dropped a sandwich. Now, that's stupid. I can only imagine how I'd feel if somebody got hurt."

Mr. Cooper picked up the pace, probably trying to get out of earshot. I watched him go, wondering how he lived with himself. He'd kicked one son out and then couldn't look after Michael after he got out of the hospital, just went on drinking like it was his reason for living. The whole situation made me angrier than I could recall being in my whole life.

Uncle Lou studied my face with the air of an adorable, aging basset hound. "It's a mess, no two ways around it. But I hope we can clear up the misunderstanding while Maxie's here."

"I hope so, too." We were nearly to the car when I gave up and asked the nosiest question of my life. "What, exactly, did Max's dad say that night at the hospital? I know Max left home right after, but—"

"Honey, I think you already know this, but…that story should come from Max. And it'd do him good to get it off his chest. When he's ready, he'll tell you himself."

Maybe, I thought.

And the prospect blazed through me in a shower of joy.

CHAPTER SEVEN

Uncle Lou drove a white vintage Cadillac. By its size, it probably dated from the '70s and got terrible gas mileage, but it was smooth riding in the back. Max's dad didn't say a word to either one of us on the way to the house, which made me wonder if he'd honestly hated me on sight, or if it was the old conflict with Max coloring his impression. People didn't always like me, obviously, but they seldom reacted with such immediate and virulent antipathy.

It took forty-five minutes to get to Uncle Lou's house, which was in Coventry, not Providence. When he turned into the driveway I realized we were there, though the line of cars should've clued me in. A white bungalow with detached garage proved to be our final destination; there was even a picket fence and a big deck out front with a ramp leading up. Neighbors and well-wishers were waiting when we got out of the car and strangers hugged me without asking how I knew the deceased. A kind-faced woman pressed

a plate of food into my hands, and I took it reflexively, bewildered.

I had some kind of fritters, a Jell-O-and-whipped-cream
salad, cold cuts, a helping of casserole that I couldn't identify.
This was the random assortment of food people showed up
with after a family death, hoping to make life easier for the
survivors. Shrugging, I ate the fried thing and settled in a
glider chair on the deck. I'd never been to a funeral after-
party before, which was what this felt like. When Eli died, I
barely held it together through the services and then I went
to bed and slept for two days. I missed nearly three weeks
of school my senior year.

Half an hour later, Carol sat down beside me. "Did you
lose track of Max?"

"He's with Michael, hopefully resolving their issues."

"Men," she said.

"Eh." I wasn't fond of generalizations. "I know plenty
of women who have a hard time articulating their feelings, too."

Too late I remembered that was how women bonded, by
being condescending about men. But I'd never participated
in that tradition. People of both genders had equal opportunity to be idiots as well as emotionally evolved. I ignored the
awkward pause in conversation, eating a bite of fruit salad.
Carol stirred, as if she might get up, but then Mr. Cooper
stumbled out of the house. From the smell, I could tell he'd
fallen off the wagon.

"Where the fuck is that bastard?" He could only be talking about Max, who wasn't there yet, thank God. "It's not
enough he crippled my Mickey, now he's—"

His brother, Jim, clapped a hand over his mouth, drag-

THE SHAPE OF MY HEART

ging him back inside. The rest of the guests swapped nervous glances, as if they were thinking about bailing, but ten minutes passed, then Jim came out of the house alone. Relief pressed a sigh out of me, and tension drained from my spine.

"Sorry, folks. It's been a rough day for Charlie."

Everyone nodded, pretending to accept the excuse, but whispers about Mr. Cooper didn't abate. *Poor Max. His dad really is an asshole.* But the rest of the family seemed okay.

Before much longer, Michael parked his Scion in front of the house, as the driveway was full. Max pulled up a minute behind; that was kind of a relief. There was no question that I was an interloper here, and the longer I sat, the weirder I felt. Plus, it was fucking hot. Sweat trickled down the small of my back when I stood up to meet him.

"You okay?" he asked, jogging up the ramp toward me.

"Yeah. You?" I noticed he'd discarded his blazer and vest, probably stowed in the bike's top box, and his tie hung loose, tempting me to tug on it. If we were dating, I'd use it to haul him in for a kiss.

"It's funny. For years I figured he hated me, blamed me for everything and that he wouldn't believe me if I explained why I couldn't be around. But in the end...he wasn't even too surprised."

"I'm guessing he knows your dad."

Max glanced around. "Where is he?"

"Drinking again. Your Uncle Jim put him to bed earlier. I think." Before I could reconsider the meddling impulse, I shared what Uncle Lou had said.

He stumbled back, his hand on the railing. "Are you serious?"

I nodded. "With one exception, your family misses you, dude."

On closer inspection, I saw that he was actually trembling. I put down my plate as Max took my hand and led me around back. It was much cooler, more wooded, less landscaping, but there was an old swing suspended on a weathered frame. He led over me to it and sort of collapsed. Max leaned forward, his face in his hands. I rubbed his sweaty back, not really understanding this reaction.

When he spoke, his words were muffled. "This is nothing like I pictured. I thought I'd have to fight everyone— that it would be all anger and blame. I was...I was braced for that, you know? I'm *used* to fighting. But Uncle Jim and Aunt Carol, Uncle Lou... They're so nice. And sad, too. Hurt, even. Because of me. Because I let my crazy-ass dad speak for everyone. Because I listened to him and cut ties without a second thought."

"You were pretty young," I said. "I think it's enough you had the courage to come back. And I admire the hell out of you for making it right with Michael. You've been on your own since you were sixteen. I mean, damn. Instead of dropping out, you graduated. Somehow. I've always wondered *how*, man."

Max straightened, but not enough to make me think he wanted me to stop, so I circled my palm up and down his back. His lashes fluttered, suggesting he liked it. "Technically, I did drop out. I raced off on the bike, ended up in a shitty no-questions-asked motel in Scranton. I worked fast food, barely squeaking by."

"Your family didn't call?" Okay, maybe they were all assholes.

THE SHAPE OF MY HEART

"I couldn't afford a cell phone."

"Email?"

"I didn't check much since I had to go to the library to use the computer, and when I did, I deleted them unread."

"But...*why*?" He could've resolved this much sooner.

"I was afraid they were trying to tell me Mickey didn't make it. Chickenshit, I know, but...it was like, if I didn't read it, then it couldn't be true. I know now, once he started getting better they got busy managing his recovery and figuring out where he'd live...because he finally told everyone else how bad it was with Pop."

"You never said anything?"

Max shook his head. "It was... I shielded Mickey from him... That was my mandate. Hell if I know why I didn't just tell Uncle Jim. But I guess, back then, I was...ashamed, like it was because of me. So I had to hide the evidence."

"What do you mean?"

"If I was better, my old man wouldn't act like that."

"You know that's not true."

"I was a dumb kid. When I think back to when my mother was alive, he wasn't that way. But I was so young, I don't remember much about her."

Working my palm up his spine, I cupped my hand around his neck, massaging the tense cords until he let out a pleased sigh. "What was she like?"

"Like I said, I was five when she died. But she spoke with an accent, and..." He paused like he was sorting his memories. "I loved watching her cook. She'd set me up in the kitchen with wooden spoons and two or three pots to bang on. Never yelled no matter how much noise I made. And... she smelled like jasmine."

Max tipped his head back, and I took the invitation, lifting the shaggy black hair to sink my fingers into it, rubbing the base of his skull in slow, gentle circles. "How come your family never tried to find you?"

"Michael said they didn't mean to lose track of me, it just happened. They figured I'd blow off some steam, come home in a few weeks. But I was too stubborn. I didn't set foot in Rhode Island until I was old enough to take the GED."

"After so much shit, you still got into college. From where I'm sitting, that's incredible. Your whole life is a colossal in-your-face to your dad."

"Not so much. The first year after I left was…rocky. I drank a lot, flirted with various addictions. Fucked any woman who'd take me home and got into pointless fights. A guy nearly stabbed me in an alley before I realized dying in the gutter wasn't how I wanted to go out."

"You turned it around, though. And your family's proud. Why wouldn't they be?" After Eli died, I got full-on hooked on prescription meds; I loved the numbness. But I didn't pull out of the spiral on my own. My mother sent me to rehab the summer after I graduated.

"I thought they agreed with him," he said quietly. "That I've always been a worthless fuckup and always will be."

"Is that what he said at the hospital?" I held my breath, wondering if he'd tell me about the most traumatic night of his life.

"I can still quote him, you know? I was sitting in the waiting room, covered in blood and powdered glass, while they worked on Mickey, afraid to hope, afraid to pray. My dad burst in and I thought, *Thank God. It'll be okay now.*

But he yanked me out of the chair and hit me so hard, I bit through my lip."

Reflexively my hand clenched in his hair, but I relaxed my fingers to avoid hurting him. On a deep, steadying breath, I resumed stroking, meant to soothe him, though it had the same effect on me. His dark hair felt like damp satin on my palm and he smelled vaguely of the shampoo we'd used earlier. There was nothing I could say, so I leaned closer, letting him know I was there whether he wanted to keep talking or not.

A few seconds later, he went on. "He said, 'I wish to God you'd never been born. What a worthless shit you turned out to be. This is why I've tried so hard to pound the ass-hole out of you, but you are fucking *un*-save-able.' Then he shoved me up against the wall and threatened to crack my skull with a beer bottle."

"Holy shit. Your dad's *insane*."

Max turned with haunted eyes, shifting so I had to move my hand or drop it entirely. I chose not to relinquish contact, sensing that he needed it. I left my hand on his jaw, the uneven scruff teasing my palm. Though I might be wrong, I didn't think he'd ever told this story before. He wore a shell-shocked expression, as if the memories were more powerful than he'd expected.

"The worst part is, I didn't even leave then. I should have. But I went all sad puppy. 'How can you…? You're my dad, you're supposed to love me.'" His mouth tightened, reveal-ing how he felt about the pathetic nature of the question.

"What did he say?" It couldn't be good.

"'It's not hard to work out, you dumb shit. If I don't love

you, it's because you're unlovable. Now get out of here. If I see you again, I will fucking end you.'"

"You took off that night." Now that I had the whole story, I understood why.

The family could only cope with one emergency at a time. While everyone sat by Michael's hospital bed, Max got farther away. And the longer the silence lasted, the more convinced he became that everyone hated him. Until Carol sent a wedding announcement email. Did I think somebody should've been on Max's side, searching tirelessly to find him? Absolutely. But sometimes the world was a cold, horrible place, and people slipped through the cracks. That didn't make it right.

"Yeah. You're really quiet. It's kind of freaking me out, I don't want this to change us. I've never laid it out completely before, and—"

"I know, you say you don't get along with your family and leave it at that. Thanks for trusting me. And no, it doesn't make a difference. You're my best friend…and I'm always on your side, Max. You can count on me for *anything*, you know that, right?"

His dark eyes shone, brightening with tears. They didn't fall; he backed away from that emotional precipice, though his smile remained soft and sweet. "I do, actually. That's why I asked you to come."

"That means a lot to me." I hugged him then, wrapping my arms around his waist.

He settled me against his chest, resting his chin on my hair. It was beyond me how anyone could call him unlovable. He radiated warmth. Yeah, the packaging was a little rough, and he didn't speak with an upscale accent, but Max hid only goodness at the heart of him. Some guys talked shit about their hookups, but I'd never heard Max comparing notes or denigrating a girl for sleeping with him.

"You got the room for three nights, right?"

"Yeah, why?"

"I was wondering if you'd mind hanging out with Michael tomorrow. We'll take off the day after."

"Not at all. I was hoping you'd get some family time."

"I didn't think it was likely," he admitted. "But Michael isn't mad. Well, he *is*, but not about the accident. He just didn't get why I vanished."

"Did you tell him everything?"

He shook his head. "Kid has enough on his plate without hating Pop as much as I do."

"So what're you guys doing tomorrow?" I figured I'd walk downtown and check out the shopping in Providence, maybe see a movie.

"You aren't coming?" He actually sounded disappointed.

"It seems like I'd be in the way. I mean, I'm not family."

Max sat back and planted his hands on my shoulders. The suddenness of the motion jolted the swing, so the chains creaked. I tumbled backward, feet coming off the ground. I didn't fight when he shifted, pulling me against his side. In slow, steady movements, he pushed off with his feet. Green shadows played across my bare legs, highlighting the pallor.

"You are," he said.

"What?"

"Family. Maybe that sounds strange. I'm not looking forward to graduation. I mean, shit, we're already splitting up. Nadia's living downstairs, and Kia might be moving in. It'll suck when I can't see you guys every day."

Mostly I didn't think about the future. I had acquaintances in the business program who had five-year and ten-year life plans. But for me, the idea of what came after college—it was all a big blur. I couldn't picture myself doing anything in particular. For a long time, I had been going through the motions, pretending I had goals, when I just missed Eli and didn't take medication that would make it stop.

You have to let me go, Eli said. *You can't be happy unless you do.*

But if I let you go, you're gone.

I've been gone for years, baby.

"Where do you go when you do that?" Max asked unexpectedly.

"Huh?"

"Sometimes in the middle of a conversation, you check out. Not here, not listening, not with me anymore."

This confession would make him think I was crazy. "Talking to my dead boyfriend."

Max's eyes widened and he glanced around his uncle's backyard as if he expected some *Medium* scenario to play out. Ruefully I smiled and shook my head, tapping my temple. "In here. We knew each other so well—and for so long—that I hear his commentary on stuff and sometimes I answer. It's weird, I know. I didn't realize anyone could tell, though."

"Trust me, I know when you're paying attention to me. And that's not the strangest habit I've encountered. When I was in Scranton, I met a guy who had a bird living in his pocket."

I shuddered. "That sounds horrible for everyone involved."

"I know, right? Anyway, the question stands. Will you come out with Michael and me?" His hand found the nape of my neck and he returned the favor, massaging until I nearly melted onto his lap.

Truthfully, he was turning me on somewhat, but I'd learned to ignore the little sparks between us. This friendship was too perfect to be complicated with sex, and making out with Max forced me to acknowledge that one night wouldn't satisfy me. Plus, he went for pretty girls—Lauren, for example—and I'd heard all about his crush from Nadia. I couldn't afford to become sexually obsessed with someone who thought of me as *family*.

We're better as friends.

"Sure. It makes sense to let him show me around. Local knowledge and all."

"Hey, I grew up here, too. I can line up some attractions that will rock your world."

I couldn't resist teasing him a bit, offering up a devilish smirk. "So that's one of your life goals? Rocking my world?"

"Better me than my brother," he muttered.

"Seriously, you don't have to worry about that." I paused just long enough for him to relax before I added, "Now. In two or three years…"

"You are not right, Kaufman. I still think of him as a goony kid."

"Better not let him hear you say that. You'll have another fight on your hands." In a casual motion, I hopped down from the swing, needing to get his hand off me. For some reason, the tingles were stronger than usual.

"Going somewhere?"

"We're finding something to eat, then you're hanging out with your family. That's why we're here, after all."

Not to make me feel things. And damn, I wish it would stop.

It can't, Eli said. *Sooner or later, you'll love somebody else. Or else you might as well have died with me.*

I wish I had. Normally, the bitterness didn't escape unless I'd been drinking. So I stuffed it back where it belonged, crouched in the back of my head like an angry tiger.

Don't say that, C. Where would this guy be without you?

I had no answer for that, but as I walked through the backyard, the longish grass tickling my bare legs, it felt like falling.

CHAPTER EIGHT

We didn't get back to Providence until nearly midnight.

I was heartily sick of this black dress—to the point that I might burn it instead of washing it when we got back. Tiredly I trudged up the stairs and keyed the code so we could finally sleep. *Damn, it's been a long day.* But the payoff had been worthwhile; Max's family had made it clear he wasn't persona non grata to anyone but Charlie, and it was apparent to me that nobody gave two shits about his opinion.

"I'm dying for a shower," Max groaned.

He dumped the bag containing his blazer and vest on the bed, and I sighed, hanging up his crumpled clothing. Not because I expected him to wear it again, but disorder bothered me. Various shrinks had communicated that I exerted this control over my environment because I hated feeling helpless. I didn't think it required an advanced degree to work that out.

"You can have the bathroom first."

Shooting me a grateful look, he went in and shut the door behind him. I didn't want to put on my relatively clean pj's while I was all sticky, though, so I wandered into the other room to watch TV. It occurred to me then that I hadn't checked messages all day. Normally I didn't make a move without my phone in hand. Braced for the worst, I turned my cell on. As expected, I had, like, five texts from my mother. She was more than Overly Attached Mom; I'd given her reasons to worry about my mental state over the years, and she was protective even before I'd lost it. For peace of mind, she preferred regular check-ins, and I hadn't been doing that since we left Michigan.

Where are you?

I haven't heard from you at all today.

What are you doing?

Are you using again? My mother prided herself on digging up the right terminology.

If you don't call me tonight, I'll have to tell your father.

Sighing, I glanced at the time. Technically, it was still tonight for a few more minutes. If I knew her, she was reading in bed, staring at her phone, after letting my dad go to sleep undisturbed. In my experience, Ma worried enough for the both of them.

I called her. "Hey, it's me."

"What in the world are you doing that you can't make time to call your mother?"

"My friend's grandfather died. I'm wearing a black dress and everything. We went to the funeral today. It wouldn't be respectful to text in the middle of the service, Ma."

"I wasn't born yesterday. That wouldn't last until almost midnight."

"We spent time with the family afterward. There was a potluck. Do you want me to text you a picture of me in this dress?" It wasn't like I didn't appreciate her concern, but sometimes it could be tedious. "I can also send you a link to the obituary. Scan a copy of the—"

"Stop teasing me. I was worried. You shouldn't be this hard to reach when classes aren't even in session."

"I know. Sorry about that. There's just been a lot going on this week. Things will settle down soon and I'll get back to my usual schedule."

"Okay. Be careful. We love you."

That got me off the hook with my parents, but before I could decide what to watch, Max stepped out of the bathroom, steam billowing behind him. The room immediately heated up, despite the air-conditioning, because he only had a towel wrapped around his waist. He seemed fine wandering around, giving me peekaboo glimpses as he prowled the bedroom. I counted his tattoos surreptitiously, coming up with four, unless the towel hid some body art. The black ink I'd noticed curving around his rib cage proved to be a black spiral symbol that looked vaguely familiar, but I couldn't place it.

"Checking out the art?" Max asked.

Startled, I jerked my head up. "Yeah. What is that?"

He came toward me, and I wished he would put on boxers and sweats, but if I said anything, he'd tease the shit out of me. My heart thumped away as he got closer, close enough for me to smell the clean scent of skin, freshly washed with castile soap. Max perched beside me on the love seat, apparently unconcerned by how his towel gapped at the thigh. A drop of water trailed down his chest and I watched it until it dripped onto the white terry cloth over his lap.

"It's a variation on the symbol for Leo."

"The zodiac sign? But your birthday's in November."

"My mom was born on August 1. This was the first tattoo I ever got." He touched the ink over his rib cage; it was all I could do not to do the same. "It's supposed to stand for courage and to remind me of her."

"That's sweet. What about the others?"

"This is just a cuff… I liked the pattern." Max flexed his arm, and the braid expanded in reaction. Then he shifted, presenting his back, along with the only colorful ink on his body. "This is obviously a Chinese dragon. It's supposed to represent power and good fortune to the worthy, so I guess you could say it's aspirational. The last is an old symbol for strength." He indicated a black symbol on his arm that resembled a tree, only more stylized.

"I like the dragon especially. The red-and-black is gorgeous." *On your skin*, I added silently. "You've never shown them to me before."

He leveled a long look on me, one that confused me as much as it tempted me to touch. "Yeah, well. I usually save the unveiling for a special occasion."

"Huh?"

"The first time I sleep with someone. Then she traces all my ink and I lay back, pretending she's the only one who ever thought to do it."

"That sounds depressing."

"It is, a little. I have personal reasons for getting them, but they're not a fetish or a separate erogenous zone."

I was torn between the urge to learn more about what

drove Max nuts in bed and the conviction that was a terrible idea. Yet I couldn't bring myself to leave yet. He was close enough that I felt the heat of his thigh against mine.

My breath quickened. "Are you planning to tell me what gets you hot? While you're nearly naked, I might add. Are you sure that's a good idea?"

"True. I might embarrass myself. You'd never let me live it down."

Smiling, I stood up. "I'll shower, you can put pants on. Then, if you still want to talk about your hot zones—"

"We'll put a pin in it. But I was wondering..."

"What?"

"Do you have any ink?"

"Just one." I pulled my bodice down just enough to show him the small red heart—tattooed over my actual blood-pumping one—with *Eli* written inside it. Since I didn't wear low-cut tops as a rule, very few people had seen it.

Max froze, then he lifted his chin, his dark gaze locking on my face. His eyes blazed with something I couldn't even identify, fiercer than desire, stronger than longing. Flutters quivered to life in my stomach, but I couldn't possibly be reading this right.

His lips parted, and it took three tries before he could speak. He cleared this throat, finally getting the words out. "You should shower."

Nodding, I practically ran to the bathroom, crazily aware of my pulse pounding in my throat, my ears, my wrists, and my pussy throbbed, too, echoing the excitement. *Dear God. I want to fuck Max.* If he was anyone else in the world, I would, if he was interested. But after Eli, I couldn't risk losing my best friend. Not again. Not when it had taken five years for me to get here…and stop feeling so alone.

I stood in the shower much longer than I needed to, conscious that I was using the same soap, the same shampoo, that my naked body was occupying the same space his had. Sighing, I banged my head lightly on the wall and let the water run down my cheeks like tears. Despite the pervasive ache in my throat, I didn't cry. I didn't masturbate either, though I was tempted.

Max had on a T-shirt and sweats when I came out of the bathroom. In my rush, I'd repeated his mistake, forgetting my clothes in the bedroom. He was lounging on the bed, fiddling with his phone, and he smirked when he spotted me barely covered in the towel.

"Close your eyes," I ordered.

To my relief, he didn't make a big thing of it, letting me dash out and snag my backpack. Then I retreated to dry off, slather on some lotion and put on clean underwear and the pajamas I'd been wearing since we left. I wondered what he made of that until I remembered he'd been wearing the same sweats at night, and that we often wandered the apartment at home in the same comfy clothes to prolong the stretches between runs to the laundry room.

God, this trip is making me mental. I ambled out of the bathroom and took a deep breath, then flung myself over Max, landing on the other side.

He laughed at my acrobatic entry and shifted over to make room for me on the bed. "Can't believe how late it is."

"What time is Michael picking us up?"

"Ten."

"Thank God. We can sleep in."

"You do that every damn day, entitled princess."

I rolled over and poked him in the side. "Are you jealous?"

"Of your sloth? Please."

I started massacring the Pussycat Dolls, making up lyrics as I went. "Don't cha wish you were unemployed like me, don't cha wish you could lay around like me——"

"Please don't ever sing again, seriously. I just died a little inside."

Laughing, I fell back onto my pillow and turned over. "Shut the light off."

"'Night, Kaufman."

"G'night."

I woke to the delicious smell of breakfast. Rolling out of bed, I stumbled into the other room to find Max setting the table with takeout. He'd brought back scrambled eggs, sweet rolls and juice, and I squelched the urge to hug him. Noticing me, he smiled and stepped into a slant of sunlight, all golden skin and liquid, dark eyes. I nearly retreated, except that would be weird enough to make him wonder what my deal was.

"You're *awesome*," I said.

"I might've heard that once or twice. Not usually for bringing breakfast."

"Yes, I get it. Women send thank-you notes for sex, you're the god of peen." Feigning a casual tone, I sat down and dug into my food.

"I might get that as my next tattoo."

I nodded. "You should put it right on your treasure trail. But make sure the lettering is classy. We wouldn't want to give anyone the wrong impression."

"You make a good point," he said with mock solemnity.

After breakfast, I got ready, pulling on leggings and an oversize T-shirt with a silver glittery skull emblazoned on it. One of these days I might grow out of this style, but part of me couldn't stand to think about it because this was how I'd dressed with Eli. My mother called it "arrested development," but I wasn't ready to say goodbye yet.

Soon, Eli whispered.

The word didn't even sound much like him anymore, more of an echo thrown back by a chasm, long after the original voice faded. Grabbing my purse, I went downstairs to look for Michael. He was just pulling up when I stepped onto the sidewalk, so I waved as he rolled down the window.

"You ready for the adventure of a lifetime?"

"Definitely. Do I get shotgun this time?"

"Fine by me. Big bro can ride in back."

Snickering, I ran around the Scion and hopped in. Max came out a few minutes later, looking vaguely disgruntled. "I go to the bathroom for two seconds and you vanish on me."

"It's a miracle you tracked me down."

Michael laughed. "Okay, the weather's nice enough that we can check out some parks if you feel outdoorsy."

I raised a brow as Max climbed in back. "Do I look like the sporty type to you?"

"Just trust me."

"Okay, but I have high expectations."

When I saw Roger Williams Park, I wasn't disappointed. It was incredibly picturesque with bridges over tiny streams, a carousel village, duck ponds and gazebos, along with beautiful landscaping. Though I wasn't a back-to-nature girl, I enjoyed walking around with Michael and Max, though I didn't say much. The sunlight felt good on my skin; it wasn't hot enough for me to sweat yet, which I suspected was why Michael had us out here in the morning.

By noon, however, I was thirsty and ready to move on. "What's next?"

"I thought I'd take you to Providence Place for lunch and shopping," Max answered.

"Just her?" Michael joked. "Also, how're you doing that? We're in *my* car. What if I have other plans?"

"Do you?" I asked.

"Nah, it's fine."

It took ten minutes or so to get back to the car and as long again driving from the park to the mall. This time I let Max have the front seat, mostly because I couldn't take the cuteness of him sulking in back while I bantered with his brother. They were a little tentative, a little awkward, but it warmed my shriveled heart to witness the progress. From the outside, you'd never guess they'd spent the past five years apart. Now and then, I caught Michael sneaking quick looks at Max, as if checking for his approval. Inside, he was still a goony kid who cared about his big brother's opinion. I had the urge to mess up their hair in one swooping move, but I sat on my hands to keep from distracting Michael as he parked.

"Joe's for lunch?" Michael suggested.

Max nodded. "Sounds good."

Joe's turned out to be an American restaurant, very manly, all gleaming oak and brass fittings. The guys ordered nachos to start and burgers for their main plates; I went with an iceberg lettuce wedge and the macaroni and cheese. If I knew Max, he'd trade me part of his burger for some of my mac. It was pretty much his favorite thing to eat.

"So what's your school situation?" I asked Michael.

"What do you mean?"

"Are you a junior?"

"Oh. Actually, I'm a senior. I've been homeschooled since the accident and I'm on target to graduate at seventeen."

"Damn. Smart *and* handsome."

Max kicked me under the table as the waitress brought our food. I jumped, more startled than hurt. "What? You're smart and handsome, too. Apparently it runs in the family."

"We get it from our mother," Michael said.

The nachos disappeared fast while they talked about Max's mechanical engineering program and Michael's interest in aeronautics. I crammed a chip in my mouth, wishing I was as excited about my future profession as these two seemed to be. But for me, the professional world seemed so nebulous that I had no idea what I'd end up doing—something I hated, probably. Eli and I used to talk about starting an indie music label, but that dream had died with him.

A few minutes after the busboy cleared the appetizer plates, the server delivered our meals. Before I could suggest a swap, Max cut his burger in half, still talking to his brother, and put part of it on my bread plate. Then he served himself some of my mac and salad while Michael stared, wearing an odd expression.

"What?" Max glanced between us.

"Are you sure you're not together? That's a very couple-y move."

"We live together," I reminded him. "So we're always sharing food."

"That's true. Never mind."

They went back to their conversation about the space program while we ate lunch, but I caught Max eyeing me with a strange expression now and then. I pretended I didn't notice because I had no idea what he was thinking or what I was supposed to do about it. In some respects it was a relief to pay the check and have the acceptable excuse of window-shopping to cover my awkwardness. *This is so strange. I've never, ever been uncomfortable with Max.* But Michael was making me really aware of how much Max and I took for granted, a closeness I hadn't even really processed consciously.

Providence Place was a fine mall with the usual high-end stores, but honestly, my mind wandered too much to concentrate on consumerism. To placate the guys I bought an antisocial slogan T-shirt at a Hot Topic wannabe store. Afterward, they looked at techy stuff and I wandered around admiring the architecture. Eventually Michael excused himself to use the restroom, so I sat down on a bench to wait.

"Didn't find anything you want?" Max asked.

"We have to cram it into my backpack and then the top box," I reminded him.

"Yeah, when you put it that way, light shopping seems like the way to go." He sat down beside me and rested his head on my shoulder. "I didn't expect it to turn out this way, but...this trip has been amazing."

"Yeah?" I reached over to pet his head, and his eyes closed.

His answer came so soft that I almost didn't catch it: "Things always are with you."

CHAPTER NINE

That night, it was hard to say goodbye to Michael, and I'd just met him. I gave him a hug, then went into the hotel to grant Max some privacy with his brother.

Waiting in the lobby, I sent my mother a text to reassure her that I wasn't doing anything stupid. I'd missed check-in by an hour, but she wasn't in a panic yet. Her rationale was this: if I had the presence of mind to send a text at the same time daily, then I must be okay. I didn't have the heart to tell her that there was probably an app with a timer that could obviate all of her micro-management.

Are you ready for school? She sent back.

Not even remotely, I thought.

But since she didn't even know I'd left Michigan, it seemed best to reply, Yep, all set. Love you. Talk to you tomorrow.

I was putting away my phone when Max came in. "You okay?"

He followed me up to our room without answering. Once we were inside, he lifted a shoulder in a half shrug. "Yes. No. Sort of? Not really."

"I'm glad you can answer so definitively." Then it occurred to me. "Do you want to stay longer? I can fly home, it's no big deal."

"That's incredibly cool of you…but I can't if I want to keep my job. Since I'd rather not go back to fast food, I need to get back, too."

"You want to, though."

"Yeah. But there's nothing stopping me from coming back. I won't even bug you for moral support next time."

"I didn't mind. We're taking off early tomorrow?"

"Six, if that works for you." I nodded, and he went on. "I was wondering if you'd mind if we pushed the whole way instead of breaking it up like before."

"Are you in a hurry?"

"I just want to get home." His mood struck me as odd tonight, but I couldn't put my finger on exactly how.

He was okay before I left them alone. Michael must've said something.

"Okay, what happened?"

"Nothing for you to worry about," he said.

That felt like a door being slammed in my face. So I pretended it didn't bother me as I went into the bathroom to get ready for bed. I didn't feel like sleeping with him tonight, though, so when he took his turn, I darted into the front room, switched on the TV and unfolded the pullout. Testing the mattress with a couple of bounces, I decided it wasn't bad. I'd just settled under the covers when Max finished up.

He came to the doorway. "You don't want the bed?"

"Nah. I'm fine."

"Is this because I didn't want to talk before?"

Damn, I hated how well he read me. I shrugged, wishing he'd go away. We needed some space anyway; this trip had confused all the ordinary boundaries.

"Don't ice me out, Kaufman."

Sighing, I rolled over to face him, quietly annoyed. "Isn't that what you just did to me?"

His face was serious as he perched on the edge of the sofa bed. "You want to know?"

"I wouldn't ask if I didn't."

"Okay, well. Michael asked me to come home. Uncle Lou has a spare room and I wouldn't have to work, I could just focus on school."

"Wow. That's an amazing offer." I could understand why he was so somber; it was a big decision, one that would affect his future in all kinds of ways.

And it'll ruin your life, Eli observed.

Max grabbed my wrist and tugged. "Come on. You won, I'm talking. Don't make me squeeze in beside you."

"You have a whole bed to yourself. Why would you?"

"Because you're not in it."

I feigned aggravation as I let him pull me up. "And what do you plan to do when we get home, genius?"

"Miss you," he said simply. Then he gave me his version of big anime eyes, so cute it should be illegal.

"You're ridiculous." I stomped into the other room and got into bed.

Max followed, shutting off lights as he went. The mattress dipped as he got in beside me. "So you now know. What do you think?"

"Oh, no. This is your decision."

"But you must have an opinion," he persisted.

In the dark he reached out unerringly to touch my cheek, turn my face toward him. The gentle touch did crazy things to my insides. If I kept feeling this way once we got home, I'd have to find reasons to stay away from him until my heart and hormones settled down.

"Honestly? I'm conflicted. Because it might be great for you here, definitely easier, and you can reconnect with your family. But I'd rather burn all my Docs than let you go. I'm…well, not exactly *ready* for us to split up next year, but resigned, I guess. Finding out you might leave sooner is like being kicked in the chest."

"My gut instinct is to say no, not now, not yet. I'm so close to graduation that transferring might not be worth what I'd save on housing, especially if I lose credits."

"I like your gut," I whispered.

"Come here." I didn't move, so Max scooted over until he could spoon me. His arm dropped over my waist and he rested his chin on top of my head. "This okay?"

"You're already doing it," I mumbled.

"I'll stop if you hate it. I'm just trying to make it up to you."

"What?"

"Making you feel shitty. Michael shocked me so much, I kind of flashed back to when I had to figure everything out alone…because there wasn't anyone to listen."

"You have tons of friends now, dude. I'm not special."

"That's completely untrue." His breath stirred my hair. "I knew you were cool the first time I saw you…and I wasn't wrong."

"Wasn't that…" I trailed off, trying to remember.

We didn't meet in class. It was the summer after our freshman year. I was already calling myself a sophomore; I recalled that much.

"We met for the first time at Scott's party. I went with Angus, you were with Amy. You thought I was gay and high-fived me."

Covering my mouth, I laughed into my hand. "Oh, shit, I remember now."

"But that wasn't the first time I *saw* you."

"Really?" He'd never mentioned this before.

"Yeah. The party was in July, but I was on campus in June, first summer session. And you were napping in the quad with your earbuds in. Your hair was streaked turquoise and blue then. And you didn't have the brow ring yet."

"Wow. I've definitely done that before, but y'know, sorry I didn't see you. Being asleep and all. But I can't believe you remember that."

"You made an impression. Had no idea we'd end up so tight, though."

I was thinking about how to reply to that when I fell asleep. In the morning, I woke to find we'd shifted in the night, my right arm and leg flung over Max in a possessive gesture. The emotional vulnerability of reaching out in my sleep sent me rolling out of bed and I couldn't get dressed fast enough. In fact, I packed my bag and got breakfast before he stirred. Since it was so early, it was just sweet rolls and coffee from a bakery down the street.

"This is fantastic." He ate as he got dressed, strewing crumbs everywhere.

Glad I'm not cleaning up after us.

I brushed my teeth after eating and checked one last time to make sure I wasn't forgetting anything. Then I grabbed my backpack. We jogged downstairs to check out. Ten minutes later, we were zooming along on Max's bike. He hadn't mentioned if we'd be taking the trip fast or slow, but I didn't know if my ass could take twelve hours on a motorcycle. But the question was answered when he took the trip in stages, letting us off to walking around every two to three hours. And we pulled off the interstate at the same motel we'd stopped at before.

"You tired?" he asked as I stumbled climbing off for the last time that day.

"Physically, yeah. Mentally, not at all."

"We could go see a movie once we check in. If you want."

"Sure. It's not that late. And I can take fifteen minutes there and back, or however far we are from town."

"Let's drop our stuff off first."

"Sounds good."

Max handled check-in while I searched for our location on my phone. As it turned out, the nearest cinema was eight miles away, no problem at all. This time we weren't around back, so we walked to the room from the office, backpacks over our shoulders. I read off the film choices as Max opened the door.

"The last one… The demon whatever."

"Horror it is." I checked the times. "There's one starting in half an hour. I think we can make it if we take off now."

Unlike last time, the room only had a queen bed. Part of me wondered if he'd done that on purpose, as there wasn't even a couch. If we didn't share tonight, someone would be on the floor. And in a place like this, I wouldn't wish that on my worst enemy.

"Bathroom?" he suggested.

"Yeah, that's a good idea."

I dodged in, used the facilities and then did what I could with my hair. Fortunately it perked right up with a little water, going from helmet-smashed to spiky with some judicious fiddling. I washed my face and put on lip gloss without letting myself wonder why. *This isn't a date. You've been living with him for six months and you've gone to the movies fifty times.* Max bounced up and headed for the door as I stepped out. He didn't comment on how I looked, but then, he never did, so it would be weird if he started now.

Before I got on the bike, I mapped our route and memorized it, just as I had from the diner in Providence. "Okay, let's go. I'll navigate."

With Max driving, we got there five minutes before the show started. The Cineplex sat off to the side in a mall parking lot but it was a huge free-standing structure with neon lights outside. Marquee lighting framed the movie posters, but since we knew what we wanted to see, Max strode up to the ticket window.

"Two, please."

Inside, I tried to give him some money but he grabbed my hands and shook them until I stopped offering. "Fine, but I'm getting the junk food. What sounds good?"

"Nachos."

"We had nachos yesterday."

"What's your point? I wasn't offering to share."

I grinned. "Good point."

At the counter I ordered vitamin water, nachos and pop-corn. *That should tide us over until dinner.*

The lobby had a few other couples ambling around, drop-ping food on the red carpet, but our theater was nearly empty, only four other people, so Max and I had our pick of seats. He blazed a trail to the second-to-last row and waited for me to precede him. It felt foreign and delicious to set-tle into the plush seat next to him. Surely we'd gone to the dollar house without Nadia and Angus, but at the moment I couldn't recall specific instances.

"I've heard this is terrible," he whispered.

"Then why are we watching it?"

"That's exactly why."

"Will you let me *MST3K* it?"

"Unless someone sits down nearby, obviously."

The movie started strong, but it went south around a quarter of the way in. I lost all sense of dread and paid more attention to Max shifting beside me than the events unfold-ing on-screen. He kept leaning over to whisper hilarious observations into my ear. It struck me then how much like this it had been with Eli. Never hard, never complicated, just sweet, beautiful and *right*. The realization startled me so much I dropped the popcorn. Max lunged for it at the same time I did and we cracked skulls so hard that I saw sparks.

"Oh, fuck. Are you all right?"

"Mildly concussed, maybe."

He cupped my face in hands, trying to see if I was bruised in this dim lighting. "I can't tell how bad it is. I'll get you some ice."

I put my hand on his arm to stop him. "It's fine. Let's finish the movie."

"Are you sure?"

"Yep. My head is incredibly hard. I could do trick videos where I break boards with it."

The producers probably didn't expect us to leave with our stomachs aching from laughter, but that was the situation when we staggered out an hour later. In the lobby I could tell Max had a contusion forming. I reached up, touching lightly with my fingertips.

"Does it hurt a bunch?"

"You can baby me when we get back."

I took that to mean *yes, Courtney, it hurts, your skull might as well be made of titanium.*

Feeling bad, I offered, "I'll give you a head rub, ice it down, whatever you want."

"Be careful," he teased. "I could ask for anything."

"I'd probably give it to you." The admission popped out before I could stop it.

Max regarded me steadily for a few seconds, and when he replied, he sounded unusually serious. "Then I'll make sure not to abuse my power."

We ate a quick dinner at a Chinese fast-food place nearby, then headed back to the motel. By this point it was dark, just the red taillights of cars ahead and the white beams of other vehicles zooming toward us in the opposite direction. I clung to Max, my arms tight about his waist. His back, God, I'd spent so much time pressed up against it this trip, and now I knew about the Chinese dragon. I could happily strip off his shirt and lick my way down his spine.

The trip had lasted long enough that we had a comfortable bedtime routine worked out now. While waiting for my shot in the bathroom, I filled the ice bucket at the machine at the end of the building. As soon as we were both ready for bed, I propped myself up against the headboard and beckoned to Max.

"One head rub, coming up. This is a limited-time offer, by the way."

"How do you want me?" The soft sweetness of the question sent a shiver straight through me, and I hid it from him like a cache of pills.

"You can lie sideways with your head in my lap or you can lean back against me, whichever looks more comfortable." Amazing I could sound so casual when my heart was beating so hard.

His answer came when he crawled between my legs and flipped around, resting his head on my chest. He was heavier in my arms than his lean build suggested, but I'd stashed enough pillows behind me. Max wriggled around a little, getting comfortable. When he stilled, I set my fingertips to his temples.

Haven't done this for a guy in forever. Haven't done this since... Eli.

Usually when I thought his name, he responded. But this time, there was only silence, broken by Max's breathing. As I widened the focus, massaging his whole head, he made the sexiest sound, somewhere between a groan and a rumble of pleasure. I pretended I didn't feel anything, no kindling heat, no desire to circle my hips. It was tough but I kept still. Just as well, because Max moved enough for both of us. He rubbed against my fingers, turning side to side, until my fingers cramped, and even then I kept rubbing.

"This is so good," he mumbled.

"I hate to make you move, but I have to pee."

"No problem." He rolled more than got up, seeming boneless, and flopped over on his stomach with a contented moan.

Okay, I had been so fucking good on this trip, but I was so done. As soon as I shut the door behind me, I pulled my leggings down and leaned back against the door. I was so fucking horny that this shouldn't take long. Touching two fingers to my slick labia, I couldn't completely strangle my gasp. The bed creaked outside, as if Max had shifted. *Did he hear me?* I was hot enough that I didn't care. *Listen, if you want.*

This position wasn't ideal, but there was no way I'd risk the tub or floor. So I had to make it work. I remembered his heat, his smell, the weight of him in my arms, and my excitement ratcheted up. All kinds of dirty fantasies spun in my head, incoherent images of Max and me, naked, straining together. I strummed my fingers against my clit, wishing for more pressure, more— I pictured his face and came, unable to muffle the whimpers completely.

Legs still shaky, I washed my hands four times, worried that the bathroom smelled of sex.

God, this is embarrassing. I hope he doesn't know. I should've made myself calm down, waited until we got home. It was only one more night.

But you want him, Eli said. *There's nothing wrong with that.*

There had been a couple of guys since he'd died, but nobody who mattered emotionally. Completely bewildered by the chaos in my head, I leaned against the mirror for a minute, as if an extreme close-up of my face could clear things up. When I ventured out, Max was asleep or pretending to be. Thankful for small mercies, I quietly crept into bed beside him. On the plus side, I was no longer crazily aware of his every movement and my mental state had caught up with physical exhaustion.

I was nearly dozing when he reached for me in his sleep, and with an ache in my throat, I let it happen. Just for tonight, I'd imagine this was where I was supposed to be.

CHAPTER TEN

Coming home was wonderful…and terrible.

The former because I had my own bed back and the latter because Max wasn't in it. But Kia was all moved in, which was a plus. She'd remembered what I said about my mild OCD and the room wasn't disorganized. It was strange seeing her furniture instead of Nadia's, all white and modern; her comforter was patterned in bright hues, reminiscent of paint splatters. Overall, Kia had great taste. I loved the abstract prints she'd hung up, both modern and aesthetically appealing. The room definitely needed the color since I leaned toward black and gray, monochrome all the way.

The first week, it was hard getting back to routine, but soon I was bumming rides to campus with Angus, just like always. People who lived closer went home between classes; I usually holed up in the library or napped in the sun in the quad. Some things didn't change. Late summer suited Mount Albion; the lush green foliage made the grounds seem stately and impressive. I wasn't paying much attention to the scenery, however, as I rushed from the coffee shop to the business building.

Since I was in a hurry, I nearly ran into someone coming up the steps. I mumbled, "Excuse me," and was ready to rush past when the girl put her hand on my arm.

"Courtney?"

Great.

I had zero desire ever to see Amy Fuller again. After I broke it off with her, she'd spread rumors about how I'd gotten her drunk and seduced her. That really hurt because I'd cared about her; I just wasn't up to the investment of time and energy that making her happy required. She'd needed constant reassurance about my level of interest and desire. Toward the end, nothing I did was enough; no words or gesture would've convinced her.

"How've you been?" The question was courtesy, nothing else. According to a surreptitious peek at my phone, I had four minutes to get to class.

"Oh, you know. Getting by."

"It was great to see you, but I have to go. Take care."

Before I could brush by, she said, "Wait?"

"I'm not dodging you, my class starts in three minutes."

"Okay, well, would you consider going for coffee with me afterward? I'll wait." A pleading look from her big blue eyes made me cave. "And I'll drive you home."

I'd always been susceptible to Amy, as she well knew. *Two minutes.* "Fine. Meet you back here."

At that point I had to run and I barely made it into my seat before the professor strode in. My mind was never 100 percent on these classes—luckily I was smart enough to make it up by reading the material on my own later—but today distraction kept showing me shiny things, making me doodle all over my notebook. As class ended, I realized I'd sketched out the Chinese dragon on Max's back. I only needed to shade it with a red marker for my obsession to be complete.

Sighing, I gathered my stuff. This was one of those big lecture halls, practically stadium seating, and I followed the rest of the students down from the back. Since it was the only class I had of this size, I didn't expect the professor to know my name, let alone call me over. It was only my third time in his class, the second week of school.

"Miss Kaufman, may I speak with you a moment?"

Nodding, I switched course, turning toward him. "Yes?"

"I've noticed you haven't done any internships, nothing outside coursework. I'm concerned that will hurt you later."

"Why?"

Professor Tompkins raised his brows at me. He was in his late fifties, fairly fit, with a bald spot he tried valiantly to cover with a devoted comb-over. Unless I missed my guess, he was a plastic surgery aficionado. There were telltale signs near his jaw and eyes. Since my mother loved having things nipped and tucked, I had practice picking up even on good work.

"I beg your pardon?"

"I'm just wondering at your interest. Did my academic advisor ask you to intervene?" Since I hadn't seen the woman since my sophomore year, I doubted it.

"No. I make it a habit to review every student I teach, even in classes this size."

"I give you a gold star for effort, but I'm good. Thanks."

With a cheery wave, I headed out, not waiting to hear how he'd reply.

Best guess—for reasons known only to him—he'd intended to offer to find me an internship in return for some game of naughty professor and undergrad, or maybe offer to mentor me, use me to grade his papers and monitor his classes in return for same. But I wasn't interested in the prize at the bottom of that box. As I hurried toward the front doors, I forgot Amy was waiting. So she startled me by falling into step.

I covered my surprise with a smile. *At least I don't have to call Angus. Or worse, take the bus.* Max would be working until six, at least, so he couldn't pick me until later, even if I begged. Not that I would. After the road trip, I needed to get my head right.

"The Pour House?" she asked.

I'd always thought that was a clever name for a coffee shop filled mostly with college students. The location was perfect, part of the small food court on campus, though unlike most of the food stands, it wasn't a chain. They had actual arm chairs, too, if you were lucky enough to snag one. I'd been known to buy juice and circle on cold or rainy days.

"Yeah. Do you want the usual?"

"I invited you, so I'm buying."

Since I didn't want to be here, arguing would only prolong the inevitable. Yet as she walked to the counter, I admired the curve of her legs, her ass and the swing of her shiny chestnut hair. Amy might be needy but she was also gorgeous, an empirical truth she found impossible to accept. It was late enough that I found us a table right away, not as cozy as a pair of padded chairs; that was better for conducting a conversation quickly. The public venue reassured me, too. If she got dramatic, I'd have witnesses about how it went down at least.

A few minutes later, she brought her skinny latte and my apple juice. "Thanks. So what did you want to talk about?"

"Us." She headed off my instinctive protest by raising a hand. "I know, that's over. But I need to apologize for the way I reacted when we broke up."

"It was pretty awful," I admitted.

And still is.

To this day, because I looked a certain way and Amy didn't, people dyke-coughed when I walked by. You'd think that mentality wouldn't survive college, but some people never outgrew the inner asshole. The last time it happened, Max nearly beat some guy into the ground and came pretty close to being arrested. I hunched my shoulders.

"It's not an excuse, but...I was so much more into you than you were me. No matter how hard I tried, you didn't let me all the way in, and it made me a little crazy." She gnawed her lip, obviously repentant. "Again, not a good enough reason. Plus, I had some things to figure out."

"I have no idea what you're talking about."

"The thing is, Courtney...I'm *not* bi-curious. I've had a couple of boyfriends, and it never felt right. I didn't even like sex until you... Until we—"

"Oh." I shifted, taking a sip of my drink to cover my astonishment. Unless I'd completely misread the subtext, she was coming out to me. *Why*, I had no idea.

"Don't look so worried. I'm not planning to make your life miserable. I'm with Elena now, and it's good." She paused, then added, "There's no wall between us."

Maybe she had a point there. In our relationship, I never really tried to love her because most of me didn't want to. The sex was fantastic, but after a while she'd picked up on how emotionally detached I was. For me, it was good orgasms and time spent hanging out while Amy was kind of falling in love. I hadn't meant to hurt her.

"I'm sorry if I made you think, if I implied—"

"You didn't. I just wanted more than you could give. When you realized and broke it off, I reacted horribly. I wish I could get a do-over. This time, I'd be mature and understanding, then when you saw me later, you'd be all, 'There's my gorgeous ex. I can't believe I let her get away,' instead of wearing the oh-no-it's-crazy-Amy face every time our paths cross."

"So basically you just want to make peace?" I could live with that. There was no undoing the damage her lies had inflicted but it didn't serve any purpose to nurse a grudge. Shining a light on my love life since Eli died didn't leave me feeling very cheerful, either. No matter who I hooked up with, I shied away, over and over again, from emotional intimacy.

"I'm not even asking for us to be friends. I just wanted to say I'm sorry and clear my conscience. Elena thinks I need closure."

"Then consider us closed. Do you mind taking me home now?"

"Not at all."

I had to give her directions, which was reassuring. If she'd honestly moved on and started a healthy relationship, she had no reason to pay attention to where I lived. Hell, maybe I could learn from her since I'd been trapped in a holding pattern for years. I thanked her and hopped out of the car outside our apartment. Max was parking his motorcycle as Amy turned around.

He jogged over to me wearing an incredulous expression. "Tell me you're not back with Crazy Amy."

"Don't call her that. She just wanted to say she's sorry."

"Sure. Then she'll be leaving dead cats on our doorstep."

"She had her reasons for being pissed when we broke up." I couldn't feel good about laying all the blame on her anymore. It would make anyone feel shitty to realize they were just a warm body in my bed and I was killing time.

"I don't give a fuck. She *hurt* you, I've heard you crying. So I don't care what she was thinking or feeling, and I never will."

"Okay, settle down. Have you been drinking Red Bull? It always makes you fractious."

He balled up a fist. "This isn't funny, Kaufman. Promise me you're not going out with her again, ever."

"Easy. She's got a girlfriend. That was…closure." Stupid word, but he relaxed visibly.

"Don't scare me like that. You deserve someone a thousand times more awesome, someone you can love like you did Eli."

I flinched a little at hearing Max say his name so unexpectedly. "I'm not sure that's possible. I mean, first love… It'll never be that way again. But maybe it'll be…I dunno, completely different but just as good."

"You don't sound hopeful."

"Meh." I shrugged, leading the way upstairs. "I'm just getting a head start on becoming a crazy cat lady."

When we got in, Angus and Kia weren't home; with

both of them trying to get into med school, they stayed long hours in the science annex, even more in the medical library studying for tests on subjects that would probably make me choke on my own bile. Noise from downstairs drew me out on the balcony, where I spotted Nadia and her boyfriend cooking out on the patio. The kid was playing with toy cars, crashing them together on the cement. She glanced up and waved, beckoning me down, but I shook my head and wandered back inside.

"I have an awesome idea," Max told me.

"Does it involve two rubber gloves, three feet of medical tubing and a bucket of fresh, warm bacon grease?"

Both his brows shot up, and for, like, thirty seconds, he seemed as if he wasn't sure if he should laugh or run. "You're a freak, you know that, right?"

"Hey, don't judge unless you've rolled around in my savory oils."

"Okay, we're backing this bus up. Idea, remember?" He was on the other side of the breakfast bar, rummaging in the fridge.

"Lay it on me." Perching on a stool, I produced a semiserious expression and propped my chin in my palm.

"I know tons of people, that's kind of my superpower. By the end of this semester, I'm finding you the *perfect* person."

The sheer awfulness of it took, like, a minute to sink in. I couldn't let on, not with him looking so happy, so excited about the prospect of fixing me up. For a few confused, horrible seconds, I thought for sure he *knew* about my weird feelings while we'd traveled together and that this was his way of making it 100 percent clear we'd never be anything but bros, no matter how many times we saw each other half-naked, talked in bed or snuggled up like puppies. Really, this was karma, considering how I'd made Amy feel. *It's not like you're in love with him anyway.* And this didn't come as a complete surprise. If Max was interested, he treated a girl much differently than he did Nadia and me. He called us both by our last names, unlike Lauren.

"Pass," I managed.

"Don't you trust me?" Hurt deepened his voice.

"It's not about that. I can find my own dates, dude."

"But...I want to help."

My jaw clenched around caustic words I wouldn't be able to unsay if they escaped. "Thanks anyway."

He seemed like he might argue, but he took another look at me and apparently thought better of it. "You hungry?"

"Nah. I need a shower, then I have some work to do."

With that, I hopped off the stool and strolled to my room as if my throat weren't tightening with every step. Somehow I closed the door quietly behind me and retreated farther, bathroom, another door. The ache swelled to horrendous proportions as if a tentacle-beast was fighting its way out of my neck. Operating on automatic, I stripped and turned on the water, climbed into the tub and closed the tropical fish shower curtain behind me. When the warm spray hit me, I broke. Dropping into a crouch, I wrapped my arms around my knees and cried.

I didn't entirely know why this hurt so much, just scrambled feelings fighting for supremacy: shame, anguish, embarrassment. *Does he feel sorry for me?* I could stand anything but that. I'd gone through a lot of shit, but through it all,

I kept my chin up. I kept pushing forward even when I didn't want to.

Sure, Max. Find me somebody to love, someone who loves me back. I cried harder.

My eyes were red as fire and the water was like ice when I finally crawled out and wrapped up in a towel. Part of me wanted to sit on the toilet and cry more, but if I'd survived losing Eli, then this was just another bump in the road. Some people were born under a golden star; obviously I wasn't one of them, but it didn't mean I'd roll over and give up.

He didn't mean to hurt you, Eli said.

The WTF of it, my dead boyfriend was right. But it didn't make me feel all better. I got dressed, toweled off my hair and then curled up on my bed with my tablet. I hadn't lied when I'd said I had assigned reading. I worked through half of it before Kia came in.

"Studying hard?" she asked, tossing her backpack toward the bed.

"Trying to. Really, I just want to go to sleep."

"It's nine-thirty."

There would be questions soon if I didn't chuck a red herring at her. "It's just been one of those days. My ex ambushed me and insisted that we talk."

"Oh, shit. Duncan's tried to make me listen, too. I run if I see him coming."

"Maybe that's a better idea."

"It's all I have time for. I'm done until I get into med school."

"What do you want to specialize in?"

"Trauma surgery."

"Wow. That's unexpected."

She cocked a teasing brow at me. "What, because I'm a woman I have to deliver babies?"

"If it's personal, you don't have to tell me. But I'm just wondering about your choice." I could've made a joke, but I wanted to get to know her better.

"My older brother was shot when I was a kid. He died on the operating table. I've always wondered if a better doctor could've saved him. Maybe not, you know? They say they did everything possible, but—"

"You wonder. It's normal."

"So I want to save people. That's all. That's why."

"Thanks for telling me."

She shrugged, setting books on her bed, presumably the ones she needed to read tonight. "You're a good listener."

"I'm putting that on my résumé." On that note, I rolled over and got under the covers.

"I can read in the living room if the light will bother you."

Lazily I waved the common cold virus at her, then hugged it to my chest. "You're fine. I can sleep through pretty much anything."

Then I pretended to drift off, though I was just staring at the wall. Angus came to the doorway, whispered to Kia, then she shooed him out. Since I knew him so well, it didn't surprise me when Max showed up a little later.

"Would you two find something to do?" Kia murmured. "Courtney's asleep."

"But…she didn't have dinner."

"She's grown. She'll eat when she's hungry. Go play a game."

"'Night, then." Max sounded confused, upset even, as he walked off.

I told myself it was for the best, but the ache in my chest kept me awake until night faded from the sky.

CHAPTER ELEVEN

For the next week, I eluded Max without half trying.

His work schedule meant that as long as I knew when he had class, I could time my returns and departures. It worked until the following Saturday. Max worked during the day and if he ran true to form, he'd be at a party or out with some girl until late, so I figured it was safe to stay home and watch TV. My luck ran out at 6:45 p.m. when he unlocked the front door and came in. The odor of burnt oil wafted from him, along with the pungent smell of sweat. He looked tired, eyes shadowed, and he hadn't shaven in a few days. I'd always liked seeing him in work clothes, matching navy pants and shirt with a stitched-on name patch. If I was his girlfriend, I'd totally steal one of those shirts. It would be dead cute with the right tank top or cami underneath.

"Hey, stranger." The only way to play this was to bluff it out. "Where've you been hiding all week? Are you avoiding me?"

He swiped a hand across his face, leaving a dirty streak; his fingers and nails were caked with grease and grime. "I was gonna ask *you* that."

"Huh. It probably just seems like we don't see as much of each other after being joined at the hip on the road trip." I shifted, patting the couch. "Take a shower and I'll throw something together for dinner. Unless you have plans?"

There, that should do it.

"No, I don't feel like going out."

"Awesome, we'll have a quiet night."

I slid off the sofa and followed him as far as the kitchen, where I rummaged in the fridge and cupboards. My heart pounded like crazy as he lingered, and when he went into the bathroom, I sighed, going limp against the countertop in relief. Then I rallied enough to set out some penne pasta. It wouldn't be fancy, but it wouldn't take forever, either. While the water boiled, I chopped up some lettuce, which was all we had for a salad, and browned the ground beef.

Need to get Angus to take me shopping.

Max took the longest shower ever so the pasta was done and I was finishing the sauce when he came back. He sniffed, seeming a little more cheerful. "Damn. I didn't realize I was so hungry until right now. I didn't get lunch."

"Busy?"

"Yeah. We had some unexpected body work and the guy threw a shit fit when Gus told him it would be at least four days on the repair, and no, we don't have loaner cars."

"Sounds like a crappy day."

He leaned against me as I served the food. "It's better now."

The words created a twinge in my heart, but mostly I was

glad to make his life better, especially when I'd all but asked
him to stay here and keep busting his ass. "Good. Should
we eat on the couch or at the table?"

"Couch. I could use some mindless entertainment."

"Co-op after we eat?"

"Sounds great."

After dinner, he stacked the plates in the sink while I put
away the leftovers. Angus and Kia would probably have
some when they got in later. Max put in his favorite shooter
and handed me the game controller. There was something
soothing about mindless violence, which a psychiatrist would
probably find worrisome. We played for a couple of hours,
long enough to soothe any lingering fears he might have
about whether we were good.

I stood up, stretching. "That's it for me. The screen's starting to get blurry."

Max sighed with mock-disappointment. "You just aren't
a hard-core gamer."

"Nope. I can live with the shame."

"Want to watch a movie instead?"

Since I'd planned to do that in my room, it was hard to
refuse. "Like what?"

"You pick."

"Then how about *Gravity*?"

"I hope you have chocolate stashed somewhere. It'll probably be depressing." But he turned on Angus's old laptop,
which we used to watch movies online, and checked the
connection to the TV.

"That's so sexist that I don't even know where to start."

He glanced at me, eyes wide, "But...the chocolate's for me."

"Fine, you win this round." I settled back, pulling an afghan that Nadia's mom had made—and she'd let us keep when she moved out—over my knees. Indian summer was still kicking during the day, but the door to the balcony was open to let in the breeze, and it was a little chilly.

Max rented the movie on my account and started it up. He switched off the living room lights, probably to increase the cinematic quality of the experience. Once the film began, I was riveted, not thinking about Max. I didn't notice him until he leaned on me, head on my arm. In the old days I'd have put an arm around him and let him use me as a pillow. I didn't this time, though I couldn't say why. Eventually he took the hint and sat up. I pretended to be oblivious, absorbed in Sandra Bullock's life-or-death struggle. Once the movie came to its gripping conclusion, I turned on the lights.

And said the last thing in the world I wanted to. "So I've been thinking about your offer."

"Huh?" Max blinked against the sudden shift in illumination, his pupils contracting against the light.

"To set me up. You know me better than anyone, so you should be good at it."

"Okay. Would you rather date a guy or a girl?"

"I'm open."

"Any deal breakers?"

I considered for a minute, acting like this didn't have disaster written all over it. "Consistently poor hygiene. Vicious streak. Extremely conservative outlook."

"Is that it? You don't want to describe your type or anything?"

"People always say this, but I swear it's true—I don't really have one. Physical traits are ephemeral anyway, while the core of the person won't change over the years."

"Some people do," he pointed out. "For better or worse."

"What is this, a proposal?"

"Funny."

"I just mean you can't fall in love with someone's butt."

He grinned. "Are you sure? Because I'm pretty sure I have."

"That's lust, Max."

"And you're opposed to it?"

How did I get into this conversation again? But it would seem suspicious if I suddenly waved my hands and retreated. We used to debate shit like this all the time. But that was before, before Providence, before I'd thought about getting naked with Max, wondered what it would be like to take it further than kissing.

"There's nothing wrong with a sexual relationship as long as both parties know that going in. Otherwise someone ends up heartbroken. That's kind of what I did to Amy, actually."

"You won't get me to agree that anything you did could be worth how she went after you. That shit was downright sociopathic."

"Your loyalty is awesome," I said, smiling. "So who do you have in mind for me?"

He tipped his head back against the couch, thoughtful. "It might be easier for me to set you up with guys. Any way you clock it, I'd be awkward as fuck trying to find out if a girl's bi, and I'm not trolling the lesbian activist group, even for you."

I laughed outright, the first true humor I'd felt regarding this train wreck. "That's fine. I told you before, I can find my own dates. But if you think you know somebody who'd be a good fit, I'm willing to meet him. Or her. Though from what you just said, that's unlikely."

"I'll get back to you. There are a couple of guys I have class with—"

"Surprise me."

"Do you want me to take a ninja pic before I talk to them about you?"

"No need, unless you plan to let them screen me the same way?"

"Fuck, no."

I could imagine the way this conversation would play out. *Are you interested in meeting my roommate?*

Why, is she hot?

She's got an incredible personality, she's so cool and funny—

No thanks, bro.

But that would probably be the least painful outcome. Better for Max to figure out what a bad idea this was on his own, then I wouldn't have to tell him how much it bothered me. A smidgen of it stemmed from the possibility that he felt sorry for me, but the vast majority came from wounded pride. I'd thought there were…mutual sparks, and that we'd chosen not to act on them. But only I was struck by lightning while Max remained completely grounded.

Depressing.

"Let me know how it goes," I said, hopping up.

"You're going to bed already?"

"It's past eleven. That's not early. Something wrong? Is your family okay? Have you talked to them since we got back?"

"Not really, and yeah. I call Michael a couple of times a week. He's training for some kind of marathon."

I grinned. "I hate to break it to you, but he got my email at the park. I've heard from him, like, six times."

"What the hell, seriously?" It was impossible to tell if he was truly agitated.

"Yep. He texts me, too." This was way more fun than talking about a potential blind date.

"Kaufman."

"What?"

"Don't string him along. He's just a kid."

I gaped at Max. "You honestly think I'm hitting on your brother? Give me some credit for not being gross and inappropriate."

"I just… It's weird, that's all."

That didn't make me feel any better. "For him to be friends with me? You are."

"Yeah, but…"

"What?"

"Never mind."

"I'm definitely going to my room, where I'll probably text Michael until I fall asleep. Don't interrupt." I stomped down the hall and shut the door behind me.

Angrily I changed into pajamas. *What the hell is wrong with him?* Half of the notes and messages his brother sent were about Max. I didn't break his confidence, though, or repeat anything about how bad it was the first year after he'd left home. Once Michael had figured out I wouldn't be spilling top secret info, he'd started asking about college, the kind of questions a homeschooled kid would have. To me, it seemed normal, nothing strange or shady.

I hated fighting with Max, though. With tension between us, I couldn't focus.

Maybe he felt the same way because he ignored my demand to be left alone, tapping on the door shortly after midnight. "You asleep?"

I sighed and got up, opening the door with an impatience that was mostly feigned. "What is it, Max?"

Even when he stepped on my feelings, it was hard to stay mad. He dug his toes into the carpet, leaning on the door frame. "I just want to say I'm sorry."

"About what?" Immature, sure, but I wondered if he even knew what bothered me about that whole Michael exchange.

"What happened before. The truth is, I was just... God, this is stupid."

"Huh?" Already losing interest, I stepped back, ready to shut the door on any more of this crap tonight, but he grabbed my arm.

"Kia will probably be home soon, and she'll kick me out before we're done talking."

Sighing, I followed him down the hall. His bedroom was smaller, barely room for a full bed and chest of drawers. He'd mounted his TV on the wall and put the game console on top of the chest. In terms of decor, there was nothing, no pictures on the walls and very few books. On second inspection, his space seemed sparse and nomadic, as if he could pack his shit and be gone in a couple of hours. The idea tightened my throat.

He clicked a music player into the dock, starting a song I didn't recognize. The hook caught me right away. "Who's this?"

"Electric President. If you like this, you'd probably enjoy Radical Face, too."

This was a lot mellower than I associated with Max, but

it was gorgeous, more suited to quiet conversation anyway. I curled up at the foot of his bed, wishing I could lie down and bury my face in his pillow. Though I probably shouldn't admit it, I missed the smell of him on the sheets as well as his warmth at my back. *He* was probably glad things were back to normal.

Are you sure? Eli asked.

I ignored him. This wasn't the time.

"So what did you want to say?" I prompted.

Max sat down, close enough that I could touch him if I shifted. "I hate admitting this, damn. But I was being childish. It hit me, like, *No way, you can't be friends with Michael because what the fuck, I found you first.*"

He was right; that was stupid, juvenile and really flipping cute. But at least he had the courage to admit it. "So I have to choose a Cooper, is that what you're saying?"

"Don't," he mumbled. "Right now you'd probably pick him…because he's not here annoying you and refusing to let you sleep."

That look, damn.

Leaning over, I ruffled his hair. "False. I'll always pick you, no matter how much you piss me off."

As the song changed, he let out a sigh, shoulders relaxing. "You don't know how happy that makes me. I actually can't sleep when you're mad at me."

Simultaneously moved and confused, I answered, "Now that I know, I have to fuck with you. Come home in a faux-rage and give you the silent treatment."

Max reacted with more alarm than I expected. "Only if you want to drive me nuts."

"Then when you ask what's wrong, I'll fall back on the classic 'If you don't know, I'm not telling you.'"

He groaned and closed his eyes briefly. "Please don't. If you start playing games, I'll lose my true north."

"Huh?" Not an eloquent response, but it was late.

"True north is a fixed point, the constant that never changes. And no matter how fucked up everything else is, as long as you're here, I can always deal." He paused, studying his hands.

They were scrubbed clean of the mechanic grime but reflected the years he'd worked with them, rough and callused, white scars on his fingers and knuckles. A purple slash marked the back of his left hand, and I remembered what he'd said about nearly getting stabbed in an alley. Meeting him for the first time, you'd take him for a laborer.

Your dad would hate him, Eli said.

Probably.

Before I could respond, he went on. "I haven't had a friend like you since I was…twelve, maybe. My dad got really bad then, drinking all the time. Uncle Jim was overseas, and Uncle Lou was having health problems. So it was on me to protect Mickey. I couldn't invite people over because I never knew what mood Pop would be in, and I couldn't leave my brother."

"I'm sure he appreciates it."

"No, that's not the point I'm making here. I'm trying to say, this doesn't come easy to me. Talking to people, making it real. You, Nadia and Angus are the only true friends I've made since I moved here."

"But you know so many people."

"Their names, sure. But they don't have any idea who I

am." Sighing, he tilted his head against the wall. "Anyway, I just wanted you to know how important you are to me."

When he came across all sweet and earnest like this, I couldn't hang on to hurt or aggravation. It wasn't his fault that I didn't attract him in the romantic sense. He'd never intentionally raised my expectations. Mentally I made peace with the idea of being Max's bro.

The heart wants what it wants, Eli said.

Were you always this annoying and unhelpful?

Hey, I'm watching my girlfriend fall for another guy. Cut me some slack.

That sounded so much like Eli that I snickered. Max's head jerked up, eyes wounded. *Shit. He just said something deep and touching. Meanwhile you're chortling.*

"You're special to me, too," I said, playing off the laugh. "But there's no need to go all scary-serious when you tell me. I'll get you the BFFs Forever necklace for your birthday."

He feigned enthusiasm, opening his eyes so wide it was creepy. "You promise? The one that says Friends on one half and Forever on the other?"

"You think I'm joking, but just wait."

"I'll cry if you disappoint me, Kaufman."

"Never. Do you prefer gold or silver?"

"I take it platinum's off the table."

"Sorry, I'm on a budget here. To buy you expensive jewelry, I'd have to get a job, and I don't plan to do that until absolutely necessary."

"Such a princess," he scoffed.

"Time for me to flounce away with my scepter and tiara. G'night."

For a few seconds, it looked like he had something to say, as if he might stop me. But in the end, he opened the door for me, then shut it with a quiet click. Angus was just coming home, and it seemed like a dick move to disappear without letting him dish about Del, so I got a drink and sat on the couch with him for half an hour, listening. Just past one, Kia came in, looking exhausted. She stumbled past with a wave and headed straight to bed.

When Angus paused for breath, I teased, "So I get the idea that Del is okay and you kinda like him."

He nudged me with his foot. "Brat. I'm ready for him to meet the family."

"Whoa, big step. Good luck."

You could use some, too, Eli pointed out.

There was no arguing with a ghost, especially when he was right.

CHAPTER TWELVE

Three weeks later, I sat in The Pour House on Friday afternoon, waiting for my first Max-driven fix-up. I was wearing a red beanie so the guy could identify me since saying "I'll be the girl in the black shirt" wasn't enough to separate me from the pack. I had juice and a muffin in front of me, but I didn't want to take a bite because as soon as I did, the lucky guy would arrive to find me with my mouth full of pastry.

I drummed my fingers nervously, until someone cast a shadow over the table. Glancing up, I registered a tallish guy, lanky, blond with a blue streak in his hair. Otherwise, he wasn't particularly memorable. I lifted my hand in a half wave.

"Jared?"

"You must be Courtney."

I nodded. "You must be wondering why you agreed to this."

"Max said you're a cool girl. I'll get a coffee and be right back." His response was lukewarm, though, and I could practically hear him inventing reasons to leave.

By the time he came back, I'd eaten half of my muffin but at least I wasn't chewing. "What did you get?"

"Double espresso." He sat down, thinly veiled contempt skating over his face as he registered that I actually ate food.

"So how do you know Max?"

"We have a couple of classes together."

Before I could reply, his phone rang. "Sorry, I have to take this."

I made a go-ahead gesture, but he lost points by doing it. While I listened to his half of the conversation, I sipped my juice. At first it was mostly monosyllabic, but then he glanced at me and said, "Nothing much. Yeah, that should be fine."

Nice.

A pause. "I know, right? Yeah, Mariah Carey looks amazing lately. I'm so glad she lost weight. It's disgusting when women let themselves go." His gaze met mine, flickered away, as if he wasn't talking to me.

Yeah, completely unrelated.

That was enough for me. I stood up, took my stuff and strode out. He wasn't worth the ten seconds it would take me to tell him to fuck off. Indignation carried me out of the student center and halfway across campus. But once I got that far, I realized I only had a bus ride ahead of me, plus the exciting job of breaking the news to Max that the meet had been worse than a dead loss. I could put off the inevitable by finding something else to do tonight, though.

I could go to the mall, maybe see a movie.

As I debated, a girl nearly barreled into me, either late

for something or running for her life. I glanced past her
to make sure it was nothing I needed to worry about and
didn't see anybody chasing her. In stepping back, I bumped
into the bulletin board behind me. The craptastic nature
of the day came full circle when I snagged my shirt on a
tack; I wriggled until my shirt tore free, then I spun, thinking about kicking the posts. A purple flyer caught my eye,
hand-drawn with an abstract band logo for Racing Sorrow;
I'd never heard of them, but that wasn't surprising. There
were, like, a hundred garage bands rattling around campus.

The poster read SEEKING NEW KEYBOARDIST, AU-
DITIONS FRIDAY, along with a number to call. Several of
the tags had already been ripped away. I took piano lessons
for eight years, but this definitely was not what my mother
had in mind when she'd said music would round me out.
Back then, she was still trying to lure me away from the
"indie influence." These days, she was satisfied if I was clear-
headed and not drowning myself in chemical bliss.

Are you thinking about it? Eli asked.

Maybe.

*It's not a terrible idea. You've been going through the motions
for a while, C.*

Dammit. Eli was right again. I needed something that
was just for me. School definitely wasn't, and it depressed
me to think about hanging out at the apartment taking out
my dissatisfaction on Max. He wouldn't relent on finding
me the perfect date if I didn't find something to do with
my time. Auditioning for a band sounded more up my alley
than a part-time job.

Shrugging, I got out my phone and dialed. This didn't
have a date on it; maybe I'd missed the window of oppor-

tunity. But the phone was already ringing, so no harm in checking.

"Yeah?" A deep, impatient voice answered.

"I was wondering if the keyboard auditions are still going on."

"We're wrapping up. If you can be here in under an hour, we'll give you a listen."

"Where's 'here' exactly?"

He named a bar three blocks from campus, one that occasionally had live music. I knew there was a piano, but on Friday night, there would probably be a crowd. A prickle of anxiety wormed to the surface, spiced liberally with excitement. It had been so long since I'd tried for anything of my own.

"I'll be there in fifteen minutes."

"Later." The guy disconnected and I took off speed-walking.

I'd been here before, so I made it in ten minutes. For a few seconds, I stared at the front of the building, finished to seem more rustic than it was. Then I rushed inside, wondering how I'd know who I was looking for. *I should've thought this through more.* It was early enough that there weren't many people here, thank God. I'd only fiddled on the piano when I was home this summer, and I'd stopped the lessons when Eli died.

A brown-haired girl in an apron tapped my shoulder. "I bet you're looking for the idiots in back." The smile belied her words.

"Thanks."

My nerves clattered like a broken strand of beads. I took a deep breath and headed toward the piano in back. Three people were sitting at a square table nearby with enough glasses to suggest they'd been here awhile and didn't tip well enough to merit frequent bussing. Various bags, papers and sheet music loaded down the vacant chair. They hadn't noticed me yet, so I scoped them out: girl with pink hair cut in a bob, guy with skull cut and a nose ring, a thin Korean-American dude with shaggy blond hair caught up in topknot.

"Hey," I said, before they could notice me staring. "I think you're waiting for me?"

"Oh, hey." The girl hopped up to clear the chair for me. "I'm Dana. I bet Ji Hoo that it was another prank call."

"I should've taken your money," the blond guy said.

He must be Ji Hoo.

"I'm Evan." The guy radiated a thuggish vibe between the hair and his tattoos on his forearms. He had on an *ouroboros* ring that wrapped halfway to the knuckle of his middle finger. By the look of his hands, he was also the guitarist.

"Courtney."

Dana waved at the seat. "Go ahead, I'll tell you a little about the group before you play. If you don't like what you hear, it'll save you the trouble."

"You want a beer?" Ji Hoo asked.

When I nodded, Evan stood to get one from the bar. He was shorter than I'd have guessed from the width of his shoulders. He rapped on the counter, his voice a deep baritone rumble as he ordered my drink. I swung my gaze back to Dana, who was talking about Racing Sorrow.

"Ji Hoo and I are both majoring in music," she was saying.

"Whereas I'm between academic engagements," Evan added. "I was, but I lost faith in the system."

"You were just too lazy to go to class," Dana said.

Ji Hoo tapped out an impatient rhythm against the table. *Betting he's the drummer.* "Do you plan to tell her about our sound at any point?"

That means Dana probably plays bass.

"I'm on it. Basically we play a 50/50 mix of original music and covers. Mumford and Sons, The Lumineers, Of Monsters and Men, Imagine Dragons—"

"I think she gets the idea," Evan cut in. "Can you sing?"

"Not well enough to front a group, but I can harmonize."

"Alto or soprano?" Dana asked.

Ji Hoo nudged her. "Five bucks says alto."

"You win." I told him.

Dana seemed pleased, at least. "Nice. I'm mezzo soprano. Ji Hoo is tenor and Evan brings the bass-baritone."

"We'll talk about that later," Evan said. "Back to basics for a minute. We're folk rock-indie, harder than Mumford. If that sounds like your thing, go play a song."

It took me a few seconds to realize they were all staring expectantly, waiting for me to respond. I bent down to check the sheet music and picked out "Ho Hey" by The Lumineers. Maybe this was a stupid idea since I'd never performed, not even a piano recital when I was eight. But at worst, I'd embarrass myself in front of the ten people currently in the bar.

Sitting down, I pretended I was home, playing in our dining room. The tinge of nerves faded when I imagined Eli sitting beside me. I delivered a simple, wistful version of the song devoid of showy flourishes. Lifting my head, I took a breath and faced my three judges.

"Can you sight-read?" Dana asked.

"Yeah, no problem."

"Then here." She brought me another song, probably meant to test my ability.

I'd never played "Radioactive" before but after skimming the notes, I gave it my best shot. Afterward, I carried the sheet music back to the table. "So…did I make the A-list?"

To my surprise, Dana laughed. "Dude, you are the list. We only got four calls total and two of those were no-shows."

Ji Hoo nodded. "Competition is fierce. You won't get rich playing with us."

"Which brings me to my next point," Evan interjected. "Whatever we get for a gig, we split four ways. So far, we've played a few shows in Ann Arbor, some frat parties here in town."

"But then Stella dropped out," Dana said. "And we really need someone in her place."

That was pretty candid, but… "Do you need for me to take a walk, so you can talk amongst yourselves?"

They exchanged a look, then Evan said, "Nope. Show of hands, all in favor of Courtney joining up?"

All three arms went up.

Dana beamed. "We rehearse Wednesday and Saturday nights in Evan's garage. He lives in an actual *house*." Her mock awe made me laugh.

"It's not like it's mine," he muttered. "I'm just house-sitting while my uncle's in the UK."

"Still, it beats the dorm," Ji Hoo pointed out.

Nodding, I said, "Agreed. I moved off campus this year, and it's awesome."

I have a good feeling about this, Eli said.

Me, too.

"Okay, so we're rehearsing tomorrow night?" It seemed like a good idea to confirm.

Evan held out a hand. He was smiling now, and the shift softened his demeanor from thuggish to slightly ferocious. I noticed he had nice eyes, somewhere between green and hazel, and his brows would do credit to an angry Cossack. With a minor jolt, I realized he was still offering his palm.

"High five? You want me to cross your palm with silver? Tell your fortune? Blink once if I get close."

He laughed. "I need your phone, funny girl."

"Right."

Evan took it and input his contact information, then I texted him. He passed along my info and it was weird but cool to have Dana and Ji Hoo checking their phones at the same time—because of me. I'd never been fantastic at making new friends. Of the two of us, Eli had been the extrovert, always collecting people. At any point, I could've left since our business was concluded, but I finished my beer while they talked about places we might be able to play.

Before I put my phone away, I saw I had a text from Max. With a frisson of determination, I put it away unread. *I can't be passive anymore. I can't build my whole life around one person. I have to* live. The realization stung, but it felt...true.

Dana stood up. "I don't know about anyone else, but I'm starving."

"Burgers?" Ji Hoo suggested a place five blocks away.

"Sounds good." I hadn't eaten lunch in my haste to meet that asshole, Jared.

"I'll walk with you and leave my car here," Evan said. "Do you have a ride home?"

Dana smacked him on the arm. "It's too soon to lure her into your car, bro."

A chuckle escaped me. "Should I be worried?"

"Nah, he's harmless. But if you *do* need a ride, I'll come along. Evan will bring me back to campus afterward."

"Oh, will I?" Evan quirked a brow.

She patted him like a spaniel. "Don't argue. You know I'm the brains of this outfit."

"And I'm the stomach." Ji Hoo was already headed out. "Are you coming or what?"

The three of us hurried after him. Dana fell into step with Evan, so I quickened my pace to catch up with Ji Hoo.

He glanced over at me with a half smile. "I'm seriously relieved that you showed up. Another week and I'd be forced to start an a cappella group."

"And that's to be avoided?"

"Nobody wants me to sing without music, trust me. But I'm a kick-ass drummer. You'll agree after jamming with us tomorrow night."

"I can't wait."

Dinner at the burger dive turned into a two-and-a-half-hour planning session. The amazing thing was they treated like me like a founding member, listening to my suggestions, even making notes occasionally. So it was past ten when we finished up and walked back to the bar. Evan suggested we go in to talk a little more and it wasn't like I had anything better to do. I drank a couple more beers, as did Ji Hoo and Dana, though Evan stuck to iced tea. By midnight, I felt ready for my first rehearsal, both excited and slightly buzzed. A rosy glow permeated everything as I followed the other three out to the car.

"If you're cool with it, I'll ride along, too," Ji Hoo said.

"I don't mind. We've been hanging out for six hours now and my gut says you're good people." With a faint twinge, I recalled Max saying more or less the same thing.

I'm putting some space between us. It's for the best.

You sure about that? Eli asked.

Shut up, you. What's your verdict about the band?

They might suck as musicians, but they're decent people.

Weird as it sounded, relief flooded through me to hear Eli agree with my assessment. One of these days, I needed to stop listening to this voice in my head. I understood that it wasn't actually *him*, but I couldn't bring myself to silence his echo. *Not yet.*

Then when, C? It's been five years.

I'll let you know.

In my distraction, I stumbled into Evan's back as he was unlocking the van. He was astonishingly solid, didn't stumble even when I bounced off him face-first. With a smirk, he opened the back door for me.

"There you go."

"Thanks. I appreciate the ride, too. I'd have to call one of my roommates out to get me. The buses stopped running an hour ago."

"Hey, anything for our new keyboardist," Dana said as Evan started the vehicle.

Ten minutes later, they dropped me off at the apartment, no trouble. My last vestige of doubt melted away. *Definitely the best idea I've had in a while.* Smiling, I strolled toward the building, the same warmth I used to get from different-colored pills trickling through me, only without the accompanying numbness. Pausing on the front steps, I watched the taillights recede.

Ji Hoo shouted, "See you tomorrow!" out the window as they pulled away.

Once the car disappeared from sight, I pushed open the door and went up to the apartment. I figured Angus would be at Del's tonight, but Kia might be home. I'd like to get to know her better, but she was pretty much always studying, and I hated to bother her. After unlocking the door, I found Max sprawled on the couch with the lights off. The TV was on, throwing shadows over his face.

He propped up on an elbow as I shut the door. For a long moment, he didn't say anything. Then his voice came out hard, angry, even. "Your phone broken? Or maybe the battery's dead."

"Huh?"

"I texted you. Three times."

I know. I saw.

"Sorry, it was loud in the bar. I probably didn't hear it."

"I thought you were meeting Jared at The Pour House."

"The evening evolved." I smiled, acting like I didn't realize that he was pissed. "And if you set me up, you can't expect me to check in, Max. No offense, but that'd be weird. Not to mention unfair to the person I'm with."

"Then you must've had fun tonight." The words came out sharp enough to cut diamonds.

Looking back, I had to admit that was true, though Jackass Jared had nothing to do with it. So I nodded. "Had burgers for dinner and then relocated to that bar near campus. Played a few rounds of darts, talked about music." All of that was certainly true.

You should just tell him, Eli piped up.

If I do that, Max kicks Jared's ass. There's drama. It's better to just let it die quietly. When he isn't so mad, I'll tell him about the band.

Eh. I heard Eli's shrug. *If you say so. You're the expert.*

"Sounds like I picked a winner on the first try," he bit out.

"Isn't that what you wanted?" I waved and headed for my room.

I heard him mumble, "Fuck if I know," but I didn't turn. I couldn't.

CHAPTER THIRTEEN

The next afternoon, I took the bus to the mall.

A keyboard player needs a keyboard. There was a small music store where I hoped to find something usable. The shopping center was unimpressive by Chicago standards, one level with Sears and JCPenney as the flagship stores. I hopped off at the stop closest and walked the last three blocks. Inside I found mostly housewives wrangling toddlers along with a handful of older people dressed for exercise; women in colorful track suits speed-walked past me, gossiping about other ladies in the coffee klatch.

With a grin, I headed for the shop; a sign in the window read ASK ABOUT GUITAR LESSONS. The guy minding the place perked up when I walked in. He probably didn't get many customers; musical instruments didn't rank high on the list of casual impulse buys.

"Can I help you with something?"

"I'm in the market for a keyboard."

He led me around, talking brands and budget. In the end, I bought a Yamaha portable. He promised the sound would be good enough for performance. But after I bought it, I realized I had no feasible way to get everything home. There was no way in hell I wanted to lug the gear to the bus stop, even assuming I could manage. Studying the contact list on my phone offered only a few possibilities. *Nadia, I guess, or Angus...* But that wouldn't solve the problem of how to get my stuff to Evan's for rehearsal tonight. *But maybe...* Hoping he wouldn't think I was an asshole, I tapped Evan in my contact list and waited for the call to connect.

"What's up, funny girl?"

I had no idea if that was a compliment but since I was about to ask for a favor, I let it go. "What're you doing right now?"

"Eating cereal in my underwear."

That started a laugh out of me. "You believe in complete honesty, huh?"

"Hey, you asked. Don't risk the question if you can't handle the answer. But I'm pretty sure you didn't call me up for that. Unless you did." I could actually hear the smile in his voice.

"Could you put some pants on and swing by the mall? I just got a new keyboard and I could use some help getting it to your place."

"Not a problem. Just chill with Dave at the store and I'll be there in fifteen minutes."

It was closer to twenty when Evan rolled in; I was fiddling with an acoustic guitar, getting a free lesson and starting to feel awkward about it. I put down the instrument and waved, picking up all the accessories I could carry.

Evan grinned. "I see how you are. So I'm a pack mule to you?"

"Do you see any saddle bags?"

"Thanks, D. I've got it from here." He made a take-off gesture at the store clerk, who reluctantly went around the counter and left us to haul everything out to the van. As he stacked my stuff in back, Evan added, "I handle transportation and since I have the most room, I store the amps and everything else at my place. If you want, you can leave your gear, too."

"That would be good. Otherwise rehearsal could be problematic. I've never really needed a car before."

"City girl," he scoffed.

"Basically. I really appreciate this." To my surprise, he came around to open my door. Evan might look like a thug, but his manners suggested otherwise.

"I might be planning to sell your shit on Craigslist as soon as you take off." He cut me an ominous look, thick brows drawn down.

"If you do, you won't have a keyboardist," I pointed out. "Don't you stand to earn more money as a working band than as a felon?"

"Your logic is my Kryptonite." He started the van and drove toward his house.

As promised, he showed me the other equipment, safe in his garage. I unloaded beside him, though he was careful to grab the heavy stuff. Evan sighed when he realized I'd bought basically everything we could possibly need for a show in one shot. He studied me, tapping one Doc Marten against the cement floor.

"What?"

"No job. You just spent eighteen hundred, easy."

"So...?"

"It means you're a rich girl. How do we know you won't just take off the minute this stops being fun? Because it's definitely work. And the rest of us need you to take it seriously. We don't expect to hit it big or anything, but—"

"Relax," I cut in. "I wouldn't have spent the money if I didn't think I could earn it back."

He scanned my face for a few seconds more, before letting me off the hook with a sharp nod. "Fine. You want a ride home?"

"At this point, it's only an hour and half until rehearsal. Unless I'd bother you, it makes sense for me to hang out here." I didn't analyze my reluctance to go home, though it absolutely had to do with the new tension between Max and me.

"If you don't mind watching TV while I shower, make yourself at home." Evan gestured for me to precede him into the house and I was surprised by how nice it was.

Wood floors contrasted beautifully with eggshell walls, more modern than I expected. The rooms were small but in all honesty, the house was cleaner than our apartment, a pleasant surprise from a guy living alone. Furniture was sparse, though, and there weren't too many personal belongings spread around. I remembered him saying he was house-sitting.

"The living room's through there. All the remotes are on the coffee table. Help yourself to a drink from the fridge if you want one." He seemed really casual as he left me alone in his front room, heading down the hall toward what I presumed to be the bathroom.

My phone buzzed as I clicked the TV on, along with the cable box. I channel surfed for a couple of minutes before picking it up. A tremor went through me when I saw Max's name. It was like I'd broken up with him even though we were never dating. Apart from Eli, I'd never felt this particular tightness in my chest.

You're in love with him, Eli pointed out.

Am not.

Lie to yourself if you want. Don't even try to fool me.

With a deep sigh, I touched the message. Where are you?

There had to be some way to get back to the old footing. Yeah, the trip had changed things, enforced a certain intimacy, but that didn't have to ruin our friendship. Reminding myself not to be a dumbass, I ignored the ache in my sternum and sent back: Hanging out with a friend.

Jared? That came back so fast he might've sprained a thumb.

Nope. I don't think that's gonna work out. See you later.

I expected that to end the convo, but Max persisted. So who're you with? He named a few people and I stared at my cell, wondering why he seemed obsessed with how I was spending my Saturday night. At that point I could've told him about the band, but I wasn't ready to explain. If we sounded terrible together, if it didn't work out, I'd rather my roomies didn't know that I'd spent so much money on an impulse, like credit card debt could fill the hole in my life.

Nobody you know, I texted.

We know all the same people, he sent back immediately.

No. We don't.

That silenced him. I was putting away my phone when Evan sauntered into the living room. His hair was so short,

I could hardly tell he'd just showered, apart from the clean, soapy smell as he passed me and plopped onto the other end of the couch. He cocked a brow.

"Everything okay?"

"Huh? Why?"

"You look aggravated."

"A little, maybe. Don't worry, it's nothing that'll impact my musical aptitude."

"Glad to hear it. Now give me the remote, I'm not watching *Hoarders*. That show is depressing as fuck."

"I treat it as an object lesson. Like, this is what can happen if you get overly attached to crap you don't need. It's also kind of…aversion therapy."

"What do you mean?"

"I have mild OCD and watching that show is—"

"Got it. You're a weird girl, you know that, right?"

With a wry smile, I nodded. "It might have come up once or twice in conversation."

Since it was his TV, I didn't bitch when Evan turned on sports. Unfortunately the game didn't hold my attention, so my mind turned to Max. Who was probably getting off work now. In the old days, before the trip, neither one of us went out on Saturday night; we just hung around the apartment, made dinner together, played video games or watched movies.

I miss him.

Evan startled me by speaking since he'd been wrapped up in the match for the past hour. "I have to go get the other two. Do you want to wait here or ride along?"

"I'll go with you." It seemed weird to do anything else.

"Come on, then."

Dana and Ji Hoo were waiting outside their dorms when we rolled by. They piled in, and though I braced for questions, neither seemed particularly interested in why I was with Evan. We talked about the set list on the way back to his place, and it felt so good to have something besides classes and Max to focus on.

"I don't know all of those songs by heart," I warned them. "Do you have sheet music?"

"For most of them," Dana answered.

Ji Hoo added, "The rest we can probably buy online and print at Evan's place."

We did that first. Well, Evan did. The rest of us went to the garage, where the magic happened. I could definitely tell it was a rehearsal space from the drum kit to the amps. With a determined nod, I set up my keyboard, though Ji Hoo had to help me.

He gave me a weird look as he showed me what to do. "If I hadn't heard you, I'd swear you never touched a keyboard before."

"To be honest, I haven't. I've only played the regular piano. There may be a learning curve but I can figure it out. When's the first show?"

Dana laughed. "Relax. We have to book one."

"So there's time. I'm relieved. I was afraid you'd tell me our first gig is next weekend."

"It is," Evan said, coming out of the house.

"Wait, what?" I gaped at him.

"Wow, you're easy. I'm kidding. I thought I'd give us two weeks of rehearsal before calling any of our usual venues."

Ji Hoo nodded. "Good idea. We might be able to play

the Omega Chi Halloween party next month. That was okay last year."

"It would be a good first show for Courtney," Dana agreed.

"How come?" I glanced between them, wondering at the rationale.

Dana slung an arm around my shoulder. "They're not a tough crowd. They drink a lot, not musically critical. The end."

"But our usual set list won't work," Evan told me. "I'll introduce you to the Greek party soundtrack later. For now, let's work on the other stuff."

"Sounds good to me."

After a few false starts while I familiarized myself with the new keyboard, rehearsal kicked off. I wouldn't call myself a pro but I didn't screw up too badly in the first few songs. Four tunes later, Evan and Dana gave me notes while Ji Hoo practiced tossing his sticks. Since I *wanted* to improve, I didn't mind the critique. The next three songs went smoothly, and it was way more fun than I expected, the way our individual instruments threaded together to form a coherent, beautiful sound. Evan had a great voice, husky and smoky. At first, I kept forgetting to sing and Dana yelled at me about shifting keys in the middle.

"You're only harmonizing half the time," she griped. "Damn. You're not competing with Evan. Think of yourself as a back-up singer."

With zero performance experience, I could only promise to try harder. I nodded at her. "I'll do better."

They all stared at me. Then Ji Hoo shook his head. "Man, you're so different than Stella."

"Is that bad?" I asked.

"It's fantastic," Dana replied. "We might take Racing Sorrow to the next level."

Evan grinned. "Hells yeah. With Courtney on board, we might even play the state fair this summer."

I had no idea if he was joking or if that was a hard gig to book, but I smiled tentatively. "Thanks for giving me a shot."

At the halfway point, we took a break and ate leftover pizza while they told me a little more about their plans to advertise and set up more shows. It felt good to be part of the collective, even if I was the noob. In the latter half of practice, I incorporated their suggestions and I managed to stay on key.

An hour later, we knocked off for the night entirely. Dana and Ji Hoo both had plans for later, so Evan drove them back to campus.

In the van, I asked, "So tell me about the name. How did you come up with it?"

Evan said quietly, "We've all got something bad behind us, you know? Without going into our sad stories, it felt right. Every morning we get up, racing sorrow, and telling ourselves this is the day we put it behind us for good."

"Wow. I love that."

"Kind of cheesy," Dana mumbled.

I shifted to meet her gaze. "Not at all."

When they hopped out of the van, I waved until they disappeared inside the dorm. It wasn't that late, not even ten, but I'd bothered Evan enough for one day. "I really appreciate the ride home. Thanks again for bailing me out at the music store. I think Dave was about to make an inde-cent proposal."

He offered a fleeting smile. "Eh, he gets lonely. You prob-ably kept him in business for another month with every-thing you bought."

"I'll consider my philanthropic quota met for the month."

"Courtney…" As he turned toward my apartment, pass-ing headlights illuminated his stark features. "I hope you won't think I'm a dick for mentioning this…"

"Now I'm worried."

"It's just a friendly warning."

His somber tone was kind of freaking me out, so I fid-dled with my seat belt, loosening it where it cut into my neck. "Go on."

"I probably should have stated this up front, but…basi-cally, we have a strict no-dating-within-the-band policy."

A relieved laugh trickled out of me. "Is that all? No prob-lem. That makes total sense. It would suck if everything imploded over a messy breakup… All that work down the toilet."

"Exactly."

"God, you made it sound like a huge deal."

He rapped his knuckles a couple of times on the steering wheel in a clearly nervous gesture before responding. "It's basically why Stella left the band. So yeah, it was a problem."

"Oh, that sucks. What happened?"

"She was crushing hard on Ji Hoo, pressuring him to hook up on the DL. He has a girlfriend, but she thought per-sistence would win him over. So she started showing up at his dorm room. A few months back, he asked me to step in."

I winced. "So that sounds awkward and horrifying."

"Pretty much. We had a huge blowup, she called me a Nazi and quit the band."

"I can see why you'd make sure I understand the group isn't my personal dating service. But don't worry, I'm here for music and friendship. I won't stalk anyone or create drama."

"If only I could believe you," he said mournfully. "But I've been burned before."

"Time will prove that I'm solid." He was kidding, but I didn't want Evan to worry that I'd hit on my bandmates. Right now, my emotional life was complicated enough, between the dead boyfriend who wouldn't stop talking in my head and the best friend haunting my heart. "Full disclosure requires me to warn you, there's been some gossip about me on campus."

Quietly I filled him in on the Amy situation, then reassured him, "She apologized and the rumors have mostly died down. I don't think it'll impact our shows, but—"

"If it does, we've got your back. Your private life is nobody else's business."

"Thanks."

We sang along with the radio the rest of the way; it was good practice harmonizing with him. By the time he pulled into my complex, I had a better handle on the constructive comments Dana and Ji Hoo had given me. Evan offered me a fist bump.

"Your voice isn't bad."

"Eh. I don't have the power to front a group. My abdominal muscles might as well be made of silly string."

"To say nothing of your diaphragm."

"Isn't that a Connie Willis novel?" I didn't expect him to

know who she was or to get the joke; it was a reference Eli would've gotten straight off. He chuckled inside my head.

Evan surprised me by laughing, too, then following with a serious question. "Have you read the *Doomsday Book*? It's one of my favorites."

"Me, too. Thanks for the ride."

"Wait, I'll walk you up. I can't believe you've actually read it. I feel like it's seriously underappreciated in genre fiction." He raved about the novel all the way up the stairs and to my front door.

His enthusiasm made me smile. "We'll put a pin in this convo and take it up later, yeah?"

"Definitely. We still need to talk about *Bellwether*."

"Can't wait. I love that one, too." I beamed at him, delighted to have met somebody I could geek out with about books.

Evan stared at me, narrowing his eyes. "You have some pizza sauce on your face."

"Oh, God." Tipping my head back, I tried to swipe it off but he shook his head.

"No, to the left. *My* left. For shit's sake, here." Just as he reached to scrape the gunk off my face, the apartment door swung open.

Max stood there staring at us with murder in his eyes.

CHAPTER FOURTEEN

Evan took a step back as I scrubbed my palm across my face, hoping to remove the sauce. Afterward, I realized it probably looked like I was wiping off a kiss. Max sucked in a sharp breath, glancing between us. If he really thought he'd interrupted something, the polite thing to do would be to say "excuse me" and shut the door.

Instead Max glared at both of us. "Who's this?"

"Evan." Wisely, he didn't offer to shake. "Who's backing out of whatever this is. I'll talk to you later, Courtney." Wheeling, he jogged down the stairs and shoved through the front doors, likely calling bullshit on my promise not to start trouble.

I brushed past Max into the apartment. The living room was dark apart from the flicker of the TV screen and if our roommates were home, they must have been in their rooms. Before I could retreat, he grabbed my hand and spun me around. I tugged but he held firm, not tight enough to hurt, but definitely communicating the fact that I wasn't going anywhere. He led me over to the couch and sat down, drawing me with him.

"Really? *That* guy?"

"What are you even talking about?" I pulled my hand back because it was hard to think with his hard, rough fingers wrapped around mine.

"Evan." Max hit out the name like it was poison. "Christ, Courtney. Is it encoded in your DNA that you can only fall for guys whose names start with *E*?"

"Do you know how crazy you sound? I'm not in love with him."

But he didn't seem to be listening, gaze fixed on his fists balled up on his thighs. "I can't believe this is happening. The minute I get close to somebody, they back off. Are you mad at me? Did I do something wrong?"

I sighed, softening at his hurt bewilderment. It wasn't Max's fault that the trip had left me feeling things we had no room for between us. And while I needed some time and space to get my head right, he had no clue why things had changed. I covered his hands with mine.

"Hey. Look at me." When he raised his chin, the sheer intensity of his dark eyes stole my breath, like my face was all he could see. "I'm not mad. And you're awesome, like always."

"Then how come you're never around? Don't lie to me, Courtney. I know something's changed, and I can't handle it. This is exactly how Lauren treated me when—"

"Do *not* compare me to her." The words came out sharper than I meant them to, because he'd spent months moping over her, wishing she'd notice him, wishing she'd take him seriously. When I was *right here*. "Our situation's completely different."

"Feels about the same," he muttered.

I froze, my heart thundering in my ears. *He can't mean that the way it sounds. He can't.*

"What?" I croaked.

Max dropped his gaze and I let go of his hands, shivering. It was hard to get my breath for the tension between us. Or maybe I was the only one caught in the net, tightening until I felt my heart beating in my lips. He didn't speak for a moment.

"I know I'm not Eli, I never will be. But why can't it be me…?"

I wet my lips. "Max—"

"No, let me get this out before you say anything. I may never have the courage again."

"Have you been drinking?"

"A little." He gestured vaguely at the twin beer cans on the end table nearby. "With Lauren, I thought everything would click and I'd be happy if I could make her mine."

"Do you seriously think I want to hear this?" *Again.*

"Bear with me." His voice was husky, unsteady with strong emotions I couldn't even guess at.

I was afraid of where he might be going with this, terrified to hope. My hands trembled in my lap, so I squeezed them until my nails bit into my palms. "Okay."

"With you, Courtney, it's enough for *you* to be happy. Like, it doesn't even matter how I feel or what I want. You know?" My expression must've told him I didn't get it, so he went on with a frustrated sigh. "It's why I tried to set you up, but when you were out with Jared last night and you didn't text, didn't call, I felt like crawling out of my skin."

"Really?" I whispered.

Impossible.

"All last night, I figured maybe you're hooking up. Maybe you're falling for Jared and he won't want us hanging out anymore. Then you show up tonight with that asshole and you're *smiling.* I don't want another guy to put that look on your face."

"I can't promise never to laugh anyone else's jokes."

"Not what I mean and you know it. Just now, you were… happy. And I'm asking, why can't I be the one who makes you feel that way? I don't *want* to find somebody else for you. I want it to be me."

He leaned forward so slowly that I could have ducked away, no problem, but I held still, barely breathing. Max brushed my hair away from my face, stroking his fingers through so gently that tingles ran down my spine. My eyes drifted half-closed. In my head, it was all throbbing drums and Spanish guitar, my ears rushing with need. I wanted his mouth on mine so bad. Not like we did the other two times—for fun or from loneliness—but our first *real* kiss.

The one that would change everything.

"Be really clear here. Please."

"I want to touch you." Deliberately, he tucked a strand of hair behind my ear, his fingertips skating lightly across the shell. "I want to date you." He kissed the tip of my nose with a tenderness other people might question.

But I recognized it. Max had shown me his hidden sweetness in countless ways, and now it was deliciously familiar. I just never expected him to focus it on me.

"What about Lauren?" Maybe I had too much pride, but there was no way I could sign on as a substitute.

He shrugged. "I wish her well. But she's not who I think about all the time."

"I am?"

"Are you trying to kill me with questions?" he demanded. "Give me an answer already. Wait, *no*, don't. Maybe you should think about it. Sleep on it. It's a huge step, but—"

"Yes."

"Yes, it's a huge step?"

I tilted my head, nestling my cheek in his palm. "Let's see what it's like to be...more."

"Does that mean I can kiss you?" he asked softly.

"You'd better." That was pure bravado.

As he closed the distance between us, I feared my heart might fracture my rib cage. He wrapped his arms around me and tilted his head, his face so close I couldn't focus on his features, so I shut my eyes. Like that was his cue, he kissed me. This time, it felt different, less *hey, he's good at this*, and more *Oh, my God, Max is kissing me like he means it*. Another beat, and I couldn't think at all.

His lips were all heat and sweetness, turning over mine with compulsive yearning. Max tangled his hands in my hair and drew me closer as I teased his lower lip with my tongue. He responded with a graze of teeth, then he deepened the kiss, melting my bones with his intensity. We kissed forever, and I couldn't get close enough. He pulled me against him hard and fell back in the same motion so I landed on top of him. Max made an approving noise in the back of his throat as he cupped my ass.

"God, yeah," he groaned.

The raw longing in his tone went straight to my pussy. Just from kissing I was already wet, and my head was spinning. "...Angus...Kia?"

"Fuck." Shuddering, he sat up, arms still around my back. "He's in his room. I almost threw down with him earlier. And she'll probably be home soon."

"Why are you fighting with Angus?" I asked, breathless.

He kissed my forehead softly. "Because of you."

"That doesn't even—"

"He was nagging me about the dishes. I said I didn't feel like it. Angus goes, 'Christ, just fuck her already, get it out of your system.' Not sure if he realized he was talking about you, but I almost took his head off."

"Oh. Well, you can apologize tomorrow. And do the dishes." My pulse might be slowing, but I was still incredibly turned on.

"You want to relocate?" He ran his hands over my hips, shifting me against him.

So fucking hard. I couldn't resist moving once, twice. "You trying to get me alone in your room?"

Max hissed in reaction, tipping his head back. "Damn right."

With a nervous smile, I rolled off the couch and followed him down the hall. By necessity, I stayed close since he didn't let go of my hand until the door shut behind us. Then he locked it for good measure like somebody might barge in at this hour. Actually, that wasn't impossible since Angus occasionally forgot that some people slept more than he did.

I'd hung out in Max's room before, but everything was different now. As he hurried around picking up laundry off the floor, I sat down on the bed. The street lights outside offered enough illumination for me to take in the wondering pleasure in his eyes each time he glanced my way. My smile widened.

"Are you laughing at me?"

"Maybe a little."

"You'd think that would discourage me somewhat..." He dropped his gaze to the hard ridge straining against his jeans.

"Turns out, no?"

"I don't know when it happened. Which sounds stupid, because I should've seen it sooner. But...I *ache* for you." Max paused, then hastened to add, "We don't have to do anything. I just... I want to hold you. I fucking miss waking up with you. Miss the smell of you on my sheets." He fidgeted by the window, and it struck me like a hammer.

Holy shit. He's nervous.

His worries put mine to rest. Smiling, I beckoned, leaning back on his bed. "Come here. You can stop talking."

"I don't know if I should. You still haven't told me how you feel. I'll be crushed if you're using me for sex." Though his words were playful, his expression wasn't, and that was Max. Effervescent on the surface, deep as an artesian spring beneath.

"I'm not. I wouldn't. To be completely honest, I noticed...*this*—" I gestured at Max "—before we got back from Providence."

His eyes widened, evident even in the half-light. "I wish you'd said something."

Startled laughter bubbled out of me. "No thanks. If you didn't feel it, too, it would've been awkward. And humiliating. I've heard the friend-zone speech enough to be positive I couldn't stand getting it from you."

"There were times when I did," he admitted. "But I thought it was just...you know. A guy and a girl in close quarters. It'd be weirder if I didn't occasionally get turned on."

"You just didn't think it was personal." That hurt more, actually.

The incidental boner. It's not you, Courtney.

"Don't look like that, please. You know I'm kind of an idiot."

I managed a shaky smile. "Yeah."

With a soft sigh, Max turned away to stare out the window. "The last night—when you rubbed my head—you got me so hot, I couldn't sleep, Courtney. And trust me, I was *very* aware who was making me feel that way by then. After we got home, I kept obsessing on how fucking good it felt when you put your hands on me."

"So the logical step when you want someone is to offer to find them a date?" I muttered the question beneath my breath but Max heard it.

He finally came over to the bed and sat down beside me. "It was for me. Remember how I said I just wanted you to be happy? That wasn't a line."

"Maybe you could take a shot at it?"

Max kissed me in a series of sexy little forays, never deep enough to sate the heat building between my thighs. Before I fell into him completely, he backed off, dusting kisses over my throat. The room tilted and I landed on my side with Max beside me. He slid an arm around me, his body half over mine. I dug my fingers into his back and shoulders, working lower until I could grab his ass and pull him against me.

"Tell me where the lines are tonight," he whispered, kissing my lower lip.

"Let me think."

He was so handsome I couldn't stand it. I cupped his face in my hands and brushed my mouth against his forehead, temples, nose and chin. Though I didn't intend to tease, he followed my mouth with his, trying to tempt me to a deeper kiss. I evaded with a teasing half smile, working my fingers through his hair to rub his head. *This turned you on, huh?* I recalled how he rolled over on his stomach when I went to the bathroom, imagined how he must've rubbed his cock against the mattress wishing I'd touch it.

"I'd probably kill somebody to find out what's making you look like *that*."

Instead of answering right off I kissed him—a deep, hot whirlwind of a kiss that left us both breathless. "I was just thinking about the last night on the way home from Providence."

"Yeah?" He was distracted, hands slipping under my shirt to explore the soft skin of my belly. I cooperated as he pulled the cotton over my head. *Wish I was wearing better underwear.* But he didn't seem to mind the sports bra I had on. His gaze fixed on the modest swell of my breasts, topped by visibly hard nipples, and he licked his lips.

"I have a confession to make," I murmured.

"Uh-huh?"

"I didn't have to pee."

"…What?" Desire blurred his dark eyes, leaving him with the most adorably perplexed expression. He couldn't figure out why I was still talking instead of touching, kissing, grinding.

I stifled a moan as he worked his thigh between mine.

"You got me so horny, I couldn't wait. I had to—"

Max swore, his intensity ratcheting from incredible to smoldering. "In the bathroom? You were—"

"Getting off. Rubbing one out. Whatever you want to call it. Not the first time, either. I've fantasized about you for a while."

"When?" The question came out hoarse, strangled even. He rolled onto me fully, so I could feel how tremendously hard he was. Then he held still, teasing us both.

"When did I start?" At his jerky nod, I answered, "We made out at that party last year, remember? And we hung out in your room afterward. You were fooling with the basketball, bouncing it off the door so people would think we were having wild monkey sex."

"I remember that."

"You were so into Lauren back then, I knew there was no future in it, but that night, I went home, imagined what it would be like."

"Tell me everything," he ordered.

You dirty boy. I had no idea he liked dirty talk, but this, I could do. "Well, I was living in the dorm back then. Madison was out, thank God. So I went to bed and fucked myself stupid, imagining you were doing me up against your bedroom door. I came so hard, Max."

"How?" he whispered.

"You mean fingers or toys?"

"Yeah." Max lay down on me and put his face in my neck, trembling with the force of his need. He pumped his hips against me in furtive movements, unconscious, uncontrollable.

"Vibrator, six inches, flexible. But I didn't turn it on that night. I just used it to fuck like you would."

My nipples were so hard they hurt. His breath gusted in my ear as he worked his hips. Even with two layers of denim between us, it felt amazing. Max levered up enough to pull my bra and his shirt off. Then we were half-naked, skin to skin, and he growled, a hot flush high on his cheekbones. His mouth was slightly parted as he hung over me, biceps bulging.

"I don't... I have no idea what I'm doing. Courtney, please—" Losing control, he bit into my neck and wrapped his arms tight around my back. His hot skin felt delicious against my aching breasts. I craved his mouth, his fingers, everything.

Never been so turned on in my life.

Somehow we wriggled out of our jeans and then there were only two thin layers of cotton between us. I expected him to roll back on top of me but instead he held himself up and slipped a hand into my panties. His eyes closed when he discovered how slick I was for him. Max stroked in perfect rhythm, edging me closer and closer. Like a bastard, he teased around my clit, working my labia until I could only moan and rub against his hand.

He kissed my belly, licking a circle around my navel while he drove me crazy with his fingers. "Sexy, sexy girl. You have to come soon."

"Working on it," I panted.

"No, you *have* to. I'm...close."

"But I'm not even touching you." Astonishment drove me upward, so my hand brushed his hard cock, and the new angle on his fingers, along with the extra pressure, spiked me into the hardest orgasm ever, even as Max called my name, shivering against me.

Holy, holy *shit.*

CHAPTER FIFTEEN

Afterward, Max stumbled to the bathroom to clean up.

Still too dreamy to move, I crawled under the covers. *If he wants me to leave, he can kick me out.* I'd pictured being nearly naked in Max's bed before, but I never thought it would actually happen. With a goofy smile, I fell into the pillows and breathed him in. His scent was clean but earthy, a hint of gas and engine oil, plus the bright lemony scent of his soap. I stroked the pillow next to me.

A few minutes later, he returned in clean boxer briefs and as he came toward me, I admired the cut of his abs along with the lean line of his thighs.

"Perving on me already?" But he grinned as he climbed in next to me.

"You love it."

"Maybe a little."

Max dropped onto his back and spread his arm around, inviting me to cuddle up against him with a smoky look.

I rolled against his side and found the perfect place for my head. As soon as I settled, he relaxed on a long breath, staring up at the ceiling with an expression that mirrored how I felt. Hesitantly I reached out and trailed my fingers down his chest, watching Max's face.

His gaze heated as he sucked in a sharp breath. "That feels amazing."

"I'm glad. I still kind of can't believe you want this. Michael will be so disappointed. He asked me to wait for him, you know."

Max's eyes snapped open fully. "The fuck he did."

"Kidding. But that does bring me to a pertinent question."

"What's that?"

"Should I tell him the next time I email? And what about our friends?"

A frown pulled his brows together. "Is there some reason we shouldn't?"

"I dunno. You might want to keep it quiet in case things don't work out."

"Hold up. Why won't it work?" His frown deepened into a scowl and he levered up, jolting me away from him.

"Don't flip out. I was only asking how you want to handle breaking the news, not prognosticating the end of *us*."

"I like *us*. Good word." Max relaxed marginally and his hands felt possessive when he drew me fully into his arms.

"Me, too. Anyway, what do you think?"

"That I want the world to know we're together. I couldn't give two shits who you tell. In fact, I'm thinking about scaling a tall building to yell about it."

That earned him a kiss on the shoulder. "Is there an elevator? If so, I'll go with you."

"I'm not worth climbing twenty-five flights of stairs?" He feigned a hurt look, executing the lost puppy air so well that if I didn't know better, I'd take him seriously.

"You are. But I might die on the way up, that's all I'm saying."

"I'll carry you."

"Hmm, that might end in a herniated something. Why don't we stay in bed?" I brushed my fingertips across his forehead, playing with silky strands of dark hair.

"Somehow you've talked me into it. So tell me about the guy who brought you home." Though Max was smiling, the look in his eyes told me he needed to know.

It was weird to imagine him feeling insecure over *me* when he was so good with women. But maybe that was the key difference, plural. To the best of my recollection, he'd never settled into a relationship, never dedicated himself to one person. Considered in that light, his vulnerability seemed more understandable; he'd never been in this position before.

"I have some news, actually." From there I told him all about the band, starting with Evan and continuing with Dana and Ji Hoo. While his expression lightened, I filled him in on the musical style and ended with the no-dating-other-members rule.

"I'm speechless."

"In a good way?"

"Obviously. This is hella cool. My girlfriend's a rock star!"

My breath caught as a shiver of pleasure rolled through me. *Girlfriend.* "Please. I just had one rehearsal and they're busy teaching me not to suck."

"Promise you'll tell me about your first show. I won't forgive you if I miss it."

"Okay, I swear. It could take a while, though."

"Understood. What made you..." He trailed off, probably unable to think of a way to phrase the question that didn't make me sound like an ambitionless potato.

"Try something new?" I offered.

"Exactly." Relief colored his voice.

I smacked his arm gently. There was no way I'd tell him that it was because I needed a non-Max-centric hobby. "In high school I was really into music. Eli and I went to concerts all the time and we talked about starting up an indie music label together."

"You never told me that." His eyes took on that deep, haunted look I'd noticed anytime I mentioned Eli.

"For the longest time I didn't see any point in talking about dead dreams. But lately I've been wondering if they could be brought back to life."

"What could?" he asked warily.

"My old plans. Eli's gone, but it doesn't mean *I* can't do things that used to make me happy. I never loved the classical stuff my parents prefer but I might have a lot of fun with the music Racing Sorrow plays. I figured it didn't hurt to try."

"That's your band?"

"Yeah." I repeated what Evan had said about the reason behind the name.

"I like it. And from what you said about the set list, I think I'll enjoy the sound, too. But even if you were playing death metal I'd come cheer you on."

I grinned. "But you'd bring earplugs."

"Probably." Sheepish tone.

"Maybe I'll write you a song," I mused.

"If you do, make sure to praise me as a sex god."

"Hmm. I suspect I'll need more empirical evidence before inspiration strikes."

Max rolled onto his side and draped his right arm and leg across my body. "Are you challenging me?"

"Possibly."

"Am I allowed an intermission?"

Smiling, I stretched lazily and kissed his jaw. "You can't go again? See, this is where being female comes in handy."

"Give me ten minutes." He ran his fingers through my hair and each time he brushed the nape of my neck, it sent fresh shivers through me. I let out a little moan. "Okay, five."

"I can't believe I'm in your bed."

Hesitating, he cupped the back of my head in his hands. "Maybe I shouldn't admit this, but there probably haven't been as many women as you think."

"In your bed? I know, you never bring them home."

"That's not what I mean. Just because I leave with somebody, it doesn't automatically mean we hooked up."

"Hey, your past is—"

"I'm being sincere here. Nadia seems to think I've banged hundreds of women. I don't care about correcting *her*, but you're different."

"I hope so. If you ever had a thing for Nadia, then you're completing the roommate trifecta, and I'm pretty sure all a woman has to do is move in and feed you a few times." I smirked to show I was teasing. "Don't they call that stray puppy syndrome?"

"Funny."

"Any stirrings toward Kia yet? Wait, I don't think she cooks—"

He shut me up with a kiss. Normally that move would make me want to kick a guy in the junk, but this was Max. I forgot about teasing him for endlessly delicious moments. When we broke apart, I was breathing hard and he had that look in his eyes again.

"Are you going to let me finish?"

"That depends."

"On what?"

"Whether you mean talking or sex."

"Both," he said. "Eventually."

"Okay, I promise I won't mess with you anymore." I hesitated long enough for him to wonder what I meant, then added, "Verbally."

"Thank God. In my defense, I liked Lauren *before* we moved in together. And no, I've never seen Nadia and Kia as anything more than friends."

"I was joking. But your earnest look is adorable, so carry on."

He kissed my nose in response. "Anyway, I just want to make sure you know you're...special to me. I won't fuck around on you."

"Wait, so this is relationship-y nakedness? Damn. I don't know if this is going to work, Max. After all, I did just join a band. I'll eventually have groupies and—"

"Really? I bare my heart and you eat it?"

I smacked my lips. "It was delicious, I regret nothing."

"You're an awful human being."

"I know."

Pulling away, he pretended to pout, so I followed him to

the other side of the bed and tickled him until he grabbed my hands and stilled them on his chest. "You were kidding, right? I already called you my girlfriend and you didn't protest. It's too late to back out."

"Obviously. I'm sure you weren't *really* worried, but I can do monogamous. You can trust me," I added quietly.

This seemed like a big deal to him, though I wasn't entirely sure why. I knew about Max's propensity for hooking up, for no-strings sex, but he'd never told me about getting his heart broken. There was the whole Lauren thing, of course, but that didn't count as a failed relationship. I studied his face in the glow from the streetlights in the parking lot, wondering why he seemed so serious. My happiness at being with him left me giddy and slightly silly, but he radiated a different vibe entirely.

"I do," he said.

"Then what's going on? You're super intense right now. Not in a scary way."

"I just feel…" He trailed off, tipping his head back on the pillows. I rolled over and propped onto my elbows, waiting. "At a disadvantage, I guess."

"Why?"

"I haven't had a girlfriend since I was fifteen, Courtney. You had Eli…and then Amy, maybe other relationships, too. You have more experience at being a partner than I do, and I'm *so* afraid I'm going to fuck this up."

Guilt slithered over me; I shouldn't have taken his concerns lightly. "The fact that you care means it'll be fine. I'm not saying we'll never disagree, but that comes with the territory. Don't let it stress you out, okay? As long as you're honest about what you need from me, we can figure it out as we go."

"I need everything," he whispered.

"Wow." I shivered a bit. "You don't have anything to worry about, you're great at this."

"At what?"

"Putting it all on the line."

He smiled slightly. "I'm really not. You're the only person in the world I can talk to like this, the one person who might believe I'm capable of it."

"That's good…because it would probably piss me off if you spread your deepest feelings around like some kind of emotional harlot."

"All my feelings are belong to you?"

"Yep. Which means I want to hear if you have a shitty day and you need a hug, or if you have amazing news and want to celebrate. I should be your first stop, no matter what. Get me?"

"I did that before we got together," he said in a quietly marveling tone. "It was—we were—all of this already, just without the sex."

"I like sex," I pointed out.

"Me, too. And it's even better with you."

"How would you know? We've spent the past hour talking. You could've fucked me four times by now."

"Complaining will *not* get you laid any faster."

"What will? Bacon sandwich? Because I'll totally fry some. Naked. And that might be painful, so I hope you appreciate what I'm willing to sacrifice for you." I made like I was going to climb over him and Max pulled me down on top.

"You know the sexiest thing about you?"

I furrowed my brow in mock-thought. "Is it my ass? I hear it's pretty juicy, if you like them big and round."

"Your brain."

"Is this where you tell me you're going to drill holes to let the demons out and then make sweet, sweet love to my skull? Because I think I have to pass."

He muffled a laugh. "Courtney. You make it really hard to be sincere, you know that?"

"Fine, tell me all about my beautiful mind."

"You make me laugh, no matter how bad my mood is. You always listen, even when you're busy or tired. And you're on my side, whether I deserve it or not. What I'm trying to say is, I'd want you if you were a dude, a robot, or a head in a jar, as long as you were still *you*."

"You win," I whispered, hugging him.

"What's the prize?"

"Me. I hope you don't feel cheated."

"No way." His arms came around me, and I snuggled my face against his neck, kissing a path toward his jaw. "You are my golden ticket, baby."

"Eh." I eased back. "Maybe not. I'm not opposed to pet names but let's find one that doesn't infantilize me."

"Fine, I'll work on it. Sweetheart."

"Better, but it still doesn't feel right."

"Do you intend to critique my sexual skills, as well?" He eyed me with a mixture of amusement and chagrin.

I grinned teasingly. "Dunno, would it push you to try harder?"

"You'll give me performance anxiety."

Wriggling on top of him, I decided that seemed unlikely. "Did you tell your dick?"

"He's *head*strong, doesn't listen to me." The faint stress delivered the joke.

I snickered as I leaned down to give Max a lingering kiss. "Ten points for a sex pun. You can't fall asleep like this. So should *I* get off or should we?"

"We already did, but you're making me curious about the sequel."

"Sequels are never as good." I kissed his shoulder.

"That's a dirty lie. What about *Mad Max 2*, *Aliens*, *Star Trek: Wrath of Khan*—"

"I've never wanted you more. Your secret geek makes me want to tie you up and lick you all over." Demonstrating, I eased down his body and ran my mouth over his rib cage to his abdomen, tasting, nibbling, nuzzling.

Max sucked in a sharp breath. "I think you might be kidding about the bondage, but you should know, you're seriously turning me on right now."

"That's the point."

"I wasn't sure you'd want to—" His voice broke on a groan when I put my mouth on his nipple, sucking lightly.

"I do, so much."

"Yeah?" His eyes burned with longing, fixed on my face until I squirmed on top of him.

Max's skin felt incredible, hot and smooth. He was so tan compared to me, a lovely contrast in the moonlight. I remembered how much he liked it when I told him how I fantasized about him. At the moment, I wasn't sure how to incorporate that without it seeming like something from a porno, but I wanted to figure out how to make talking natural.

Oh. Maybe…

"I want to make you come again." His cock throbbed against my stomach in reaction. *Yeah, definitely on the right track.* "But how? Should I use my mouth, tease you, until you can't take anymore and you—"

"Yes, that. Do that." He worked his hips against me, getting hotter as I spoke. *Phone sex with him would be amazing.*

"Or I could strip off your underwear right now and climb on. It feels like you're ready to be fucked. Hard and fast, gentle and slow?"

I pretended to consider while Max ran desperate hands over my back, stroking, urging me on. He cupped my ass and kneaded, licking his lips as he gazed up at me. At any point, he could've taken control but he seemed to be waiting for me to decide. I liked his hungry patience; God, I was so wet, partly from the orgasm he'd given me before, but mostly from the incredible rush of tenderness and desire flooding through me right now.

"You feel so fucking good," he whispered.

Lowering my head, I went back to my original plan of kissing him all over soon. I tasted every inch of his throat and shoulders, his chest, his sexy-as-fuck abs. Max knotted his fists in the sheets as I lowered the waistband of his boxer briefs and licked the curve of his hip. His thighs came up, taut as steel beams, and I used the leverage to strip off the fabric entirely. Then he was naked for me, his cock long and lean, throbbing visibly.

"Delicious."

"It feels like you're making love to me." His voice was husky, thick, not just from sex.

I paused, glancing up. "Is that a problem?"

"Nobody ever has before. It's *so good*."

His emotional nakedness stripped me to the bone. Before I knew it, I was naked, too. Max fumbled in his bedside drawer and got out a condom. I rolled it on for him and then pulled him upright. It felt like we needed to do this together. Sinking onto his lap, I watched his face as he pushed into me, an agony of pleasure, the brightest sunrise in his parted lips. Max wrapped his arms tight around me and I held him just as hard, wrapping my legs around his back, too. I'd never had anyone inside me like this, not ever, sexually, emotionally; he was everything, everywhere, and we strained together, fighting for more, deeper, better—*yes*.

"Like that?" he breathed. "Oh, fuck. Courtney."

My breasts rubbed against his chest while he pulled me into him. He worked my ass in his hands, cupping, squeezing, and I was so hot, unable to stop thinking, *Max, this is Max inside me, Max*— We came together, shuddering, and I remembered how the French called this the little death. Yet my heart beat on, for him.

Always, for him.

CHAPTER SIXTEEN

The next morning, it was late when I rolled out of Max's bed.

I woke alone, my clothes still strewn all over his floor, mingling with his dirty laundry. Which was gross but also kind of weirdly sweet. *You are in so deep if you think his sweaty socks are adorable.* After getting dressed, I could *not* resist the urge to straighten up his room.

It wasn't that I was trying to mother him, but if he expected me to spend time in here, there would have to be some changes or OCD would make my head explode. Quietly I tiptoed around, sorting his clothes by clean and dirty, and yeah, I did the sniff test, which should've made me want to dump Max immediately. The fact that it didn't struck me as worrisome.

After I put his laundry in the hamper, I tucked it away in the closet, then I started on his clutter. I organized music, movies and games as made sense to me, expecting him to burst in any minute and ask what the hell I was doing. *It's helpful*, I told myself. *I'm helping. He'll see that, right?* Making the bed properly only took a couple of minutes, then I dusted his bedside table, chest and shelves, though I couldn't call myself satisfied until I vacuumed in here.

I ventured out, not cautious exactly, but I still froze when Max came down the hall toward me. "You look guilty."

Biting my lip, I gave up on the idea of *ever* keeping a secret from him. "Uh. Surprise?"

"Wow. I haven't seen the carpet in three months. It's still beige, huh?" That wasn't a horrible reaction, I guessed. He seemed more amused than upset.

"If you want me to have sex with you in there again," I whispered, "then it has to stay that way. Last night was an aberration...and it was dark."

"Hey, I picked up some dirty clothes last night."

I grinned, going on tiptoe to kiss him on the cheek. "You only got the first layer, it's like you're trying to make topsoil or something."

"When you put it that way, it sounds supergross. Let's do laundry later." Max followed me to the kitchen, wrapping his arms about my waist to snuggle me from behind.

Angus was making pancakes in the kitchen. He cracked a huge grin, pointing his spatula at me. "Somebody got lucky last night."

"Was it your mom?"

"Doubtful. She prefers sculpting and charity work. *Don't* try to change the subject."

Opening my eyes anime wide, I protested, "I'm not. I'm genuinely concerned about your mother's sex life."

"I already told him we're together, don't let him give you

a hard time." As Angus ladled out another hotcake, Max kissed my ear.

I shivered slightly. "That's your job?"

"Got that right."

"I can see you washed the dishes. Did you apologize, too?" It seemed best to confirm, though if Angus was still mad at Max, I suspected I'd know by now.

He nuzzled my neck. "Of course. For *some* reason I'm in a fantastic mood today." Releasing me, he ambled over to the fridge and spelled out You Drive Me Wild with the fridge magnets. Not content with that, Max added I Want You.

Angus sighed. "Clearly we need some PDA rules. If I *ever* come across you two screwing around in the common areas, I will hose you down like dogs."

Laughing, I said, "That's fair. I'm pretty sure we can confine our lust to Max's room."

"Speak for yourself. The minute Angus goes to Del's, we're doing it in his bed."

"I hate you *so* much," Angus muttered.

"Wrong. Or you wouldn't be making enough food for everyone." Max went over to mess up Angus's hair, something he *hated*.

"Get off me, you asshole." Angus hip-checked him into the counter while flipping a flapjack. I considered that fairly impressive multitasking.

"God, y'all are loud." Kia stumbled out of our room wearing a cranky look. "I don't care who's hooking up with who, I need actual sleep." She brightened up when she realized breakfast was in the works. "*Ooh*, pancakes."

Turning to her with a smile, Angus ordered us around

like a boss. "They're almost ready. Courtney, can you get the eggs out of the oven? Max, set the table."

"Wow, this is fancy." When Nadia lived here, we did this sort of thing a lot more often, as she and Angus were more domestic than Max and me.

"I figured we should try talking to each other once a week or so."

Kia smirked at Angus. "Boy, you sound just like my mama. If you guilt me about family time, I won't even notice I left home."

Though she was joking, I could tell it was a nice surprise for her to wake up to a home-cooked meal. I got the pot-holders and delivered an egg casserole thing to the table. It had bacon in it, but since Angus was health-conscious, it would be turkey, not pork. I was mostly lapsed, religion-wise, but sometimes I felt bad for abandoning most of our family traditions. But this wasn't time to think about pa-rental disapproval and disappointment.

Max had plates, silverware and napkins laid out, so I added margarine and syrup. Kia sat down wearing a bemused look as Angus delivered the pancakes.

"Do you need something?" she asked him.

I laughed.

Angus shook his head. "I used to cook more before things got so...*good* with Del. In fact we used to eat dinner together whenever we could."

"You know that's kinda weird, right?" But it didn't stop her from digging into the food.

"What is?" Max asked.

"Building a little surrogate family when people are only

together to make rent and may move along as soon as the lease runs out."

Okay, it was weird for me to be the one fielding this since I wasn't typically superemotional, but… "That may be true, but if we get to be friends instead of just roommates, then I can count on you. And vice versa. Even after you go your own way, I'll still come when you call. I'd do the same for Nadia, she's downstairs now, and I don't see her as much as I did when she was in my room, but when she left, it didn't change anything."

"And if Lauren needed me," Angus put in, "I'd be on the first plane to Kansas."

From behind my hand, I corrected, "Nebraska."

"Lack of geographic accuracy doesn't negate my point."

"Sustained," Max said.

Angus grabbed his spoon and started singing Diana Ross, "I'm Gonna Make You Love Me," while I harmonized on backup. Max couldn't carry a tune in a bag, but he chimed in on the chorus after hearing us run through it a couple times.

"Okay, I'm starting to get it." Kia glanced between us, her smile warm if slightly bewildered. "How much time do I have to put in? Because I already don't sleep a whole lot."

"This is enough," I answered.

"What is?"

"Hanging out on Sunday morning, goofing with us and eating pancakes."

She grinned. "It's a tough job but somebody's gotta do it. Angus, these are fab, seriously. Everything is. The last time I ate this well, it was in a restaurant."

Beaming at her, he said, "Flattery will definitely get you fed more often."

"Why doesn't that work for me?" Max wondered aloud.

"Because you're a pig who refuses to do the dishes on time, drinks from the carton and leaves wet towels on our bathroom floor."

"Are you gonna let him talk to me that way?" Max nudged me with his knee under the table, rubbing his leg against mine.

"But…that's all true. So…uhm. Wow, Angus, you sure are painfully honest. Stop it right now, seriously. Max is a fragile flower who needs lying kindness to bloom. Or something."

Kia asked, "Are you *sure* you two are really a couple? I mean, I noticed your bed was empty last night and all but if I'd fucked with Duncan like that—"

"Duncan was a douche canoe," Angus cut in. "The polar opposite of a dreamboat."

I nodded. "Never met the guy, but from everything you've said, I tend to agree. Sounds like he didn't have much sense of humor, either."

She sighed, her fork hovering in midair. "The stories I could tell. I can't believe I wasted two years on him."

"Why did you?" Max wanted to know.

"At first, it was the status," she admitted.

"Huh?" That wasn't what I expected to hear.

"He was fine, drove an expensive car. And when I walked in at his side, I felt like somebody. With Duncan, there were never any lines, no club we couldn't get into. He didn't think anything of hopping in the private plane and flying us somewhere for the weekend."

Wow. Racking my brain, I couldn't remember much about her ex, except that he came from a conservative family in the Bible belt. And obviously he had money, based on what she was saying. "Yeah, I can see how that would be appealing at first."

Max made a game-show buzzer sound. "Wrong answer. Your not-at-all rich boyfriend reminds you how much cooler it is to *earn* things."

God, it seemed like he might never get tired of claiming ownership like that, and to be honest, it gave me a happy little thrill, too. The sweetness rushed over me until I could barely think, so I just reached for his hand under the table while offering a half smile. Kia cleaned her plate quietly, obviously pensive, and Angus was good at reading the mood. I suspected we all understood that she had more to say.

"Eventually, though..." I prompted.

"I got sick of his entitlement, the way he was raised to believe the world revolved around him and never questioned it. In his mind, I should've been happy just *being* with him, like an accessory. He treated my dreams like nothing, like it's vanity that I'm busting ass to get into med school. And let's not even get started on the way he tried to vet my friends."

"Sounds like you're still pretty pissed off at him," Angus said.

"I guess I am. Little boys have *no* place in my life, and he wasted *so* much of my time. Though there were moments I thought maybe he'd grow up fast enough to make it right."

"I'm not making excuses for him, but it can be hard to break away from family expectations," I said quietly. "I did it, but every time I go home, I hear about how far I am from where my parents want me to be, all the ways I'm letting them down. And what's worse is, they're not trying to be assholes. It always comes couched in genuine concern."

Kia tilted her head. "My mama's not like that. My dad,

either. They're both crazy proud of how well I'm doing. Sophomore year, I almost flunked out from skipping school so much. I didn't think there was any way I'd get to college, so why even try? But my mama put me in a volunteer program at the hospital, trying to show me how many people had it worse than me."

"And that's when you realized you wanted to be a doctor?" Max asked.

She grinned, slightly sheepish. "Hells no. I was mad for six months. I had to deliver and read mail, feed people who couldn't hold a spoon, and I wasn't even getting paid."

"So what was your big defining moment?" Angus wondered aloud.

She'd told me about her older brother, but I was curious what she'd say now, plus he'd asked Kia, not me. So I kept quiet.

"When I was a kid, my older brother was shot. Died on the operating table. That's part of why I started skipping school. Darrell was smart, you know? He would've had a bright future."

"I'm sorry," Angus murmured.

"Me, too. So anyway, fast forward to the volunteer program. They asked me to deliver a message to the ER, something that wasn't even on my to-do list, as I worked mostly with elder care and long-term patients. But I liked the woman in charge, so I didn't bitch. Ended up at the desk when a GSW came in. Blood everywhere, and I couldn't stop thinking about Darrell. But the doctor on duty was so calm, so capable, and she got *everything* under control so fast, brought order to the chaos. I wanted to *be* her."

As it turned out, she'd only told me part of the story. I

liked learning the rest. "And now you're making it happen. Fuck Duncan for not getting it."

"I'll drink to that," Kia said.

We raised our OJ glasses and toasted. To lighten the atmosphere, I changed the subject. "So I have news."

Max shot me a curious look but he already knew. Everyone was excited to find out about the band, and I promised to keep them posted about our schedule. "But I'm pretty sure it'll be weeks, if not months, before I'm good enough for an actual performance."

Kia tilted her head. "You want to be a rock star? Sex, drugs, all that. Is that why your parents disapprove?"

Maybe it was time I stopped clutching my dreams to my chest, hiding them like faded prom corsages I'd pressed in an old scrapbook. "Actually..."

Hesitating, I remembered sitting at Eli's bedside while we created the business plan. I still had the notebook with the figures written neatly in Eli's best accounting style, including studio time, marketing, production and engineering fees, PR, artwork, website design, accountant and legal fees, packaging, remixers and session musicians. At one point, I knew exactly how my future looked—with Eli beside me every step of the way. We'd been together since we were kids; there was no reason for me to imagine anything else.

A wistful feeling stole over me, not the anguish that left me hollowed out like a Russian stacking doll. For once, thinking of him didn't bring his voice to life in my head. A few months back, the silence would've made me melancholy. Yet the idea of losing Eli's echo seemed inevitable now, not a fate worse than death. Maybe I was getting better. Despite my mother's compulsive fear, I no longer had the urge to eat sleeping pills and dream my life away.

With a small smile, I told everyone about my indie music label idea, omitting Eli entirely.

There were only Max's fingers wrapped around mine, encouraging me to continue, warm and rough, completely real. *He's here, he's healthy. He cares about me.* To anyone else, those might seem like small things but from where I'd been, the brightness felt miraculous.

"Not to be crass, but that'll require start-up money," Angus pointed out.

I nodded. "I have some in savings from my grandfather. So far, I haven't touched it because my parents are paying my way. I know that makes me a princess." Ducking my head, I couldn't quite look at Max and Kia, who had things much tougher.

"I guess that makes me a queen," Angus joked.

"Yeah, *I* go home to Chicago over the summer, I don't get sent to Europe for three weeks." I teased him a little. "And didn't they pay for Del to go this time?"

"God, it was incredible. You haven't lived until you've had morning coffee on the Seine. We found a lovely café on the Quai d'Orsay, all Belle Epoque with fabulous hammered silver—"

"You realize some of us have never even been on a plane," Max cut in.

"Seriously?" Angus asked.

Since Max tended to joke around, I understood Angus's skepticism. But I'd learned to read him over the years, and he wasn't kidding about this. I hadn't known this either, though. No reason for Angus to feel bad. But on closer consideration, it made sense. Leaving home at sixteen didn't exactly offer a ton of vacation opportunities. For years he'd focused on working and getting his GED. After that, it was probably a constant battle to make tuition payments.

"Yeah. My old man wasn't big on family trips when we were kids."

It would've taken away too much time from the drinking, I thought.

Before the others could dig into his past, I stood up, positive he didn't want other people knowing as much as I did. "I'll wash up. Kia, feel free to go back to sleep."

She smiled at me. "I have some reading to do, but thanks. You, too, Angus."

When she went into our room and closed the door, I felt like we were a few steps closer to being actual friends. That brightened my mood.

As I started clearing, Angus kicked my happy up another notch when he hugged me. "You're the best, you know that? Del's coming over later and I wasn't sure how I'd get this place cleaned up fast enough to still have time to deliver my usual level of hotness."

"Please, you're fantastic even when you're sweaty-gross from housework."

"That's enough of that," Max said, elbowing between us.

"You're not allowed to be jealous when Courtney flirts with me," Angus complained. "It's harmless fun...and great for my ego."

"Bullshit. I can be, all the time if I want. I'm jealous of her sheets."

"You're so weird." When Max came into the kitchen

with a load of plates, I kissed him to show my approval of his brand of bizarre-love.

"That's my cue to shower." Angus headed down the hall with a wave, pointedly not looking back, which prompted Max to shove me up against the fridge. His lips tasted like pancakes and maple syrup. *Yum.*

"Whew. Stop distracting me, I promised to clean."

"I could be convinced to help."

"I'll make it worth your while," I promised.

He waggled his brows as he pressed closer, teasing but not. Before sex, he'd totally tidy up the apartment to make me happy—on his day off—despite hating these chores. That was his way of showing devotion, so adorable, impassioned, sincere…and *mine. He's mine.* Heat swept over me, not just a desire for sex, but deeper and fiercer, a hunger for everything Max, as if I could somehow absorb his sweetness into my bones.

Please, I thought. *Please, Max. Don't ever stop feeling this way.*

CHAPTER SEVENTEEN

I was lounging on my bed, half-heartedly reading assigned statistics material when the front door slammed.

Things had been…interesting since Sunday. I had to argue with Max about whose bed I'd be sleeping in every night, but I wasn't ready to move into his room. That felt too fast and I definitely wouldn't get enough sleep if we didn't impose some limits. So right now, I was restricting us to weekend sleepovers because he had work and school, too. That didn't mean I wouldn't fool around, obviously. Max had been annoyed for two days, giving me his trademark puppy eyes, but I was iron woman; I just needed a titanium bustier to prove it.

Maybe for Halloween…

My door flew open. Not a big deal because it wasn't closed tight anyway. I'd shut and lock if I was feeling antisocial. Max strode into the room, still grubby from working at the garage all afternoon. "This might sound odd, but…I want to take you out."

"Like garbage? For an airing, maybe? Also, hey, honey, how was your day? You look all grimy and what-not. Makes me want to loofah you."

"Is that a verb?"

"It is not. Frankly you look like you could use a sound loofah-ing. Was it a bad day?" I hopped off the bed and closed the distance between us, clutching the front of his jumpsuit to pull him in for a kiss. I'd die before admitting this, but his gray work coveralls, complete with MAX patch, were so retro they were adorable. If my ass wasn't bigger than his, I'd steal a pair. Sometimes he just wore a work shirt and pants, but for really dirty jobs he busted these out.

"I haven't even washed my hands yet. Can't touch you."

"Even hotter," I whispered.

He smelled like he'd been working on cars in the late summer heat, but his scent was so familiar that I didn't mind. I kissed him deeply, savoring the hint of salt on his lips. Max exhaled slowly, fingers curling into fists at his side as he resisted the urge to reach for me. I pulled back with a teasing smile.

"You're heartless. Unless you actually plan to loofah me."

"Is anyone else home?" It never left my mind how quickly the others could get fed up. Angus and Kia never signed on to live with a couple, and sex always complicated any dynamic.

"Yeah, Angus is in his room." Judging by his glum tone, Max realized that shower sex dreams had to wait.

"So you want to take me out, huh. For an official first date?"

"Yeah. Is that dumb?"

"Well, no. Dating is what people do. Well, those who are dating."

"So will you? Go out with me."

I grinned up at him. "Technically, I already am. We do everything backward, you know? But it sounds fun. When?"

"Friday night, clear your schedule, because you're all mine."

"Okay. Can't wait to see what you have planned for us." Giving him a little shove, I followed him toward the door. "Come back when you're clean."

"Fine. But just so you know, I'll be all naked, soapy and wet, thinking of you. When nature takes its course, you have only yourself to blame."

"Blame, my ass. I'll take credit. Also, pics or it didn't happen."

Max grinned. "You serious? I'll totally—"

"Get out." I shut the door in his face before he tempted me to be wild, irresponsible and inconsiderate to poor Angus, who probably didn't want to listen to us banging in his bathroom.

Still, I went to the bathroom and splashed cold water on my face. Max lit me up from normal temperature to white-hot in ten seconds. Somehow, I didn't think he was what my mom had in mind when she bugged me to get over Eli, get out there and meet a nice boy. With a faint sigh, I texted her my usual reassurance that I was sober and doing homework. She replied instantly, making me wonder what she actually *did* with her time. Before I was born she'd worked but never since, not even after I left home. I had some vague memory of clubs and coffee klatches, but that left her way too much opportunity to obsess over my life choices.

I opened the text. When are you coming home again?

Since I was there a month ago, I could be forgiven for the impatience as I typed back, Winter break probably. Talk to you later.

My phone beeped again but I didn't read the message. The time on the screen reminded me I had fifteen minutes to get to Evan's. So I banged on the bathroom door.

"Did you change your mind?" Max yelled. "Because I already started without you."

From Angus's room came a muffled groan. "God, why?"

Ignoring him, I called, "Then stop. I need a ride."

"I can take a break if it's not far," Angus offered.

That would've been fine, except I heard Max cussing and dropping things in the bathroom. I smirked at Angus. "I think that means he wants to go."

"He's weirdly possessive about you. I mean, he knows I won't try anything, so…"

"Her time is mine," Max said flatly.

"Dial it down and let's go."

"I'm hungry," he complained, following me out of the apartment and down the stairs.

"Whose fault is that? Angus could've driven me to rehearsal." But that would've meant missing out on *this*. A surge of warmth went through me as he handed me his spare helmet. Once he got settled, I swung on behind him and wrapped my arms around his back.

"Is it so wrong that I want to be with you?"

"Nah. It's adorable. I don't even mind when you growl to

warn other people away. But if you even *think* about peeing on me, all bets are off."

"Gotcha, no water sports. Hold on tight, angel."

"Really?"

"So that's another for the no pile?"

"I'm afraid so, champ."

Max made a face over his shoulder at me. "You're not even trying. Didn't you call me 'sport' the other night?"

"Yeah, I'm bad at this. But I'm great at sex, so that's a win for you. All the orgasms, none of the embarrassing nicknames. Cuddle monkey."

"I won't rest until I've dubbed you something permanently precious."

"You could call me precious, as long as you can do the sinister dog laugh."

"I have no idea what you're talking about."

"It's an old cartoon, Eli used to watch it online. I'll show you later."

"If Eli loved it, I can't wait," he said wryly.

I can't believe he's jealous of me, Eli said. *He's already had sex with you more than I have. Plus, y'know, he's got a pulse.*

"Cut it out." The weird thing: I was talking to both Max and Eli, how trippy was that.

"Where am I going?" I gave him Evan's address and he started the bike, roaring off with a certainty that told me he knew the way.

It had been a while since I rode with him; I strangled a possessive impulse to demand he never let anyone else on the back of his motorcycle. Maybe I'd been watching too much *Sons of Anarchy* but it felt like that privilege should be reserved for me. Hell, next time he came out with some crazy hands-off statement, I'd even say so.

Since it was getting dark at this hour, cool wind rushed over my skin, adding another layer of pleasure to the ride. Too soon, he pulled up at Evan's place, but there were no lights inside and I didn't hear anything from the garage. Hopping off the bike, I yanked off my helmet.

"I bet he went to pick up Dana and Ji Hoo. They'll be here any minute."

"Do I get to meet them?"

"Do you want to?"

"Well, yeah. I'm curious about your new bandmates. I can't wait to hear you play."

"I'm nothing special," I muttered.

"That's completely false."

Raising a brow, I said, "Anyone could achieve equal proficiency after the same lessons."

"Not what I'm talking about, Courtney."

"Oh." Since I was thinking about music, I didn't connect the dots. His sudden sweetness brought heat to my cheeks, and dear God, I *never* blushed. It was kind of my deal to be out there: unshockable, edgy and outrageous. "Well, I meant instrumentally, though I really do love music. I have a great ear, I think, I just don't have the talent to back it up."

"I won't argue the point until you play me something. Which had better be soon." He made a mock-threatening face and kissed the top of my head. "But honestly, if you're on point with that personal assessment, it's an even better argument to run with your indie label idea. You know music, you love it, but you don't want to play for a living. So it'd be perfect if you could help make other people's dreams come true and create something beautiful at the same time."

My throat tightened. "Yeah. It would."

Before he could answer, Evan's van pulled into the drive-way. The garage door opened—I assumed by remote—to reveal the rehearsal space, but he didn't pull in. We needed the space. Evan looked wary when he hopped out and spotted Max, who made me smile by strolling over with his hand extended.

"Sorry, man. We got off on the wrong foot the other night and I owe you a big apology."

"You thought I was hitting on your girl?" Evan guessed.

Max lifted a shoulder in a vague gesture. "Something like that. But we cleared the air and everything is cool. I hope you don't think I'm a complete dick."

"Nah. If you were, you wouldn't admit to your mistakes. It's all good."

At that point, I introduced Dana and Ji Hoo, wanting to make Max feel like I wasn't trying to keep him out of this part of my life. Dana totally elevatored him, and when I raised my brow at her, she grinned. "Hey, I can window shop."

"I'm standing right here," Max pointed out.

"How cute, he thinks he can complain when we objectify him." Dana slung an arm around my shoulders and led me to the garage. "You can spill all the juicy stuff after he leaves."

"You mean his weird sexual fetishes? Oh, I'll talk about that now. Four lemons, a sack of ferrets and a pint of rum. Oh, and he wouldn't say no to a rubber hose—"

"I...feel like I need to get back in the van," Ji Hoo said, tipping his head heavenward.

"Me, too," Max muttered.

Clearing his throat with an amused glint in his eyes, Evan cocked his head at our instruments. "Should we get started?"

"I guess that's my cue to take off." Max bent to kiss me. "What time should I pick you up, Princess Leprechaun?"

Dana shot me a horrified look. "Should I even ask?"

"Please don't."

"You don't have to go," Evan said unexpectedly. "If you don't mind making like scenery for a couple of hours, I'm fine with you hanging out here."

"I dunno, I'm pretty fucking hungry," Max answered.

"Last time we got pizza. Not sure if that's the usual?" I glanced at the others for confirmation; Dana and Ji Hoo were nodding.

"Then sure, I'll chill over here if that's fine with everyone?" Max ambled over to a lawn chair in the far corner and sprawled in it, giving us plenty of space to practice.

"Don't tell my girlfriend," the drummer said, heading over to his kit. "These two hours are the only time I get away from her."

Dana chucked a ball of wadded-up paper at him. "You say that like it's a bad thing."

"Eh, I love her but she's a lot of work." Ji Hoo got out his sticks, clearly done talking about his relationship issues.

Conscious of Max watching me, I set up my keyboard and plugged everything in. This time I didn't need any help with the equipment. This was so weird and new, but it felt right to have Max here, making him part of this new chapter in my life. I didn't want him to feel like I was shutting him out or leaving him behind. For his part, he was respectfully quiet as we kicked things off, launching into the first song on our set list. After a while, I got so into the music that I forgot we had an audience.

So an hour later, when we paused for dinner, he startled me by bounding to his feet and giving a raucous two-finger whistle. "For serious, that was awesome. I'd pay to hear you play."

"That's the dream," Evan said.

"How much?" Dana wanted to know.

"Ten whole dollars." When Max bit his pinky, Ji Hoo cracked up.

"Okay, I'm calling for pizza. Pick up or delivery?" Setting her bass down carefully, Dana went to rummage through her bag, then produced her phone with a flourish of triumph.

Evan thought for a few seconds. "I'll just go get it."

"You're my hero," Ji Hoo said.

"Who said I'm buying? Show me the money." Evan collected crumpled bills until he had enough for two pies. With three guys eating, it was unlikely they could fill up on one while leaving any crumbs for Dana and me.

After checking our preferences, she got one plain cheese and the other loaded with meat. It wasn't like I was picky. Ten minutes later, Evan took off with Ji Hoo, leaving the three of us chilling in the garage. Dana set up a couple more lawn chairs, making me wonder why she didn't go in the house. But maybe she felt weird when Evan was gone. Since I'd opted to ride along with him before—for the same reason—I could relate. Presumably, though, she knew him better than me, and certainly longer.

"So how did you guys meet?" she asked, sitting forward with her elbows on her knees like this would be an awesome story.

"How did we meet, or how'd we get together?" Maybe I was being pedantic, but since Max and I were friends first, it wasn't like he'd spotted me in a club and broken speed records to reach me.

"Both, either. I'm just being nosy. If you prefer we can have a staring contest instead."

"Pass," Max said. "We met first at a party a few years back, but I'd seen her around campus before then."

Dana grinned. "Oooh, he *noticed* you."

I flipped my non-existent long hair in an exaggerated fashion, pretending to fling it over one shoulder. "Well, obviously. I'm memorable. Junior year, he got an apartment with some friends but I was a second-stringer. They subbed me in when one of the girls moved home."

"Hey, I suggested you to Angus," Max protested. "But Lauren and Nadia were kind of a package deal, best friends and all."

"And back then you wanted to bang Lauren, so…" I pretended to duck as he came toward me, but he bent down to kiss my nose instead of getting defensive.

Oddly, his casual response made me feel better, like the past was really…past. It was a little weird for me sometimes, sleeping on Lauren's side of the room, being with Max, like I'd stepped into a role she'd rejected. But God, that wasn't healthy, especially when I hadn't been this happy since before. Before Eli died. Before the pills and the white forgetting fog that scared the shit out of my mother and made my dad not want to face me.

Max went on quietly, eyes on mine. "We lived together for six months before I realized she wasn't just my best friend…that to me, she was also all the love in the world."

"Holy shit," Dana breathed. "Is it just me or did it get *really* fucking hot in here?"

I exhaled slowly. "You're not wrong."

"Want to take a walk?" He offered a hand like a knight of old, and I took it, not minding the chivalry when it came from Max.

Tonight, he was rugged, two days of scruff darkening his jaw, and his black hair fell in shiny, shaggy waves, disheveled by the helmet. A dark blue T-shirt didn't quite hide the ink on his arms, and I thought about the ones I couldn't currently see as longing coiled in my stomach. God, it hadn't even been that long, but the lightning kept striking again and again. He kept his hand wrapped around mine as he led me out of the garage and around the side of the house. Where he promptly pushed me up against the wall and kissed me until I was ready to fuck him in Evan's backyard.

"Where's this coming from?" I finally managed to ask.

"I don't think you realize how sexy you are when you're playing. Like, serious fucking intense hotness, Courtney. I love the way it lights you up."

"Wow." For once, I had no clever comeback. "Really?"

"Yeah. I might have to go with you to your shows and keep the pervs and groupies away. I'll get a Security shirt, just in case." Now he was obviously teasing me, but from the look in his eyes, I could see that he meant it—that he thought *any* guy would want me.

Based on my life experiences—and what had just happened with Jared—that definitely wasn't true. Leaving only one rational explanation.

Max was nuts. About me.

CHAPTER EIGHTEEN

Friday afternoon, I sat in class, daydreaming, thinking about the band and Max, not necessarily in that order.

The professor's voice rolled over me in waves, white noise similar to the ocean. Around me other people seemed more engaged, but I couldn't get interested in statistics. My entrepreneurship class was more intriguing; even marketing had its moments, but this one sapped my will to live. I'd just gotten a B on my first test, though, so it seemed likely that I'd manage to graduate with a business degree like my parents wanted.

After my last class, I rushed out of the building, anticipation quickening my step. Tonight was my first date with Max, and I couldn't wait to get home to see him. That eager mood lasted just long enough for me to enjoy the sunlight on my face, then I spotted Max across the quad with Jared. I would've been happy if I never saw that asshole again, and from Max's expression, the shit was about to hit the fan. He spat something, then shoved Jared hard.

Worried, I ran toward them, closing the distance fast enough to hear Max snarl, "Say it again, motherfucker, I dare you."

"What, that the girl you set me up with is a complete butterface? That's true, bro. Except you only say that when her body's banging, and damn. I wouldn't hit that with a hammer. Cause when I say 'dat ass' about whatshername, it ain't a good thing."

Max hauled his arm back and cracked Jared right in the mouth, hard enough that the guy staggered back a few steps and had to grab a tree to avoid going down. Two more punches came in hard, stomach and jaw, so Jared doubled over wheezing, but when he came up, he had rage to burn. I envisioned this escalating quickly if I didn't do something, but part of me wanted to watch him get his ass kicked, so I wrestled with conscience and schadenfreude.

"I catch you talking about her again, and I will fucking *end you*." Max ducked away from a wild swing.

A crowd was gathering, but nobody tried to break it up. Instead six people got out their phones and started filming. If I knew human nature, this would be on YouTube later tonight, uploaded with a title like DUMBASSES FIGHTING. There would be awesome comments about their technique and dissatisfaction that nobody ended up spewing blood from an orifice, then the internet trolls would start arguing and someone would get called a Nazi before the whole thing got shut down.

"What the fuck! You sucker punched me, asshole. Over

some homely bitch." With an angry growl, Jared rushed Max, tackling him hard enough to drop him.

On the ground, the battle got ugly with elbows to the face, palms in the throat, while they rolled around, snarling curses. Jared was insane, and he seemed to know some wrestling holds because he was doing better close-up. Fighting an arm lock, Max slammed his head into the side of Jared's face and fought to get a knee onto his chest. In retaliation, Jared smashed four knuckles into Max's cheekbone, splitting the skin. At the sight of blood, my good angel won, mostly because I was afraid Max might get really hurt.

So I yelled, "Campus security's heading this way. You might want to take off before the awkward questions start."

As he sprang to his feet, his mouth smeared with blood, Jared shot me a look of pure loathing. "I should've known you'd show up to make my day worse."

"It's my goal in life," I said lightly. "Fuck off now, thanks."

Jared glared; if he had psychic powers, my head would be exploding like a melon right now. "This isn't over. Not by a long shot."

"Don't even think about it," Max growled.

With one final hate stare, Jared bailed, apparently buying the idea he was about to be busted, even though he was technically the victim in this scenario. If he wasn't a total idiot, he'd realize he had the legal high ground here and could make Max's life uncomfortable by pressing charges. Near the science complex, he turned and yelled something but I couldn't make it out, then he rounded the corner.

Max watched him go, hands still curled into fists at his sides. "Dipshit is probably carrying. I can't believe I was dumb enough to ask you to meet him." Turning to me, he took my hand, his expression serious. "What happened exactly? How did the date go?"

"About like this," I said quietly. "He made it pretty clear I don't meet his standards so I clocked out early. Ended up auditioning for Racing Sorrow and hanging out with the band last Friday."

"So that's why you were so late. It was evil of you not to text me when I thought you were with that guy."

"You have terrible taste in men," I told him.

Bending to kiss me, he whispered, "But awesome taste in women. So that makes up for everything, huh?"

"Almost." I touched his cheekbone. "Does it hurt a lot?"

"Kinda."

"Nobody's ever fought for me before. Is it unenlightened to say...I didn't hate it?"

"Probably. But I won't tell. You ready to go?"

"Yeah, but...is that why you're here?"

He nodded, leading me toward the parking lot. "I've memorized your class schedule like a good boyfriend. I'm here to pick you up."

"Wow, are you writing a manual?"

"Obviously. *The Dummy's Guide to Dating*."

"I'm pretty sure someone already wrote that."

"The title's a work in progress." Twining his fingers through mine, he swung our hands slightly, giving me a soft, sweet smile, at odds with his battered face.

"You took a hit in the mouth, too, huh?" His lower lip was slightly swollen, a bruise forming just below.

"Worth it. Do you plan to kiss it better?"

"Would you want me to?"

"Always."

If he kept it up, I might actually blush again and I was *not* that girl. "So tell me what you have planned tonight."

"It's a surprise."

"Come on, I have to know how to dress or I'll be the idiot in stilettos on the nature hike."

Max laughed. "Like you even own a pair of heels."

"You make a good point. Maybe I could've sold that better with 'I'll be the moron at the fancy restaurant in combat boots.'"

"Closer," he admitted, "but you look hot in anything, so don't worry. And no, I'm still not telling you."

"And you say I'm cruel." But I was smiling as I put on the helmet and climbed on behind him.

The bike started with a roar, and Max drove away from campus toward the apartment. By the time we got home, I'd worked up a fine resentment. How the hell was I supposed to get ready for something when I had no idea where we were going or what—

"Stop with the cranky face," he said as he parked.

"Make me."

"If we go down that road, all my carefully laid plans will go to waste."

"Are you saying you'd use sex to improve my mood?"

"I'd have sex with you for any reason." Max grinned as I hopped off the motorcycle, and I struggled against the urge to grab him by the ears and kiss him until he couldn't breathe. "Is that wrong?"

"Not from my point of view."

"Okay, I'll give you a hint. Dress like you usually do."

"That helps. Let's get you upstairs, bruiser. Before we go anywhere, I'm taking care of your war wounds."

"Really?" He gave me the softest, brightest smile.

Linking our fingers, I led Max upstairs. Kia was on the couch surrounded by charts and papers, feet propped up. That was a pretty unusual sight this early; she glanced up at Max's face and cocked her head. "Somebody threw down, huh? Want me to take a look?"

That made sense since she was studying to be a doctor, but before I could answer, Max shook his head. "Courtney's got me covered."

Shooting him a surprised but pleased look, we went down the hall to the bathroom he shared with Angus. I flipped down the lid of the toilet. "Here, so I can reach you."

"It's funny because you're so tiny and adorable."

"Say it again, I dare you." As I got out the first aid kit, I pretended to threaten him with a bottle of iodine.

"I wouldn't dare."

Maybe I should've let Kia do this. But Max wanted medical attention from me, despite my inexperience. So I held a clean washcloth under the faucet, then wrung it out and dabbed the blood away. Under the bright lights, his face looked even worse, yet…he was also the most beautiful person I'd ever seen. His thick lashes fluttered against his cheeks, a strange, dreamy smile curving his mouth.

"What's that look for?"

"Since I left home, I've gotten into plenty of fights, but I never had anybody take care of me afterward before. It's… nice."

My throat tightened. "Don't make a habit of it. You're too pretty to let assholes use your face as a punching bag."

"Yeah?" He smiled up at me like I was sunshine, rainbows and pot of gold, all wrapped up in one. The feeling that swelled in my chest nearly stole my breath.

"Definitely," I managed to say.

With exaggerated care, I finished cleaning him up and applied antibacterial ointment to his cuts. For his bruises, I dug out the arnica cream, though Max seemed skeptical. But he still tilted his chin up, letting me coat the sore spots. As the last step, I carefully applied a Band-Aid to his cut. Once I finished, he stood up and wrapped his arms around me. His chin rested on top of my head briefly, then he rubbed his undamaged cheek against my hair.

Max whispered, "Don't give up on me, okay?"

"Are you nuts, why would I?"

"Because you really don't belong with somebody like me."

"Smart, self-sufficient, handsome and hard-working?"

"You know what I mean."

"I really don't." Stretching up, I kissed him lightly on the mouth. "But I promise letting you go isn't remotely on my to-do list. You're pretty damn special. Now I need to wash up and change. Meet you in the living room in ten minutes?"

"I love that about you," he said.

"What?"

"The way you treat me like I matter." The quiet words spoke volumes on the way his family had made him feel. While they might be patching up the cracks in the foundation, it didn't mean the damage didn't run deep.

"Max—"

"You're the only person in the world who knows exactly who I am."

"I could say the same."

His smile widened and he gave me a look so sweet and intimate that it curled my toes. With a mumbled excuse, I hurried to my room before he could tell I was blushing. Again. Something about Max brought out my inner ingenue; I suspected it was his utter sincerity. With other people, he was kind of a clown, and it made me incredibly happy that—for some reason—this amazing guy had chosen me. While he might not be impressed with himself, I could only admire his determination. In his shoes, I'd be addicted to something and probably hooking to pay for it. Which might not be an optimistic self-assessment, but I'd already chosen pills over dealing with Eli's loss and for the rest of my life, I had to remember how easily I could backslide.

After some inner debate, I changed into clean jeans, concert T-shirt, hoodie. He'd said I should dress like I normally did, after all. Then I spiked my hair and put on some red lipstick. I'd never been one for endless primping, but it looked like I was due for some fresh streaks. Maybe I'd go back to blue this time. Thoughtful, I peered at myself in the mirror, something I didn't do a lot. Big nose, small mouth, sharp chin... I had what might honestly be called a witchy face.

Pretty eyes, Eli said.

You're biased.

I always thought you had cat eyes. Sexy.

Thanks, I thought, but it was a reflex more than an actual conversation. Most of my attention was fixed on putting on eyeliner. I brushed my teeth last and went into the living room, where Max was already waiting. Kia was ignoring him to focus on her work, and the old Max would've played around, begging for attention. This one seemed to get everything he needed from me because he sat quietly, hands on his knees. It was a small miracle to find him still, no TV, music or video game to distract him. I wasn't sure what it meant but it was good, right?

His gaze met mine, pure smoky heat. "You look great. Ready?"

"Yep. See you later, Kia."

"Don't do anything I wouldn't do," she said without glancing up from her reading. "Wait, since I don't do anything but study, change that up. How about, do everything I don't?"

"Sounds like I'm in for an awesome night." Max grinned and set a hand in the small of my back, guiding me toward the door.

Smiling, I let him. "Bye, Kia!"

He didn't speak until I was strapping on the helmet. "It's weird how nervous I am. I was going for original but I hope I didn't cross into cheesy."

"I love cheese," I told him.

"That makes me feel marginally better."

Max got on the bike and I climbed on behind him, wrapping my arms around his waist. The motorcycle zoomed off, warm wind rushing against my skin. At first I wasn't sure where we were going, but then I started recognizing landmarks. Each turn brought us closer to the private place Max had shared with me before, the spot that offered him respite from the world. Like before, we parked and walked in, but when we pushed through the bushes to the small clearing overlooking the river, everything was different. He'd set up a red-and-white blanket, complete with picnic basket. Overhead, the sky was darkening to a shade of bruised plum, and the moon cut through in a crescent of silver. Glimmers of starlight caught the water, just a hint now, though it would be a flood of brilliance in an hour or so.

"I want to give you the world," he said. "But for now, will you settle for a corner of it?"

In answer I sang the chorus of "I Only Want to Be With You." At every bar mitzvah I ever attended, the terrible DJ always played this song, and I never imagined I'd have reason to sing it. But from Max's grin, it was a good choice. Obviously relieved at my reaction, he set out the food carefully packaged in plastic containers: cheese, fruit, cold cuts and crackers. There was also a bottle of wine with plastic glasses.

"Ten points for pure ambiance," I said.

"That's not all."

Max delved into his pocket and came up with an iPod, which he connected to a small flexible speaker. In seconds, the soft strains of my favorite song filled the silence—"Big Strong Girl" by Deb Talan. It was incredible to realize all the nights we'd hung out, talking music, hadn't rolled over him like ocean waves, leaving the sand fundamentally unchanged. No, it was more like Max had been soaking me up like a sponge.

"You are killing me," I whispered, oddly on the verge of tears.

"In a good way?"

I managed a nod. "The best. Thank you for all of this."

"So you like it?" Tension seeped out of his shoulders as he offered his hand and pulled me down onto the blanket beside him. It was thick and plush but I could still feel the blades of grass prickling through. Judging by the pile of stones nearby, he must've spent at least an hour clearing the area.

"This is perfect. I'm not much for consumer culture anyway."

"I figured I needed to do something special—and memorable—for our first date."

"Mission accomplished. You hungry?"

"Starving," he admitted, but from the look in his eyes, he wasn't entirely talking about the food.

All in due time.

To repay his effort, I put together a cheese-and-meat cracker and offered it to Max. Without hesitation he ate from my fingers, which felt more significant than it should, maybe. I mean, he was my best friend in the world, and we'd slept together, made each other come. Yet it still moved me when he trusted me that way. It felt strangely as if I'd tamed a wild creature to my hand. Realizing he'd treat nobody else this way brought an ache to my throat.

"I can't believe you did all of this. It must've taken hours."

"It was definitely more labor-intensive than dinner and a movie."

I swallowed hard. "More special, too. I know what this place means to you."

"Then you know why I want you here?"

This might sound dumb, but... "When Lois Lane visits Superman's Fortress of Solitude...he's symbolically giving her the keys to his kingdom."

Smiling, Max wrapped his arm around my shoulders. The rush of the water lent this space a private, sacred air. "Something like that. For so long, it's just been me against the world. But since I met you, Courtney...I haven't felt alone. The first time I brought you here, I suspect I already

felt this way about you. I just hadn't put the pieces all together." He offered a wry smile. "I'm bad at puzzles."

"So what's the plan for tonight?" I leaned my head against
him as tenderness flooded through me.

"We eat. Listen to music. Stargaze. Talk about life, the
universe and everything." As I identified that as a Douglas
Adams reference, he went on, stealing my ability to think.
"And when you're tired of that, I make love to you."

CHAPTER NINETEEN

The sky gradually filled with stars as the MP3 player worked through my favorite songs mingled with Max's. Truthfully our preferences weren't as far apart as some people I'd dated. He liked older music along with a variety of indie artists, and I'd always been all about music I discovered myself. There was an indescribable thrill in unearthing a beautiful sound, akin to finding buried treasure.

By the time the songs started looping, we'd finished the food and were working toward the bottom of the wine bottle. I had a nice buzz on and Max was looking mellow. He drew me into his arms, settling me in front of him, so I leaned back against his chest. At first I resisted because I figured that couldn't be comfortable for him.

He tightened his arms around me. "Stop squirming, woman."

"Why, you don't like it?"

"Maybe I like it too much."

"There's no such thing."

In response he kissed the curve between my neck and shoulder. "The nape of your neck is so fucking sexy."

"It is?" I'd never heard that before.

"Yeah. I didn't realize I liked short hair on a woman until we got together. Now I'm constantly fighting the urge to nibble. Right here." He trailed his fingertips just beneath my hairline, sending a shiver through me.

"So don't," I whispered. "Fight, that is."

He chuckled softly and then his mouth grazed the sensitive skin behind my ear. Growing up in the city, I'd never fooled around outside, so the prospect sent an eager thrill through me. Arching my neck to give him better access, I closed my eyes as heat burgeoned with each graze of his lips. When he switched to teeth, a soft sound escaped me.

"Oh, God," he murmured, right in my ear. "I could stand to hear that again."

"Keep it up. Out here I can be as loud as I want."

"Challenge accepted."

Though I was ready to fall into the longing, an old question niggled at me, and it wasn't idle curiosity. Max had said hurting women during sex was a hot button for him before we got together, and I needed to know why, since I wasn't opposed to rough play, but I didn't want to trigger any flashbacks, either.

"Can I ask you something, knowing it may impact the mood?"

His lips stilled on my neck. "Now I'm worried."

"It's about something you said. I made a sex joke about not being able to walk—"

"Oh. I figured you might bring it up eventually. You're

too attentive to just forget." He wrapped his arms around my shoulders, settling me against him. "That's both amazing and alarming. I bet you know what my favorite cereal is."

"Lucky Charms," I said promptly.

"My point exactly. I guess you already know this, but… my first year away from home completely sucked. The motel I stayed at charged by the hour, and I got…friendly with the girls who worked there."

I had no idea if he was telling me he'd slept with hookers, so I just kept quiet, glad he couldn't see my face. Nothing could make me stop caring about Max but a frisson of fear surfaced about what he might tell me. It seemed like he was waiting for some kind of response.

"Yeah?"

He went on. "They were good to me. I was living on fast food because it was free, completely rudderless and half-crazy worried about Mickey. Charlene used to bring me tuna casserole because she said I'd die of malnutrition eating only where I worked. And eventually I got to the point that I couldn't choke down a burger without wanting to hurl."

Quietly I covered his hands with mine. He clutched like this was unexpectedly hard to talk about. "She sounds nice."

"Most of them were. It was weird, but…they mothered me."

Picturing that, I had to smile. Trust Max to charm a bunch of working girls into wanting to take care of him. "I'm not surprised."

"In return, I paid attention, listened for trouble when I was around. One night after my shift, I heard screaming. Didn't even think about it, just ran up and kicked the door in." I felt a tremor run through him. "There were three ass-

ANN AGUIRRE

holes with Charlene, and it wasn't a package deal. Her eyes, she couldn't even see, and she was bleeding—"

"What happened?"

"I got the shit kicked out of me, but the assistant manager called the cops, and they prevented it from turning into a murder scene." From his bleak tone, I couldn't imagine how bad it was. "There was no way I could stay down and watch them finish gang-raping her. So no matter how much it hurt, I got up again. I couldn't see, couldn't fucking breathe, and I could only think, *Fuck, at least life with my dad trained me for this. I know how to take a punch.*"

"Oh, Max." My heart ached; I'd never imagined his hot button could possibly be this bad.

"What happened afterward?"

"The police rounded us all up, asked questions. I bailed before they realized I was underage and limped off to a free clinic. And I had to pay for the fucking door." Wry tone.

"Wow. When you say life completely sucked, you weren't exaggerating."

"Later, one of those assholes tried to stab me." He showed me the scar on the back of his hand. "And that was when Charlene had a come-to-Jesus talk with me. It was her way of thanking me, I think."

"That's when you started thinking about the future?"

"Before then, I was just trying to survive. I figured I'd die alone in some shitty room." He paused, kissing the top of my head. "I'm not telling this to make you feel sorry for me. But…it does affect some parts of my psyche, if I can say that without sounding like a weirdo. I'll never want to tie you up. I'll never be into anything that will hurt you, even a little."

"That would be a problem if I wanted you to."

"You don't?"

I shook my head. "Don't worry, we're good. But I'm glad you told me. I feel like I understand you better now."

"How so?"

"The way you are. You've seen too much of women being disrespected so you're trying to make up for it." What other people saw as Max being a player, flirting with everyone, was more like him paying compliments to offer some good to balance the bad in the world. A lot of women wanted to sleep with him as a result, and sometimes he did. But libido didn't drive his behavior; that was kind of interesting.

"That's not how I'd characterize my behavior freshman year," Max said.

"No?"

"Honestly?"

"Preferably."

"I came to college on my own. No parents dropping me off. No car load of stuff." His words conjured a poignant picture. "I...asked Charlene to come with me, but she couldn't. She said I was better off without her, not that I necessarily agree."

"Do you still talk to her?"

"Freshman year, I called her but she stopped answering." His tone told me it bothered him. In his experience, people only got close, hurt you and bailed. No wonder he'd freaked out over me pulling away. "Before I left, she told me not to look back."

I fought the urge to turn and hug him. That wouldn't make it easy for him to keep talking, though. I suspected the fact that I couldn't see his face helped. "So...college?"

"Yeah. I had exactly what I could fit on my bike. And I was scared. Nervous. Lonely. So I figured it would be better to seem overconfident, you know? I kept trying to connect but I never got past a few hours in bed. A few months of that and word got around. 'Don't take that asshole seriously, he just wants to hook up'. Which wasn't necessarily true, but—"

"It's hard to change a reputation once the damage is done." I knew that especially well. To this day, it hurt that *anyone* could believe I'd take advantage of someone who wasn't coherent enough to consent to sex.

"So anyway. You asked." He let out a deep, shuddering breath. Then he continued in a wondering tone, "You know...I think I saw some of Charlene in Lauren."

"Huh?" That seemed really odd and unlikely.

I felt him nod against my head. "Nobody else ever noticed, but to me, Lauren always seemed like she needed saving."

"Interesting. I didn't know her that well." For the first time in forever, I could talk about her with him without wanting to chew through my own arm. I'd played confidante so often, listening to his ideas on how to make her realize he was serious.

"I got beat up over her, too. Another thing she has in common with Charlene." Rueful tone, as he carried my hand to his mouth to press a kiss into my palm. "You're the first woman I ever fought for when I wasn't in rescue mode."

"That's good because I'm not a damsel. I can take care of myself." Privately I wondered about the Lauren-related altercation, but I'd already gotten all the truth I could handle tonight. Changing the subject seemed like the best option. "So...did I ruin our first official date?"

"Nope. But I need to move."

"Am I crushing you?"

"Nah. I just need to see your face."

Max shifted me forward and we wriggled around until I ended up in his arms on my side. He drew me closer by draping a thigh over mine. I slid my arm across his waist, conscious of the sound of the water, the insects chirping, but also of the warm rush of his breath over my face and the thump of his heart against mine.

"I've never told anyone about that," he said softly.

"I'm glad you did."

The idea of Max being hurt filled me with a wild and impotent rage. I couldn't get the image out of my head: three grown men, pummeling him, kicking him, blood everywhere, and Max staggering to his feet, again and again. Beautifully unbreakable. I could learn so much from him— so much about determination. Shame trickled through me that I'd hit one hurdle and given up so quickly, taken so long to find my spark again.

"There's nothing I won't answer, if you ask me."

"Ooh. How can I resist? Have you ever thought about being with a guy?" It was the kind of question that told you a lot about the person answering it.

"I've kissed one," Max said unexpectedly.

I propped up on an elbow, simultaneously surprised and slightly turned on. "Really?"

"Last year at one of Josh's parties. You know how he likes to play Suckface Trivia?"

Vaguely I recalled him as being Angus's ex-boyfriend, the

one who'd cheated. I'd never participated but he'd enjoyed rounding up the drunk and/or high people and orchestrating random, interesting make-out sessions. Sometimes it got unexpectedly heated between apparently incompatible partners. I was curious about Max's experience.

"You were drunk enough to get a simple answer wrong?"

"Yep. It was a crappy night and you weren't around." His plaintive tone made me kiss the top of his nose.

"So who did you kiss?"

"Josh."

"Wow, was Angus pissed?" This must've been before the cheating confession.

"Nah. I didn't French him or anything."

"Cheek or mouth?"

"Mouth."

"How come?"

He lifted one shoulder with a shy smile. "I didn't want to wimp out."

"How was it?"

"It was fine. But no sparks, if that's what you're asking. I hate to disappoint but we're not a bi couple. Though I was dead serious when I said I'd want you even if you were a guy. I'd figure out how to make it work."

"You'd be gay for me?"

"I'd be anything for you," he whispered.

"Talk like that will get you in my pants."

"That's the dream."

In answer, I sat up and pulled my top off. I was prepared tonight with a pretty set of matching underwear. Nothing supersexy, but the black satin looked great against my skin, plus it was probably a surprise under the cargo pants and concert T-shirts. Max stared up at me, his mouth open, then he ran a fingertip between my breasts, lingering over the tiny bow between, and then he traced my bellybutton, admiring the small silver ring with a delicate touch.

"This working for you?"

His throat worked. "In a big way. Your skin is…glowing. Moonlight. Here. And here." He kissed where he touched, bringing back the shivers.

"Please get naked," I said. "I want to fuck you in the worst way."

"God, yes." He was down to boxer briefs in, like, fifteen seconds.

Not that I was counting. Okay, I was totally counting.

If anyone had told me I'd be naked in the woods with Max Cooper, I would've said they were bananas. But I couldn't be happier about it. He knelt before me, almost like a penitent, but his dark eyes blazed as he lowered his head to the tops of my breasts. He didn't need to push for me to fall back. I'd fantasized about this before, but it was so much better than my imagination to have Max's mouth on my nipples, his black hair slipping over my skin. He used lips and tongue with only the barest hint of teeth to get me writhing on the blanket, clutching his head as I stared up at the ocean of stars. I'd meant for us to get to the fucking because his emotional honesty revved me up, but it seemed I was getting foreplay, the extended cut. Pleasure crashed through me, so much tension in my thighs and calves that I might actually cramp up. As if he sensed it, Max shifted lower, an arm across my stomach to hold me still. He licked down my ribs, which tickled a little, then he nuzzled at my navel, toying with my ring.

"You like that?" I managed to ask.

His voice came out hoarse. "It's incredibly sexy. Like you."

"Mmm."

He didn't linger long. Soon he was driving me crazy with his mouth on my lower belly, so close, but not close enough. Impatient, I touched my breasts, not to tease him, but because it felt good, but he stared, riveted, forgetting momentarily to keep kissing me.

"Never saw a woman take the reins before?" I teased.

"You are *so* hot."

"I just know what I want."

"What's that?" He shifted to my inner thigh, licking upward, until I was shivering in anticipation.

As I opened my mouth to answer, he parted my labia with gentle fingers. I gasped out the answer, lifting my hips. "You. For so long, it's been you."

"I can't stand the thought of anyone else looking at you." As he spoke, he kissed. Licked. Nuzzled. I arched with a whimper that blossomed into a full moan. "Touching you. Courtney, you *have* to be mine."

"I am."

"Mine." As he growled it, he sucked on each of my lips in turn, teasing me.

The next shift made me see stars. "That's it."

"Here?" He increased the pressure, working me with lips and fingertips, until my pulse pounded in my clit. I tingled and ached, a sea of heat rising with each movement.

"No," I gasped. "Courtney. That's the endearment. You always called me Kaufman before. So...I don't need anything else. Just my name."

"You want me to say your name?" Max hooked a finger inside me, lowering his head to rub his tongue against my clit.

"Yeah. *Yes*." The last word came out in a near hiss, more in response to the steady rhythm in my pussy than his question.

"Courtney." He spoke the word straight into my core and it shouldn't have turned me on as much as it did. I went white-hot as he licked harder, faster, while finger-fucking me slowly. Like I was too tender for words, he eased another inside, so it was better and fuller, but still not enough. I wanted his cock so bad that I couldn't think or breathe.

I raised my hips, only thinking about the orgasm. "Faster."

"Are you close?"

"Mmm."

"Then…" He stopped, prompting a snarl of frustration. "Dammit!"

But when I heard the crinkle of the condom wrapper, my interrupted sex-rage abated. I helped him roll it on, noticed how incredibly hard he was, but he didn't let me touch him for very long. Though I'd love to study his dick close up for several hours, it wouldn't be tonight. Max was actually trembling when he rolled on top of me.

"Sorry. I keep trying to rock your world, but I can never wait. Maybe next time—"

"No, this is good. It's good now. Please. *Please*." I urged him forward as I opened my legs and he pushed home in one thrust.

Immediately, I lifted my hips, breathless at the feel of Max. There was no way he could be just a warm body to me, faceless pleasure. There was too much of his soul twined with mine, so each time he moved, I felt him so deep in me that my heart pounded with his. He wrapped his arms around, holding me so close he could barely move but somehow it made the sporadic, desperate lunges feel even deeper. His belly slid against mine, his cock slick as he thrust. I held onto him as hard as I could, need spiraling.

"Come on." A hard thrust. Two fingers on my clit. "Take it, Courtney." Max groaning my name into my mouth sent me over, a ferocious orgasm tightening my thighs.

He throbbed but he didn't come. Somehow he held on for three or four more strokes, then he let go, collapsing on top of me as the waves rocked him. I held him and stroked his back until our shivers subsided. Eventually he groaned and rolled away, seeking blindly for the light blanket folded on top of the basket. Still unsteady, he pulled it over us and I snuggled into his side.

"So…you said you might crit my performance," he said dreamily. "And I'm in a receptive mood. Any feedback?"

"Yeah." Evilly, I paused long enough to get him to open his eyes.

"Uh-oh."

"Don't worry about not being able to wait. There's no time minimum on good sex. And because it's you, it's consistently amazing."

His arms tightened. "Keep talking, it's making me feel like I can fly."

"Hey, no jumping off high things. I need you beside me."

"For you, I'll desist."

He kissed me so tenderly it brought to tears to my eyes. The whole world was washed in silver and gold—moonlight and Max's skin. God, being this happy scared the shit out of me. For the first time in forever, I had something precious to lose. From deep down inside me, a tiny, cynical voice that didn't belong to Eli quoted an old Robert Frost poem:

So dawn goes down to day.
Nothing gold can stay.

CHAPTER TWENTY

Band rehearsals, school and Max kept me busy through September and October.

When Halloween rolled around, I was nervous because we got the Omega Chi gig, and it would be my first show. The others said it was no big deal, but my stomach roiled as I helped Evan unload the van. Racing Sorrow didn't wear costumes but they did coordinate, so we were all in red-and-black in varying combinations. I had on black jeans, a red tank top, black leather jacket, red Converse. Dana laughed when she saw me because she'd gone for a similar look, only her jacket had silver studs on the shoulders.

"Admit it, you two compared notes," Evan teased.

"At least we're not pimptastic," Dana shot back.

"Hey, I am rocking this look."

We both shook our heads as Ji Hoo hopped out of the van in red skinny jeans and a black T-shirt. Evan wore black pants and blazer, black dress shirt underneath, with pops of color from his red combat boots and porkpie hat. Most guys couldn't pull off that outfit but he gave it a certain panache. Taken together, we formed a cohesive group and I was happy we could manage it without resorting to matching jumpsuits.

"Let's get set up." Ji Hoo tended to be the most focused and he quietly put a stop to the playful bickering, a reminder that I had to be serious.

Yeah, this was just a frat party, but they were paying us four hundred dollars to play. I'd never earned money on my own before. Which made me sound really spoiled—and I probably was. In high school I spent all my spare time with Eli, and my parents never suggested I do anything else. Maybe that should've tipped me off as to how bleak our chances for a happy ending were. Most parents would be nagging about the future, but my folks never suggested I should back off, possibly because they'd realized I would go ballistic.

They knew I was dying, Eli said. *You were the only one who wouldn't accept it.*

You had remissions before. But my heart wasn't in the argument. As he'd said, he had been gone for five years. The fact that I was still clinging said something sad about my mental health. I took a deep breath. And for the first time, it felt *wrong* talking to him when I had Max for real, as if I was silently admitting that he wasn't enough—that I couldn't share certain things with him. And that felt…disloyal.

You're almost there. Eli sounded sad.

Tipping my head back, I stared up at the tangle of tree limbs waving in the wind. The scrape of dry leaves lent the night an oddly funeral air. In some ways, this was like burying my boyfriend all over again. While he might've died, he was never really gone. I fought the urge to cry. *God, I'm so crazy.*

"You okay?" Evan set a hand on my shoulder. "Nervous?"

"Somewhat." Managing a smile, I followed him into the frat house.

After the show, I promised Eli.

It's up to you, he answered. *But you've known you have to move on for a while.*

Hearing that swelled the knot in my throat. Dread quickened my pulse and sweat broke out on my forehead. I had been treading water for five years, not drowning but not swimming, either. It was a weird situation, no question, but I didn't think I could play alone. Once I got through the performance, then I'd see about quieting the voice in my head.

The downstairs was huge and open with a loft area immediately upstairs. There must have been bedrooms up there, too, but it didn't impact us. We took the forty-five minutes before the party started to set up and do the sound check. Acoustics were decent due to the ceilings, but I doubted anyone would notice unless we absolutely sucked. Max had said he'd swing by later; he was the kind of guy who could wander into a party and it never mattered if he'd been invited.

By the time people started arriving in costume, we were ready to go. The blond guy in charge of entertainment paid Evan and he nodded at the rest of us. *That's my cue.* I came in as Ji Hoo set the temp and we worked through our first set as more and more people arrived. Few of them paid any attention to the music, more interested in yelling and drinking, but that was fine. We were still getting paid. I saw what Evan meant about this being perfect for my first show, though. It was highly unlikely anybody would notice if I fumbled a few keys. The rest of the group was focused and professional, though, and I followed their example.

Ten minutes in, and people started dancing. That was kind of a rush. I'd been at parties with live music before but I never wondered how they felt while I was rocking out. Good thing I played the keyboard, which let me sit down, because I had no moves. Not that I ever let it stop me from having fun, but there was no way I could do the cool spins that Dana was pulling off with her bass, somehow not stumbling on cables in the process.

Mostly I focused on playing, not paying much attention to the idiots running around, but something made me glance up and I found Max standing in the crowd, just watching me. I smiled, somehow didn't screw up and lifted my chin in silent acknowledgment. He answered with a smile so big and bright that my heart clenched. While the set wrapped up, a few girls came over to him and I saw him shaking his head, nodding toward me, ridiculous how happy it made me.

"We're taking a fifteen minute break," Evan said, after we finished the song.

A few guests actually protested as we stood up. Max threaded through a cluster of drinkers to catch my hand. I laced our fingers together as he led me toward the door. Until I got outside, I didn't realize how hot I was, the brisk air chilly on my sweaty skin. Shivering, I rubbed my hands together, and his arm circled my shoulders.

"How're you doing?"

"It's fun. We sound okay?"

"Yeah. And I love watching you."

"Pervert."

"You know what I mean." He shifted, pulling me back against him so his chin rested on the top of my head and his arms wrapped around me from behind. "I feel like I should get you a present to commemorate your first show, but…"

Though he didn't finish, I knew he must be feeling bad that he couldn't afford to get me expensive jewelry. I wouldn't wear it anyway. "I don't need anything."

"Come on, tell me your wish list. I'll put a pin in it for later. What do you want?"

"From you?" Tilting my head back so I could just see his profile, I pretended to consider. "Many things, and most of them are *so* dirty."

"Be serious. I'm not in a position now, but someday I will be." To me, the words sounded like a promise.

"Okay. I'd love for you to pick up an old car and restore it for me, top-notch cherry all the way. If I'm going to be an indie music mogul, I need a ride that says I'm the real deal."

Max set his hands on my shoulders and turned me to face him slowly. "Seriously? Because I can do that. We're always getting tips on good rebuild possibilities at the garage. It wouldn't be fast, though, Courtney. Like my bike, it could take years."

The sweetest ache tightened my throat. "I'm counting on that."

His smile grew like a ray of sunlight streaming through the clouds, and Max pulled me fully into his arms, rubbing his hands over my back. "Are you saying what I think you are?"

"If you're asking if I'm in for the long haul, then the answer's yes. I don't connect to people too well, but when I do, I don't let go."

"Thank God," he whispered.

I slid my arms around his waist and rested my cheek on his chest. "You're really impressive, you know. Don't think I haven't noticed."

He kissed my forehead. "I don't want to brag but I can take pretty much any broken thing and get it going again."

"I know," I said. "You did that with me."

"...What?"

Embarrassed, I closed my eyes before answering. "I wasn't alive before, Max."

"Sure you were." He sounded...uncomfortable, but I couldn't risk a look at him to gauge his expression, not if I expected to make it through this confession.

"I was more like a wind-up girl. Not living, just...there, going through the motions. You reminded me who I used to be...and that I still have dreams."

"Courtney." The softness as he said my name told me he remembered that it felt like an endearment.

Max bent to kiss me, and I stretched up to meet him. He cupped the back of my head, long fingers on the nape of my neck, and now that I knew he found it sexy, it seemed hotter to me, too, skin on skin, his mouth moving on mine. I tasted his tongue as someone stumbled out of the house to barf in the bushes. With a wry laugh, I pulled back.

"Maybe not here."

"Yeah. You have a show to finish."

I followed him back inside, where Evan and Ji Hoo were already waiting. A minute later, Dana joined us, so they shut off the canned music and we played our second set. Nobody seemed to find our sound life-changing, but they danced and drank; we got paid. It was almost two when we broke down the equipment and loaded the van. Max hung around to help out, hauling the amps with no hint he'd already worked a full shift at the garage before showering and checking out the show. From what I'd seen, he definitely wasn't there to party. He'd come for me.

He must be exhausted, Eli said.

Probably.

"It's late," Evan said. "If you want, go on home with your boyfriend. I'll put the van in the garage and unload in the morning."

"Are you sure?" Truthfully, I was pretty tired, but I didn't want to seem like a slacker.

"Yeah, it's not a problem. How do you think I keep these guns?"

"Thanks, man." Max slapped him on the back, then steered me toward his bike.

I'd heard that born performers got a natural high after a show, boosted by the love of the crowd. Either I wasn't made for this or the audience hadn't been receptive enough, because instead of buoyant, I mostly felt sleepy and sad. I remembered the promise I'd made to the voice in my head, and while it was past time, it was also the end of an era. Thankfully, the motorcycle precluded conversation because I had no idea how I'd explain this to Max if he noticed something was wrong.

I shouldn't be upset.

He parked the bike around the side of the building and I climbed off, handing him my helmet to stow. When he reached for my hand, I stepped back. "Give me a few minutes."

He frowned, the expression illuminated by the amber glow of the parking-lot lights. "Is something wrong?"

"No, I'll be up in a minute. It's okay."

To my relief, he didn't push. "If you're sure. But if you're not in my bed in fifteen minutes, I'm coming to find you."

"I hope so."

Max touched his brow to mine gently. "It's a promise."

Once he left, the side lot seemed especially dark and quiet. This late, it was cold enough to see my breath and my leather jacket didn't offer much insulation. I rubbed my hands together, then stuck them in my pockets. This seemed so bizarre, just lingering on the sidewalk, eyeing the gravel on either side that passed as landscaping around here.

So I guess this is it, Eli said.

My eyes filled with tears. Over the years I'd cried for him *so often* but I'd never felt like I was losing him. But now when I closed my eyes, I couldn't picture his face anymore. I'd have to open up the album and remind myself how thick his brows were, if they were more brown or ginger. I could only recall the freckled explosion of his cheeks and his blue, blue eyes.

I'm sorry, I don't want to forget you. I hate that I am. But I remember more now how I felt when you died than how it was when we were together. Tears spilled over, hot as acid streaming down my cheeks. The wind chilled them immediately, and I scrubbed them away with an impatient swipe of my hand. *Part of me will always love you. But we're done talking now. Goodbye, Eli.*

And you'll always be my first love. Take care of yourself, C.

In my mind's eye, I could almost see his face, but it was blurred by too-bright light, shining on his blond hair like a halo and then he went, leaving me. My head was so, so quiet, just my own thoughts, and the odd, muffled noises I made in trying not to cry. Failing, I crouched on the sidewalk and wept, hugging my knees until it hurt.

Shit-fucking-shit. I didn't expect it to be this bad.

As I looked now, there was no way I could get in bed with Max without freaking him out, so I got out my phone and sent, Don't wait up, I'll see you in the morning. Then I trudged over to the workout room. At this hour, no sane person was using the equipment. I wasn't dressed for this, but it was the only idea I had. The buses weren't running and I had nowhere else to go. After taking off my jacket, I climbed onto the treadmill. I started at a run, like I could escape these feelings, but after five minutes, to keep my lungs from exploding, I slowed to a walk.

This is how I do it. One day at a time, one step at a time. It's fine. It's been over forever. You didn't lose him all over again. This is closure. So just walk one mile. Then one more. In the morning, it'll be done.

I had no idea how long I stumbled on, hands on the frame, mindless, streaming sweat; I only glanced up when the door banged open. Max froze when he spotted me, slumping against the doorframe. He looked like utter shit, dark circles under his eyes, two days of scruff on his jaw. His mouth was red and chapped, probably from hours of walking around, looking for me. Sorrow twisted into remorse when he rubbed a palm against his chest, as if finding me safe resulted in an actual physical ache.

I stopped moving, let the conveyer belt dump me off the end of the machine. I had no idea what to say when he was so ferociously quiet. "Hey."

"We're right upstairs, you know. I've only seen you i[n] passing and you haven't texted me in a week and a half. You[r] silence is starting to hurt my feelings." I was mostly joking, but there was a touch of truth to it.

She winced. "Sorry about that. I tend to focus on whatever's in my immediate field of vision. I need to work on that."

"I'm willing to let you make it up to me."

"Yeah? Come on in. Ty's in Sam's room, helping him pack. We're going to the zoological society in Ann Arbor later."

I raised a brow. "The kid needs to pack for that?"

"You'd be surprised what a five-year-old thinks is mandatory for a day trip."

"Probably." I followed her into the apartment and sat down on the red L-shaped sectional. "So…I was wondering if you had Thanksgiving plans."

Her smile dimmed. "Yeah, we do. We'll be with Ty's parents. They want us to spend the night because his sisters are both flying in. Did you plan to invite us over?"

"No, actually. I was hoping you wouldn't mind hosting *us*. See, Max's brother is coming to visit and our apartment isn't wheelchair accessible."

Her eyes widened to the point that it was comical. "Max has a brother? He never talks about his family. One of these days, I'm going to pick your brain and learn all his secrets."

"That will never happen." Though I was smiling, my tone was firm.

"Gotcha. Well, we won't even *be* here on Thanksgiving, so if you want to eat here, it's fine with me. I need to talk to Ty but when he finds out why, I'm sure he won't have

"You scared the shit out of me, you know that?"

"Sorry." If I tried to explain, it would probably sound crazy. "You didn't have to stay up searching. I can take care of myself. I wouldn't do anything dangerous."

"Yeah," he bit out. "I did. I can't lose my true north, Courtney. So I will always, always come and find you. No matter how long it takes."

Now my chest hurt, too, different than saying goodbye to Eli. "I should have told you I was going to Nadia's. I didn't mean to keep you up."

"Like I could sleep when I didn't know where you were, if you were okay."

"I will be."

"What happened? Did someone fuck with you at the party?" By his grim expression, he was already planning to kick that person's ass.

That won a faint smile. "No, it was fine. And I guess I owe you the truth, after worrying you so much. I'm sorry." Quietly I summed things up for him, then added, "See, there's only room for you in my heart and in my head. I wanted to be all yours. And now…I am."

His throat worked. Finally he came up with "Holy shit."

Then he came from the doorway in a rush, sweeping me into his arms and hugging me so hard it hurt. "You didn't have to do that…but I'm not sorry you did. It ate at me sometimes to watch you check out, wondering if you wished—"

"I don't. I'm with you, Max. All the way." The tightness in my sternum gave way to sweetness, the warmth of him spreading through me.

"Will you please come to bed now? I hope you're satisfied, by the way. I'm too fucking tired for sex."

"Why would that satisfy me?"

"You're the one who stayed on the treadmill until almost five in the morning."

"Damn. I had no idea it was so late. Early? Yeah, let's go."

At home I showered quickly, quietly, using their bathroom so I didn't bother Kia. Then I crept into Max's bed, where he was already asleep, sprawled on my side of the bed. In the morning, I didn't wake until almost noon, confirmed by the brightness streaming in the window and a quick look at my phone. There was a new lightness in my heart. For a few minutes, I just watched him sleep, stroking his hair.

I love you, I thought. *Only you.*

Shifting, Max kissed me without opening his eyes. "I like this."

"Me, too." Since I'd checked my email when I'd glanced at the time, I was bursting with news. "Guess what?"

He pretended to think, nuzzling kisses against my neck. "You want to be my love slave and live only for me?"

"Tempting. But no."

An exaggerated sigh. "I'm sad now. Why must you crush my dreams?"

"Because I'm minoring in it. You want to guess again, or should I—"

"Just tell me."

Propping up on my elbows, I beamed down at him. "Okay, I'll tell you. Michael's coming for Thanksgiving!"

Max's expression was priceless.

♥

CHAPTER TWENTY-ONE

A week later, I was knocking on Nadia's door to request a favor.

I felt bad that I hadn't spent much time with her since she'd moved out, but her life was different now. Not only did she work full-time, she was also juggling a serious relationship and a kid. Maybe it was wrong of me, but in some ways, it felt like she'd leveled out of my league. She'd probably tell me not to be stupid if I admitted it out loud, but there was no doubt that her problems were much different than mine.

She swung it open in a rush, hair up in a messy bun that she had the curls to pull off. I'd always admired her height, and she had fantastic legs. But personality-wise, she was too much of a type A to attract me. Which was good because sharing a room with her might've been awkward otherwise. I found relentlessly goal-oriented people exhausting.

"Hey," she said, smiling. "Long time no see."

a problem with it. It would probably be easier on the guy's pride than having to be carted around."

I nodded. "That's what I was thinking."

"So what's he like?"

"Max's brother?"

At her nod, I answered, "Looks a lot like him but he's buffer in the chest and shoulders. Very handsome, great eyes. Kind of hawkish whereas Max's are all dark and soulful. He's an athlete…" I considered, trying to remember what else I'd learned about him on the trip that wouldn't breach Max's confidence. "He's homeschooled and smart. Curious about college. Interested in aeronautics."

"Damn. I wish I could meet him. But we've already committed to Ty's parents."

"That's right," Ty said, coming down the hall with Sam's backpack in one hand. "No take-backs. You'll break my mom's heart. Hey, Courtney." He threw a smile my way.

Tall, lean and ginger, he wasn't my type, but I could see why Nadia had fallen for him; they made sense to me as a couple. He was definitely happier than he'd been when I first moved in to the building, and she was less…wired when he was around. When I first met her, I thought she'd have a heart attack before she was forty with her constant running around and overly scheduled life. Since I hated committing to anything—even classes—my willingness to rehearse twice weekly was kind of a huge deal. A rehab shrink said that my aversion to planning related to my reluctance to move on, which contributed to my OCD issues, as well.

"That's not what she's asking, anyway." Nadia summarized my request.

Soon Ty was nodding. "Not a problem. We'll leave the

keys. Use the dining room, kitchen, whatever you need." He paused to survey the hallway with a frown. "Not sure this place is fully accessible, though. The doorways may give him some trouble, and the bathroom definitely isn't designed properly."

Belatedly I remembered Ty was studying architecture, so this was definitely his wheelhouse. "But the living and dining room should be fine, right?"

He nodded. "I'll rearrange the furniture a little before we leave Wednesday, open up some wider pathways. Michael can spend the night here if you want, if he decides it's doable."

"Thanks. He said a hotel would be easier because the room will have the right facilities, but we'll offer, just so he knows he's welcome."

Nadia wore a half-frustrated look. "I wish we could all hang out like before. But...I'm a step ahead now, huh?"

Sam opened up the trunk in the middle of the room and pulled out a basket of blocks, ignoring the rest of us. Ty glanced down at him, wearing a conflicted expression, then he pulled her toward me.

His look deepened to a sort of bemused tenderness as he wrapped an arm around Nadia's shoulders. "Why don't you have Thanksgiving here with your friends? You can eat with my family next year, but once everyone graduates, you may not have this chance again for a while."

Her look brightened immediately. "Are you sure? But your sisters are coming."

"Come over Thursday night. You can go shopping with them on Black Friday while I watch sports with my dad and Sam."

"That's perfect." She bounced onto her toes and hugged him tight around the neck.

Taking that as my cue to head out, I definitely had a good feeling about the way the Thanksgiving bash was shaping up. A few days later, I went grocery shopping with Angus, excited about seeing Michael again, as if he were *my* little brother. Since I was an only child, that was a strange feeling…but cool, too. He sent me messages as he traveled, updating me as to where they were. I suspected he also wanted to see Max, and I couldn't blame him.

On Wednesday, we started cooking, and at noon on Thanksgiving Day, Michael called to let us know he was near the apartment complex. Max dropped the knife he was chopping onions with and ran downstairs, excited like it was Christmas morning. I fought a stinging in my eyes and a tightness in my throat when I realized this was the first holiday in five years where he'd had any family around. I finished up chopping and added the onions to the celery in a pan. I wasn't a great cook and Angus shooed me out when he realized I'd moved out of the preparation phase. So I hurried downstairs to greet Max's family.

It wasn't just Michael, but Uncle Lou, too. He looked older than he had at the funeral, though it had only been a few months. The veins in his hands seemed more pronounced, his face thinner, his body more frail. He hugged me, and I responded, at first out of surprise, but his warmth prodded me toward affection; he smelled of peppermints and camphor, his shock of white hair like dandelion fluff blowing in the brisk November wind. When I stepped back, he grabbed Max and I leaned over to give Michael a hug, too.

"We're so glad you could make it," I said. "It's great to see you both."

"Congratulations on hooking up with Courtney," Michael said, elbowing Max.

He grinned. "It was your idea, bro."

"I see how you are."

"We brought wine," Uncle Lou said.

Michael added, "Plus cheese and crackers."

I headed toward the building and opened the front door while Max lingered with his family. Since I'd known him, I had rarely seen him this happy. Usually there was a shadow beneath his smile—not today. Waiting for them to come, I cherished the sweetness of seeing him like he was meant to be, completely at ease and…happy. He directed them through the front foyer and down the hall toward Nadia and Ty's apartment. When he passed by last, I put a hand on his arm.

"Hang out here. I'll help Angus and Kia cook. We'll be down when the food's ready. No more than a couple of hours. He's been working on it since nine this morning."

"Are you sure?" His gaze flickered after his family while his smile brightened, so I knew it was the right move.

"Completely. It's no problem."

He kissed me quickly, then jogged down the hall as Uncle Lou knocked. I waited until Nadia answered, and afterward, I hurried back up to resume my role as sous chef. Kia was largely uninterested, though she did make a nice fruit salad. And two hours later, we started ferrying dishes down to Nadia's apartment. Inside, the decor impressed me, as she'd gone all out; somebody had obviously visited a party store and bought up turkey-day stuff, between orange horn-of-plenty paper plates, matching cups and napkins.

Max had his uncle and brother watching sports while he helped Nadia set the tables. They'd put up an extra card table and, as promised, shifted the sofa to provide a pathway that Michael could navigate without problems. I let out a silent sigh of relief, as I knew how much Max wanted this to be perfect. Judging by his smile, things were going great.

"Is your place this nice?" Michael asked as we sat down to eat.

"It's not as well decorated," I admitted. "But the layout's the same and the carpet might even be cleaner."

"Just wait until you have a five year old," Nadia muttered.

Uncle Lou shot her a surprised look, probably wondering how old she was when she'd had him, but nobody clarified the situation. Nadia got testy when people said things like *He's not actually your kid.* When she moved in with Ty, she'd gone all in. I moved the conversation along by complimenting Angus's turkey.

"It's really delicious," I said. "Better than my mom's, even, and last year I ate at home. I wasn't living with you guys then, anyway."

"Don't remind me of those dark times," Max joked.

"If you two are gonna start with the sweet talk, I'm taking my plate upstairs." Kia threatened to stand up, but Angus yanked her back down.

He frowned at us. "Are you people completely uncivilized? We haven't said what we're thankful for yet."

That wasn't something we did at my house. Mostly we listened to my mother talk while my dad and I pretended to listen. She had a good heart and better intentions; unfortunately, she showed her concern via nagging. Supposedly it was for our betterment, but a lot of what she said left me feeling shitty.

"I'll start," Max said. "I'm thankful to have my friends and family together this year. And I'm thankful for Courtney."

Warmth glowed through me. "I'm thankful to be alive and healthy…and for Max."

"Well, that was adorable," Kia muttered. "I'm thankful I got six hours' sleep last night."

Michael picked up from there. "I'm grateful I'm talking to my brother again."

A fond smile lit up Uncle Lou's face. His gaze was bright as it lingered on Max and Michael. "I'm thankful for the food and for my two clever, handsome nephews."

Nadia glanced around the table, her expression hard to interpret. "I appreciate the fact that my boyfriend understands how much I miss all of you…and that I got the chance for us all to have Thanksgiving together one last time."

Angus gave her a half hug. "Stop. If you get emotional, I will. And you know it's not the last time. I won't stand for it."

"But you'll all be graduating. Moving on. *I* may still be here, but the rest of you won't." From Nadia's expression, the prospect of being left behind bothered her; while she didn't seem to regret choosing Ty, with her type A personality, it would be odd if she didn't twitch a bit over the delay in her life plan.

I understood.

"Let's make a deal," I said, mostly to cheer her up. "In five years, we promise to have Thanksgiving again. No matter where we are, we figure out who's hosting and we travel as needed to make it happen. Agreed?"

"I'm in." Angus put his palm out and Nadia covered it, then Max and me.

Kia stared at us all before sighing and dropping her hand on top of the pile. "Lord, y'all are just determined to bond with me, huh?"

"You know it." Angus tugged on one of her braids.

"I'll tell Lauren. I think she'll want to come, too," Nadia said.

"Is she still dating your brother?" I asked.

"They broke up." She sounded really sad about it, so I didn't pry.

Angus stepped in, thankfully. "Wait, I didn't go yet. I'm thankful that my parents love Del as much as I do, and that he's so supportive."

"How come he's not here?" I wondered aloud.

"His family really wanted him to come home and...I didn't want to miss our last year together." Considering how much he'd protested when Nadia said basically the same thing, that spoke volumes on how much Angus loved us all.

We're family, I thought.

Uncle Lou took off his glasses and wiped his eyes, visibly moved. I froze, wondering what I should do, but Michael was already on it. He put a hand on the old man's shoulder and asked, "Are you okay?"

"I'm just...glad," he said.

Max asked, "About what?"

"That you found a home," Uncle Lou said simply. "You don't know how worried I've been about you all these years."

Protecting Max was second-nature to me now. Since nobody else knew his family secrets, I reached across the table for the mashed potatoes and added a heaping spoon of them to my plate. "Did you make these with extra lumps, Angus? I can count three in this serving."

He mock-threatened me with his fork. "Next time you make them, and they'll come out like wallpaper paste."

"In five years, I'll be a better cook."

For the first time, I imagined what the future might be like, what I could be doing—my job, my boyfriend. *Max and I might be married by then.* Twenty-six would be old enough to start thinking about it, anyway. I intended to focus on my business for a couple of years after school and he had to finish restoring my car before I'd accept any proposals. I didn't realize I was smiling until he reached for my hand under the table. When I glanced over, he squeezed gently, his fingers stroking over mine.

"Thanks," he whispered.

"No problem," I answered softly.

I'll always have your back.

After the meal, we watched football, which bored the crap out of me. Kia excused herself to take a tryptophan-induced nap upstairs; it was impossible to mind, knowing how little sleep she got. So while the guys yelled at the TV, Nadia and I sat in the dining room, nibbling leftovers. She wore a wistful look as she studied Angus and Max. Uncle Lou was dozing while they argued over somebody's chances at getting to the Superbowl.

"Hey, we made a pact."

She started, glancing at me. "I know. I'm just feeling it today, you know? How it's all winding down."

"I get it. I can't believe I'm about to graduate—that we've

been here four years. I didn't want to ask in front of the guys, but…is Lauren okay? Should I call her?" I had never been close to her, mostly because I secretly envied how much of Max's attention she'd demanded without even trying.

"Honestly? I don't know. It's up to you. She and I don't talk as much as we used to, though I'm trying to get back to where we were. Max seems like he's over her, though. I'm glad you guys got together."

I flicked a glance his way, admiring the sheer beauty of his profile. "Me, too. I…always liked him. But I didn't think… I'm not his type."

"He's clearly nuts about you." Nadia nudged me, grinning.

"It's mutual."

Before she could respond, Uncle Lou stirred and rubbed his chest. Max leaned over and peered at him, obviously worried. "You okay?"

"Touch of indigestion. That's what I get for eating so much."

"If you're sure."

"We should hang out more," Nadia said. "That's on me. I'm not too busy to make time, it's just easier to be lazy and hang out with Ty."

"Plus you can't get enough of him," I teased. "Before, there were all these codicils and regulations. Now he's just yours."

"That's kinda true," she mumbled, blushing.

I grinned. "If you could see your face right now."

"Shut up."

"It's awesome, I'm glad you're happy."

We talked until night fell, then Nadia had to go to Ty's

family, our cue to break up the party. Max hugged his uncle and brother, like, five times, though they were coming back the next day. He intended to show them the garage where he worked and give them a tour of campus, something college students usually did before enrollment, and I knew exactly how much of a big deal this was for Max. I fought the urge to wrap my arms around him and never let go. *Don't let him down. Don't hurt him.* But I couldn't say those things out loud—and I didn't think Michael and Uncle Lou would. I just had this crazy need to keep anyone from hurting Max more than he already had been. *Whatever it takes*, I thought.

Back then I didn't realize I'd be the one to make him bleed.

CHAPTER TWENTY-TWO

Saturday morning, I woke up next to Max and rolled out of bed quietly.

Tiptoeing to the kitchen, I made breakfast in silence, early enough that he shouldn't catch me. And since it was his birthday, I was hoping to surprise him with breakfast in bed. Later, we were planning to hang out with his family and show them what little there was to see in Mount Albion. Max had planned the agenda, but I suspected he didn't realize I remembered what day it was. His gift was wrapped and in my closet.

Thanks to Angus, our kitchen was fully stocked with housewares we rarely used, so I set up the tray and put Max's present on it. Then I slipped into the bedroom and perched on the bed beside him. It was past nine, and we were meeting his brother and uncle at eleven, so we had time. For a few seconds, I just watched him sleep. His lashes were incredibly long and lush, black crescents against his tan cheeks.

I resisted the urge to touch his lower lip, such a soft, beautiful curve. Looking at him, it was hard to credit everything he'd been through; nobody had given him a hand, either. Everything he'd achieved, he'd done it on his own.

Eventually he stirred, eyes fluttering open. Before he even woke fully, he was smiling up at me. "Can't get enough of me, huh?"

"Never. Happy birthday, Max."

"Shit." He sat up in apparent astonishment, rocking the tray beside him.

I put it across his lap and he slow-blinked at scrambled eggs, toast and coffee. It wasn't fancy, no adorable strawberry roses and hotcakes shaped like hearts, but the smile that bloomed made me feel like I'd accomplished something awesome. Max picked up the gift I'd wrapped in silver foil and blue ribbon. For a few seconds, he just held it and stared.

"What?" His nonresponse was making me nervous.

"You know how long it's been since anyone remembered my birthday?"

A pang of guilt shot through me. Last year I'd had so many problems with Madison in the dorm that I hadn't even thought about it; I'd raced back to Chicago without a second thought. On the surface, Max seemed to have friends all over the place, so I'd figured somebody—probably his roommates—would throw him an awesome party. But to my best recollection, Nadia and Lauren went home for Thanksgiving and Angus was probably preoccupied with Josh.

"I'd be a crappy girlfriend if I didn't," I said gently.

He treated the wrapping paper like it was pressed platinum, carefully unfolding each corner, until I started feeling nervous about his reaction to what was inside. When he got to the jeweler's box, I held my breath. But he didn't hesitate, just opened it up to reveal the most rugged dress watch I'd been able to afford. As he pulled it out of the case, I turned it over to show him the engraving on the back. I'd waffled over the inscription for ages, nearly exhausting the clerk's patience. In the end, the message was simple: *I love you.* And then our initials intertwined in pretty script below.

"Wow," he breathed. "It's beautiful."

Leaning forward, I kissed him, and the breakfast tray prevented him from yanking me down on top of him. "Glad you like it. Now eat. We're meeting your family pretty soon."

"Do you think that's why they came?"

"Part of it, probably." I hoped so, anyway.

Max shared his food with me, offering every other bite. My own cooking even tasted better when he was holding the fork. Afterward, he got up and folded the wrapping paper, then stashed it in a heavy textbook. I didn't say anything but I felt pretty sure he intended to keep it. The moment was too sweet for teasing, though, so I just hugged him and went to take a shower. Today, it would be nice if we could do it together, but out of respect for Kia and Angus, I restricted myself to separate bathrooms. Our roomies were still asleep when we headed out—or maybe in Angus's case, he wasn't even home. Still, I tiptoed so Kia wouldn't lose out on a rare occasion to sleep in.

On coming downstairs, I saw Michael's Scion already parked by the curb, though we were five minutes early. He broke out in a huge grin when he spotted Max. *Missed your brother, huh? Please remember what day it is.*

My wish came true when Michael handed Max a birthday bag as soon as we hopped in the Scion. The truck was crowded with Uncle Lou in front and Max and me huddled on half a backseat, but I didn't mind snuggling. In fact, you could even say it was a perk. Uncle Lou passed another package back once we got settled. Max's dark eyes were shining like it was Christmas morning.

"Don't just sit there," his brother ordered. "Open them."

He stared at the presents for a few seconds before peering into the gift bag. "Dress socks, sweater, cologne. Thanks, bro. Next time I take Courtney somewhere nice, I'm all set."

Nudging him, I grinned at Michael. "I'll take pictures."

"Mine next," Uncle Lou prompted.

He unwrapped a really nice set of headphones, amazing quality. I knew for a fact that Max's earbuds weren't nearly this nice and they should be more comfortable, too. I read the spec and gave an approving nod.

"If he doesn't love these, I'm stealing them."

"Hey," Max protested, pulling the box away from me. But his eyes were smiling. "These are awesome, thanks, Uncle Lou."

"Glad I got it right. I had no idea what you like or need these days." The old man sounded sad about that.

Before I could decide what to say, Michael turned on the wipers to smear away the light mist that wasn't quite rain. "Where to first?"

"Campus. Turn right here." Max gave directions until Michael made it to the student center. On the Saturday after Thanksgiving the place was virtually deserted, giving us complete freedom to show them around.

We went to the engineering sciences building first, where Max spent most of his time. He gave a quick tour and I hung back, letting him bond with his family. Michael was full of questions and I remembered he was interested in aeronautics. Since I knew less than nothing about those programs at Mount Albion, I fell into step with Uncle Lou, who was looking a little tired, frankly. Road trips must be tougher at his age.

"He seems really happy," he said, glancing at Max.

"I hope so."

"You have a lot to do with that. When you came to Providence, I could tell you cared a lot about the boy. But I wasn't sure then."

"Of what?"

"If you love him."

I swallowed, suddenly worried that this was about to get deep. Somehow I managed a noncommittal reply. "Oh?"

"But I'm positive now. And grateful, too."

"For what?" This was so weird.

Instead of answering directly, Uncle Lou wore a pensive look. "Did you know Max is like a tree?"

"Huh?"

"He looks strong, doesn't he? All his life, people have leaned on him, even when they probably shouldn't have. But without strong roots, even the strongest oak dies. Either it happens slow, rotting from within, or it falls at the first wind."

"I have no idea what you're talking about." It seemed disingenuous to pretend I didn't know he meant Max and me somehow, but I wasn't getting the analogy.

Uncle Lou offered me a gentle smile and a warm pat on the shoulder. "You're his roots now, Courtney. Thank you for saving him."

That seemed like an overstatement, but I couldn't speak for the pleasure washing over me. If his family considered me essential, then maybe I was. Smiling back, I linked arms with the old man and caught up to Max and Michael. It took half an hour to go through the building because Max kept pausing to tell stories, and his brother didn't seem to mind. The weather was brisk outside, but it didn't stop us from covering the whole campus. Max had so much to say that my heart tightened. I doubted he even knew how happy he looked, finally able to share something about his life with the people he thought he'd lost.

Eventually, it was late enough to think about lunch. So I suggested the burger place a few blocks from school. From what I remembered, the sidewalks were good, no access issues. Everyone agreed so we headed that way as fat, wet snowflakes drifted down. One stuck to Max's cheek, then melted a second later, trickling down to his jaw like a teardrop. As the other two pulled ahead, I stretched on tiptoes to kiss it away.

"All good?" I asked.

Wordless, he nodded and threaded our fingers together. Lunch was good, if greasy, and the rest of the day he directed Michael around town. Toward evening, we drove out to the body shop where he worked; the sign out front proclaimed Rutger's Garage. Max introduced Michael and Uncle Lou to the guys, all of whom were in their thirties and forties. At first I hung back, as I hadn't visited him here before, but he drew me forward and told everyone I was his girlfriend. Happiness filled my chest like bubbles, each one popping in a shimmer of color that made me feel like I'd found magical rose-colored glasses.

"That's pretty much it," Max said, as we climbed back into the Scion. "From this point, we can do whatever you guys want."

We had the keys to Nadia's apartment if they just wanted to hang out and watch movies. Their furniture was better than ours anyway. Fortunately, as it turned out.

"I'm pretty beat," the old man admitted.

"Back home it is." Michael turned toward the apartment complex, and I was impressed when he only needed one word from Max to find the place again.

Better sense of direction than me.

We watched an old comedy, something Uncle Lou could enjoy, too. Halfway through, I made popcorn in Ty and Nadia's kitchen, feeling a little weird about it. But they'd said we should feel at home. Around ten, Michael said he needed to get back, and I didn't argue. Max hugged them both and walked them out while I cleaned up the apartment.

I was sitting at the bottom of the stairs, elbows on my knees, when he came in on a cold gust of wind. When he spotted me, his expression melted in such pure joy that my breath caught. It was ridiculous the way he made me feel.

"Good birthday?" I asked.

"There's only one way it could be better." He waggled his brows.

"That could be arranged."

Before he could reply, I raced up the stairs ahead of him. Since his legs were a lot longer, he caught me before I got to our door. He wrapped his arms around me from behind, nibbling the curve between my neck and shoulder as I fought to get the door unlocked. Shivers coursed through me as I struggled to unlock the door.

"Want me to do that?"

"Um. Maybe."

With a cocky grin, Max took over. He kept his hands to himself as we stepped into the apartment. Since Kia was on the couch watching TV, I silently praised his forethought. She flicked us a half smile, then went back to whatever she was watching. I took a step and decided it looked like *Scandal*.

"You should call if you're gonna be late. Kept me up half the night worrying." The way her smirk widened into a grin told me she was messing with us.

"Sorry," I said, playing along.

I swapped a glance with Max, silently asking if we should sit with her for a little while, much as I'd rather head straight to his room. She sighed without looking at us.

"I heard you two in the hall. Just go."

Choking back laughter, I murmured, "G'night," as Max mumbled something, pulling me after him, one hand wrapped around my wrist.

"We only have an hour," he said.

My eyes widened. "I had no idea there was a deadline."

"Definitely. Any later and it won't be birthday sex anymore."

"That would be a terrible disappointment, huh?"

"You have no idea."

He backed me into his bedroom door, the one we'd pretended to have sex against last fall by bouncing a basketball while we took turns bitching about our problems. Then he kissed a hot path down my neck. *Mmm. Things have changed so much.* Closing my eyes, I tilted my head to grant him better access. At this point, Max knew that was the quickest way to drive me crazy.

"Then we'd better hurry." My voice came out breathless.

"Are you reading my mind?"

Max spun me, hands on my hips, and walked me toward the bed, his lips never leaving my shoulder. His thighs grazed mine, back and forth, with each step. Beneath my T-shirt my nipples tightened, and he yanked the fabric over my head. I didn't let him look long before I pulled his shirt off, too. Relatively speaking, it hadn't been that long since I could see him this way, anytime I wanted. Gently I trailed my fingertips down the center of his chest, admiring the way his muscles jumped. His abs tightened when I got there, and a little sound escaped him.

"You're giving me ideas," he whispered.

"Good ones?"

"*I* think so."

I offered, "We could give them a shot."

"Quietly."

"That goes without saying." Leaning in, I kissed his collarbone. God, he had such great shoulders: lean, graceful and strong from working at the garage. Anytime I saw them, I just wanted to bite him. "So you'll have to try not to moan. Try hard."

His throat worked, and his voice came out shaky. "Okay."

"Tonight's for you. So I need you naked."

I didn't have to say it twice. His pants hit the floor, then his boxers, and Max was on the bed, waiting, so hot I could hardly look directly at him. He crossed his arms behind his head, likely to prove he was leaving everything to me.

What a rush.

When I went for the lamp, he shook his head. "Leave it on."

Biting my lip, I hesitated. Usually I didn't because while I was confident I could rock somebody's world, I felt less assured they'd want to watch me do it. *But it's his birthday.* So I shrugged and peeled off my clothes, letting Max stare as much as he wanted. If anything, his erection swelled further, sending a jolt of pleasure through me.

"How do you want me?" I asked, kneeling on the bed beside him.

"All the ways."

I teased, "But we only have an hour."

"Then start by kissing me." An unexpectedly romantic answer, but that was Max.

Taking the lead, I cupped the back of his head in my hand and took his mouth. For a few seconds, he held still, just letting me, my lips moving on his. His breath misted hot and sweet as he opened for me, his tongue touching mine. Sparks shot through me at once, as I registered his moan. *We're kissing. Just kissing.* But it felt like so much more.

After that, I forgot whatever plan I had. There was only Max and I couldn't touch him enough; I had to taste him everywhere. Countless minutes later, I didn't even know what I was doing, when his hand came down roughly on my head. I was between his thighs, licking frantically, and he kept trying to pull me up.

"Enough." He sounded dazed. "Or it'll just be a birthday blow job. I'm pretty close to a happy ending here."

My hands shook as I rolled the latex on, then he tugged me on top of him. Usually I hated this position, but for him, I'd do my absolute best. And it was no more than a couple of minutes, focused on his face, his dark eyes and the pure pleasure that made him bite at his lower lip, until I didn't care how I looked moving on him. He held my butt, working me against him. The finish came hard and fast, him first, me a few seconds later. I came so hard that my thighs locked and I was a little afraid I might be hurting him. His groan reassured me when I toppled over. Max just lay there panting, his face soft with pleasure.

Right. This is my show.

After taking care of the condom, I came back to bed. "Were we quiet?"

"Dammit. I have no idea."

"Me, either." Wearing what had to be a stupid-looking grin, I passed out with him stroking my back.

The next day, we met Michael and Uncle Lou for brunch. I loved seeing Max with his family, but it was hard watching them say goodbye later. He hugged them both so hard that I had to look away, wishing I was this close to my folks. But between my dad's silent shame over my weakness and my mom's overprotective clutching, it was so hard to talk to them.

"Take care of yourself," Uncle Lou cautioned. "And Courtney, too."

"See you soon," Michael added.

Max nodded. "I'll visit, I promise."

After that, they got on the road home. I stood with him on the front walk, waving until Michael's Scion turned out of sight. When Max turned to me, his expression was layered, a complex mingling of pleasure and regret. Without speaking I twined our fingers together and waited for him to speak. It took a couple of minutes and then he surprised me. Tugging on my hand, he led me toward his bike.

"Let's go for a ride," he said.

No particular objections sprang to mind, so I strapped on my helmet and climbed on behind him. Max didn't say any more as he started the bike and drove away. His turns didn't strike any familiar chords, giving me no clue where we were headed. This time I was clueless until he pulled into a rutted parking lot, one we'd visited the day before.

"You're taking me to work with you?" I asked.

"Not exactly." Gently he pulled off my helmet and took my hand. "This way."

The body shop didn't seem to be open on Sunday, and he circled the building to reveal about ten parked cars in various stages of restoration. A couple had FOR SALE signs in the front windshield, but most had parts missing, flat tires or were coated in primer. I faced Max with a puzzled cock of my head.

"What's up?"

He paused beside a small vehicle that needed a hell of a lot of work, but it was small and adorable, rather like a Corvette, only…cuter, which probably wouldn't win me any fans with car aficionados. The body had rust spots and the door was crumpled on the passenger side. I walked around it, wondering if my suspicions could possibly be right.

"This is an Opel GT," Max said. "And it's yours."

"Oh, my God, are you serious?" Squinting at the car, I could easily imagine how cool it would be, years later.

"You told me what you wanted. Now I just have to make it happen."

I threw my arms around Max's neck. "It's amazing, thank you."

He leaned down to kiss me, I thought, but instead he rubbed our noses together. The sweetness of it curled my toes. "You didn't give me any parameters, but when this showed up, I could totally see you driving it."

"Me, too. You're incredible." It was past time to make this move. "Okay, so...I've met your family. You want to come home with me for Christmas?"

He stared for a few seconds. "Are you sure? I mean, I'm... me. You come from a good family and everything."

By which he meant they had some money. But *big deal*. The Kaufman family honor had never prompted me to change my mind about anything, ever.

So I nodded. "Absolutely. They need to know I have somebody special. Let's not do things halfway."

Max rested his chin on top of my head. "How bad can it be, right?"

But in all honesty, neither one of us had *any* idea.

CHAPTER TWENTY-THREE

The next day, I called my mom as soon as I woke up. "Hey, it's me."

"What's wrong?" she demanded.

"Nothing. How's everyone doing?"

There was a long pause. "Are you sick?"

"How does that question even make sense?"

She thought for a few seconds, then asked, "Do you need money?"

"Wow. I'm a terrible daughter, huh?"

"No...but when you deviate from the pattern, there's usually a reason."

Okay, the woman knew me pretty well. "You're not completely wrong. The reason I'm calling is, I want to know if it's all right for me to bring someone home during the break."

"...Someone?" She sounded cautious.

"My boyfriend."

I caught a relieved puff of breath before she responded. Yeah, she was glad I didn't say *girlfriend*. Stifling a sigh, I waited to hear her verdict.

"Are you coming for all of Hanukkah?" Excitement percolated in her tone, and I felt bad about disappointing her, though it wasn't really a major holiday.

"Sorry. We have exams until the nineteenth. I was thinking we'd leave on Saturday afterward."

"How long do you want to stay? Before you get touchy, understand that I'm only asking so I can buy groceries."

I'd talked to Max already, and he'd managed to get some time off from work. Since he'd never asked for any vacation time, regardless of the holiday, his boss didn't mind. So he had a full seven days from the start of winter break. We'd head back on the twenty-sixth, and he'd probably end up working on New Year's. As for me, rehearsals were canceled until school started back in January.

"A week?" I suggested.

"Understood. Does he have any special food requirements?"

God, she was easy to read. At this point she was hoping I'd say he was kosher, but I pretended not to get it. "He's not allergic to anything, if that's what you're asking."

Mom forced a cheerful tone. "Ah, well, that's good. I'll tell Daddy you've got a plus one this year. And I'm *really* looking forward to meeting him."

A little shiver went through me, imagining the interrogation that would ensue and what answers Max might give. But it was too late to back out. *It'll be fine.* I chatted with her a little more before hanging up and catching a ride to campus with Angus. My professors were all distracted by the twinkle lights or something, so my classes for the next few weeks were mostly review sessions led by the TAs.

The days melted away in a rush of cramming for exams, band rehearsal and stolen moments with Max. He was spending more time at school, finishing up a project, and when he wasn't in the engineering department, he was holed up at the garage. I suspected he might be working on my car, but I didn't want to ask. It seemed…presumptuous.

The second week in December, I played a dorm party with Racing Sorrow, and afterward, we went out drinking. Max still wasn't home when I got in, so I texted *Miss you*. And went to bed.

Finally I stumbled through my tests and emerged like a zombie on the other side. I doubted I'd be graduating with honors, but I'd done enough to stay on track for graduation. *So weird, only one semester left*. On Friday, I did my laundry and started packing. Since we were going on Max's bike, I had to travel light.

Around ten that night, he propped himself against the door frame in my room and watched me trying to decide what to bring with me. I had some clothes at home, but most of what I'd left behind had been purchased by my mother…and consequently, my closet was full of dresses I wouldn't wear even if I lost a bet—Young Miss stuff mostly, with pleats and ruffles.

"All set?" he asked.

I narrowed my eyes, cocking my head. "Huh. You look a little like my boyfriend. He disappeared like, three, weeks ago. But *he* wasn't so thin and hollow-eyed."

"Did you report him missing?" Max ambled into my room, flopping onto my bed with a quiet groan.

"Thought about it. But his occasional texts kept me from fearing the worst."

"You're heartless," he complained. "Do you have any idea what I've suffered for you?"

"Not unless you tell me."

As it turned out, he'd been putting in overtime, taking shifts for the guys who would be covering his week off. *So, not working on your car. Dumbass.* It never occurred to me that he'd have to work extra to make up for going home with me. I put down my backpack and went over to the bed; Max shifted over so I could sit beside him, and he sighed in pleasure when I brushed the hair away from his eyes.

"That feels good."

"I'm sorry, I had no idea it would be such a huge deal. I've never had a job." I felt like such a princess saying that.

He smiled wearily. "It's okay, it was worth it. I've repaid all the guys now, and I'm free to take off in the morning."

"You look like you've done nothing but work and study for weeks."

"Feels like it. Come here." Max drew me into his arms and I could actually feel the difference in him.

He'd always been lean, but now his ribs dug into my side and his shoulder bone poked me when I rested my head. I sat up, staring at him with what had to be a very worried look. "You know I want to make you, like, a gallon of mashed potatoes, right?"

"The kitchen's too far," he mumbled. "And your mom will fatten me up, I'm sure."

"If you get sick, I'll be really pissed." Seeing him like this was...scary. It was hard not to make the mental leap to how Eli had looked the last few weeks of his life. He hadn't started that way, either. I remembered when he was healthy and in remission.

"I'm fine. Don't worry, Courtney."

"Have you *seen* yourself lately?"

He flashed me a tired smile. "Pretty hot, huh? I don't know how you're holding back."

Since he seemed disinclined to take my concern seriously, I changed the subject. "Are you all packed?"

Max nodded. "Make sure you dress warm tomorrow. It's only three hours to Chicago, but it'll feel longer if you're freezing."

"Maybe I should get a leather biker jacket. Think I could pull it off? Black leather, silver studs…?" I was mostly teasing, but he surveyed me through a tangle of thick lashes, as if seriously considering the possibility.

Then he said in a low, rough voice, "Definitely. Get the boots, too."

I went breathless. "Okay."

With some effort, he got himself to his feet. "Come on. I'm so fucking tired that I could pass out in your bed, and I suspect Kia wouldn't be amused."

"She's already gone home for the holidays," I said. "But your bed is bigger."

"True." When Max draped his arm around my shoulders, it felt more like he needed physical support than a gesture of affection.

"You sure you're okay to ride tomorrow?"

"I'll be fine. Just let me sleep for ten hours and feed me something good in the morning."

"If you're sure."

He fell face-first on the bed and I finished packing. The

apartment was quiet at this hour; Angus must have been at Del's place, and nobody else seemed to be stirring, either. Usually on a Friday night, I heard music in the complex, doors slamming, cars pulling up and roaring away. But it appeared that a bunch of folks had rolled out for the holidays already. I tiptoed back to Max's room and climbed in beside him. Since I was pretty tired, too, I passed out right away.

In the morning I made the huge breakfast Max wanted with pancakes from a box mix and scrambled eggs. When he came out of the shower, he looked better. Though he was still thin, he'd lost some of the heroin chic he was rocking last night. One night couldn't erase dark circles like those, unfortunately, but he could rest up at my parents' place. Since I was thirteen, we'd lived in a condo within a few blocks of Lakeshore Drive, three bedrooms, which allowed my mom to keep my room as a shrine and still have a spare for guests.

He ate with flattering gusto, considering half the pancakes were burned on one side; it took me half the batter to get the skillet temperature right. I watched him for, like, five minutes, letting my own food get cold.

Max glanced up with a question in his eyes. "You're not hungry?"

"No, I am. Sorry."

I can't believe you're mine.

Hurriedly I finished up, then I got my stuff so he could pack our bags into the top box. As instructed, I layered up with a hat, gloves and scarf, and then we took off on our second road trip. For obvious reasons, I was more nervous. Last time, I was just doing a friend a favor. Meeting my parents, well, it was a huge deal; there hadn't been anyone significant since Eli died.

An hour and a half into the trip, Max called, "Do you want to take a break?"

I shouted no. We rode straight through, mostly because I was eager to get there. Sitting in a rest-stop food court sipping coffee would warm me up, but it would also add to my agitation. Probably I was on edge because I'd basically *never* done this. Eli didn't require an introduction; we'd gone to nursery school together, and our parents were still close.

Once we hit the city, I gave directions until my voice was hoarse. Just past one in the afternoon, he pulled up in front of the building. Max stared up at the imposing glass and steel shining in the wan winter sunshine. People at school didn't know that much about my background since I tried not to come across as a privileged asshole. Even now, I didn't have the heart to tell him that my dad owned the building—and that it wasn't the only one. He'd started off as a stockbroker, but he was so good at gauging the market, he'd started investing his own money, and by forty, he'd made his first million.

"Holy shit," he said quietly.

Feeling like an asshole, I took a breath. *It'll be fine.* "The garage entrance is over there."

I'd definitely led him to believe my folks were upper-middle-class, no big deal. Some money, normal affluence, and he was already self-conscious about that divide. God only knew how he'd react to this.

"Okay, just tell me where to park."

I guided him to one of the VIP spaces designated for my family's use. That earned me a sharp look, but he didn't say anything. Honestly I had no idea how to act because it wasn't like I hid this from him on purpose. I didn't consider my dad's money mine; I had my own dreams. There was no way I'd conform to parental expectations to earn an inheritance. And both my mom and dad *knew* that; I'd made it completely clear when I left rehab that I was done letting them write the checks that dictated my behavior. They were only paying for college because I hadn't cared enough to argue when they pushed me toward a business degree. Now that I was *alive* again, I suspected it might even come in handy when I started my indie label, which was why I hadn't changed my major.

"We're going to the penthouse, aren't we?" Max said, as I swiped my card in the elevator, then pressed the PH button.

I swallowed. "Yeah."

"You don't think you should've prepped me a little better?" His voice was tight, mouth flat and pale. When he glanced down at his jeans and work boots, I registered his uncertainty.

But we're both in jeans and hoodies. I'd never matched the Kaufman ideal of elegance, either. So I didn't see what difference it made. Max might put on a Boss suit and shiny shoes, but it wouldn't change anything about him. More to the point, I didn't want him to pretend to be somebody he wasn't, not even for my parents. But maybe he didn't get that.

"Would it have helped?"

He didn't answer as the floors ticked away, eventually opening into the foyer. I registered his shock. *Yeah, the condo takes up the whole top of the building.* The place was huge with phenomenal views, three bedrooms, three baths and a study. At this point my dad didn't do anything except own property

and invest money. I didn't remember my mom *ever* working. When I lived at home, we'd had a daily housekeeper
because we all agreed it would be intrusive to have someone
stay in the condo with us, though there was a small maid's
room near the laundry.

"We're here," I called.

My mother rushed out to greet us in a blue-and-white
print dress with too many ruffles down the front. She had
a belly, which she blamed me for, and the style made her
look even more like a pigeon, emphasizing her round middle, thin legs and small feet. In honor of meeting my boyfriend, she'd broken out the diamonds, too, something my
dad must've bought recently since I hadn't seen the set before. Her steps faltered when she spotted Max, and her smile
froze into a ghastly, polite rictus. A flickered gaze up and
down told me how profoundly disappointed she was in what
I'd dragged home.

It was too much to hope Max didn't notice it. But he
stepped forward to extend a hand anyway, and she shook
it while I performed the introductions. "Ma, this is Max
Cooper, my boyfriend. Max, my mother."

"Nice to meet you," he said.

"You don't look like a Cooper."

I cut her a horrified look, but before I could respond, he
answered evenly, "Maybe not. My mom was from Paraguay."

"Was?"

His voice was level. "She died when I was five."

That distracted her from the inquisition, at least. "I'm
sorry. But look at the two of you, your faces are so red.
And Courtney, your hands are freezing. Did you fly in on
a broomstick?"

I smirked. "I got the nose from you, Ma."

"And I had mine fixed years ago." It was true, she had a short, straight nose now that made her face…forgettable.

Max spoke up, slightly testy, because he hated it when anyone talked shit about the way I looked. Apparently, even my mother. "We came on my bike, actually."

Her brows shot up. "As in…motorcycle?"

Oh, man. Strike one. But I didn't want him to lie to make a better impression, so I nodded. "You wouldn't believe how much fun it is to ride."

"I'm sure," she said tightly. "But did you know the nurses in the emergency room call them widow makers?"

"I'm careful."

"And I always wear a helmet," I assured her.

Max shrugged out of his leather jacket, revealing his Mount Albion hoodie with the faded lettering. He'd likely had the thing since freshman year, but it suited him. He was so damn handsome that when he dressed up, as he had for his granddad's funeral, it made me feel like hyperventilating. She took our coats and hung them up in the closet, fingering the leather of his jacket with faint distaste, like there was grease on it. I immediately wished I'd already bought the coat I joked about last night, for solidarity if nothing else. But I couldn't give up so easily. Max was great, and if she gave him a chance, she'd see that.

Her pause was telling. "You're old enough to make your own decisions." The look told me that I was making bad ones. "Come and sit down, both of you. Are you hungry?"

She rambled on about the snacks the housekeeper had prepared, which was a welcome break. I was too tense to want lunch, though. So I perched on the pristine white leather couch, marveling that she'd redecorated yet again. This time, the room was all silver and white, beautiful but cold, an impression reinforced by the wall of windows behind us. The usual Hanukkah decorations were out as well, including the menorah. Max seemed nervous, not leaning back fully, and sitting with his hands tightly laced, a full foot away.

I told myself, *It'll get better. She had to know I wasn't bringing home a hot young banker fresh from J-Date.* Ma offered, like, four kinds of drinks before accepting that neither of us wanted anything. Afterward, I realized I should've asked for tea, just to distract her.

Because once she sat down with a glass of lemonade in hand, she got right back to being nosy. "So it's just you and your father? What does he do?" The question was so obviously intended to make him feel inadequate, that I almost got up right then.

"Ma," I warned.

Max wasn't playing her game, though. He smiled sweetly and said, "Drink and collect disability checks, mostly."

She choked on her drink, staring with wide, watering eyes. That wasn't the kind of thing anyone she knew would freely admit. Instead it'd be talked about in whispers with lots of headshaking, but hell, why should Max feel bad about it? He wasn't his father.

He went on. "But I have other relatives. My little brother's pretty great. So are my Uncle Lou, Aunt Carol and Uncle Jim. They're all fine, upstanding members of society, so I have a fair shot of *not* ending up in the gutter."

It seemed like he'd won that round, but I hated that this week was likely to be so uncomfortable and adversarial.

CHAPTER TWENTY-FOUR

"Max, wait."

But he wasn't listening to me. When I didn't immediately hand over the backpack, he brushed past me without a word and strode toward the foyer. I chased after him while my mother stood frozen in shock. After grabbing his jacket from the hall closet, he called the elevator without looking at me, and I had the awful feeling he blamed me for how this had gone down. As the doors opened, I tried to step on with him but he shook his head.

"You came to see your parents. So stay here and do that."

"I wanted *you* to meet them."

"But you didn't tell me the whole story, did you? Wonder why not." Max didn't relent, so I tried to push closer and he actually walked me back, just before the doors shut in my face.

It felt like someone was squeezing my heart with a pair of pliers. The fact that something *I* did made Max feel this way? Unbearable. If I'd known it would turn out this way, I never would have brought him home. And in hindsight, I definitely should've told him the truth about my family's status, but…it was pretty hard to reveal out of nowhere. How would that conversation even go? *By the way, Max, my parents have a lot of money. So be prepared for them to act like assholes and live in a penthouse.* Maybe if I'd said that, though, this wouldn't have happened.

My mom's heels clicked as she came toward me. "At least he isn't stupid. That's to his credit. But I can't believe—"

"You acted that way to a guest I brought home," I cut in furiously. "He wasn't here because he's hoping to get something from me. Max doesn't even like me to pay for dinner when we go out. And he's definitely not on drugs, Ma. That was *me*, remember? Because I couldn't cope. I was weak and losing Eli was just too much."

The elevator dinged, and I had some hope it was Max coming back up, regretting his quick exit, but the door opened to reveal my father instead. As usual, he was dressed in expensive slacks and a tailored button-up shirt. He'd lost even more hair from the last time I saw him, which he covered with a yarmulke at all times. Privately, I thought he did it out of vanity more than religious conviction, as my mother had more real faith than my dad and me put together. That was part of the reason why she cared so much about me marrying a nice Jewish boy, though some of that stemmed from snobbery.

Ma glanced between us, visibly troubled. "Do you think I can ever forget that? I—"

"Drove out the most important person in my life. You judged him in one look." My knees went shaky as fury flooded me. "I've never been *so* ashamed to be part of this family."

"What are you saying?" Dad demanded, stepping out of the elevator to stare at us. "Apologize to your mother right now."

"I won't. She gave permission for me to bring Max home, and then she treated him like garbage, made it crystal clear he wasn't welcome."

My dad hesitated. Typical. Apart from market fluctuations, he wasn't a decisive man and usually found it easier to let my mom handle things. But if he took her side blindly... I bit my lip, so angry that I had to clench my hands into fists to keep them from trembling.

"Is that what happened?" he asked Ma.

"He looked a little...ethnic. So I inquired about his background," she said. "Then I pulled Courtney aside to talk to her in private and he came to eavesdrop. Is it my fault he didn't like what he heard?" She made a face. "That proves my point. Bad manners, bad upbringing."

"Was it the one that came roaring out of the garage on a motorcycle?" Dad asked.

As soon as he said that, I knew how this would go. He wouldn't take my side. To my parents, everything about Max represented "the bad element" and it didn't matter how hard he'd worked to get where he was. If they ever saw his tattoos, their heads would probably explode. Which meant this argument was completely pointless. Resigning myself to that fact, I wheeled and stalked down the hall to get my bag. There was no point in being here when I was so upset.

"Where do you think you're going?" Ma called after me.

"Back to Michigan."

"Out of the question. We've got parties to attend, I promised the Cohens that you'd come. Their son is home from Princeton. You remember Joseph, right? He—"

"I don't care what promises you made," I said, shouldering my backpack.

When I realized how this week would've gone, relief spilled through me. Imagining how shitty Max would've felt while my mother threw eligible Jewish guys at me prompted a shudder. *Glad you had too much pride to stick around. I'm done, too.*

"You can't just storm out." Dad stepped in front of me, boxing me in between my mom and the wall.

"Do you plan to physically restrain me and lock me up?" My expression had to be hard as I looked between them. "Because that's the only way I'm staying."

I took a step forward and his hands clamped on my shoulders. He wasn't a big man, but he still had six inches on me, and my mother pushed closer. Her eyes shone with a frantic gleam but I couldn't tell if she was about to cry or if it was something else. She put a hand on my cheek, and I started to get worried. They didn't seem to realize how far across the line they were.

"I'm worried about you," she said quietly.

"Because I'm dating someone you don't approve of? Guess what, I'm also in a band."

That shocked her into backing up a step. I took advantage of the opening to yank away from my dad and push through the gap to head for the elevator. My mother ran after me, pulling on my arm to hold me. My dad followed slower, his face serious and heavy with dismay. I could practically read their minds—I was either crazy or on drugs. Either way, I needed an intervention and to go back to rehab.

"You can't leave," my father said.

"Watch me."

"Courtney, don't do this," my mother siad. "We'll talk about it some more. Maybe if you tell me about him…" But I saw right through that tactic; she didn't care to learn about Max. She just wanted time to nag and wear me down, list all the reasons why we made no sense as a couple.

"If you meant to get to know him, you would have treated him like a person who matters. You would've shown us both some respect."

"What's that boy done to earn it, other than seduce my daughter? I'm supposed to be glad that you brought home some—"

"Whatever you're about to say, don't," I warned. "Or that'll be a bridge you can't cross back again. I'm serious, Ma."

"You both just need to calm down," Dad put in.

She spun on him. "You stay out of it, if you're not helping."

"I only saw a jacket and a helmet," he protested. "What am I supposed to say?"

"Tell her to stop this nonsense."

My father was trying to play peacemaker. "How can I? Is it fair to judge somebody this fast? How much do you know about him? Maybe a background check…"

Silently I winced. They wouldn't like Max better when they discovered he'd dropped out and earned his GED. They'd only see it as more proof of his unsuitability, whereas to me it proved how strong and determined he was. I ignored the both of them and got my jacket out of the closet. *Worst Hanukkah ever.*

My mother's voice went shrill when she realized I was serious about taking off. "If you walk out now, Courtney, we're cutting you off."

I glanced at my dad, wondering if he'd go along with this. He wore an uncomfortable expression, heavy silvery brows knit in a faint frown. "Why don't you just stay for dinner? We'll have something nice, talk it out. There's no reason to be rash."

"Talk to your wife. I thought she cared about being a good hostess, but I guess her manners depend on how many zeroes are on somebody's tax return."

"You can't talk about your mother that way."

I shrugged. "I would've said she can't treat people I love that way. Sad. Looks like we're both wrong, huh?"

His jaw tightened. "I don't like the way you're acting over this boy, Courtney. You don't sound rational."

My brows shut up, as incredulity swamped me. "I'm supposed to sound logical when I'm mad? Nobody sent me that memo. And I'm *not* staying for dinner. Talk to you later." I didn't want to add that last part, but I was trying not to leave them in a dead panic.

"You walking out like this tells me there's a serious problem," Dad said soberly.

A sigh escaped me. "I'm clean."

"We can't take that chance. I'm not giving you the money to buy whatever you're on." Tears trickled down my mother's cheeks. "This time, you have to get sober on your own."

I couldn't believe this was actually happening. "Whatever. You want my credit cards?"

Pulling out my wallet, I handed them over. "The bank card is mine, you can't touch what I have in checking. The money in savings from Granddad is mine, too. Otherwise, I'm cut off. I got it."

"That means no more wire transfers. No more tuition payments. No more rent money." My dad seemed to think he could make me heel like a bad puppy by reminding me.

"That's fine. I'm an adult now anyway. I'm sure I can get by. My roommates do." They didn't know Max was one of them; that would surely make the situation worse.

As I thought about the payment cutoff dates, I realized they'd probably already paid for my last semester anyway. So I just needed to earn my keep for a few months before looking for a real job or implementing my studio startup plan. The latter was more risky, but in my heart, it was what I wanted to do.

"I don't think you realize how difficult this will be," Ma said. "Or what you're giving up. To me, that's even more proof that you're—"

"Maybe I *don't* know. But I'll learn. Obviously I won't be sending a daily update text anymore. If you're cutting me loose, that means I'm off the hook. So be sure to tell the Cohens that you've given up on me." I flashed a sweet smile. "I bet your friends will be impressed to hear how well you dish out the tough love on your disappointment of a daughter." Stepping around my parents, I pushed the elevator button and then handed over the passcard that let into the condo. "I won't be needing this either, huh?"

My parents stared at me as the doors closed and the elevator jerked, carrying me away. The lobby was deserted when I reached it, apart from the doorman. Not surprising.

Max would be long gone. Or maybe he was waiting for me somewhere? Surely he knew I wouldn't stick around. So I got out my phone as I went out the front doors. Pain pricked me when I saw no new messages. *But maybe he's on the bike.* I remembered how he'd left me once in Providence, but he didn't go far. *So maybe...*

I sent, I'm so sorry. Where are you?

Outside the wind was bitter cold, ripping through my jacket. I got my hat, scarf and gloves out of my backpack and bundled up. I'd always loved living near the Magnificent Mile, so while I admired the familiar beauty of the city as I walked, waiting for my phone to ping, I was also quaking inwardly. *Max seemed pretty angry when he left. At you, not Ma.*

A few blocks later, I still had no messages from him and I found myself at the bus stop. Briefly I considered getting a cab, then I shook my head. *I'm poor now.* I remembered the train and bus schedules from growing up in the city, so I stopped here. Max could contact me if I was on a bus, which seemed smarter than wandering aimlessly in the cold. I still hadn't heard from him when the 156 arrived, so I got on, planning to head for Union Station.

Out of habit, I put in my earbuds and listened to music while staring out the window. Somebody sat down next to me but I didn't turn. Instead I just watched the winter cityscape pass by with a heavy heart and a knot in my throat. If the silence went on too much longer, I might cry, though right now I was fighting it. *I handled this all wrong, huh?* For the first time since I'd said goodbye, I missed Eli's voice in my head.

My phone was still dead quiet as I hopped off the bus at the Adams & Canal stop. Union Station was only a block

away, but I walked slow, hoping I wouldn't need a ticket—
that Max would text or call, giving me a chance to apologize
in person. When my cell buzzed just before I went inside,
I nearly dropped it. Pausing, I opened up my messages. It
was a text from Nadia, wishing me happy holidays. Sighing, I sent back, You, too.

Soon, she replied, I'm going home for Christmas. See you
next year!

Union Station was enormous, imposing on the outside,
and there were tons of people scurrying, probably trying
to get somewhere last-minute for the holidays. I hovered
outside, not wanting to admit this was necessary, but my
fingers were numb even through my gloves by the time I
admitted defeat an hour later and trudged inside. The inte-
rior was gorgeous, historical elegance, but I didn't have the
heart to admire anything; it had been years since I'd been
here. My mother preferred to fly. The last time—when I
was twelve—I'd gone with my dad to Milwaukee for some
reason, probably business-related.

I sat down in the central waiting area, staring at my phone
like I could make it respond magically. Because it seemed
prudent, I also checked the schedule, and I could still get
a ticket for the last train to Ann Arbor. There wouldn't be
any buses running when I got in, though, so I wouldn't have
a way back to Mount Albion. Since I needed to be careful
with my money until I found a job, I pondered the best so-
lution. A hotel was out of the question, since the train ticket
would cost me eighty bucks. *Nadia's gone. Kia's gone. What
about Angus?* I tried calling but it rang a bunch of times, then
I got a perky message about him being castaway somewhere
tropical with Del. *Why didn't I know he was going to Jamaica?*

Though I was scared to dial, I called Max. A
mail. *It didn't even ring... He must've turned it o*
doesn't want to talk to me right now. I suspected he
spend the week with my parents, as planned, but
how could I? Closing my eyes against a hot rush
loneliness clutched with icy fingers, exacerbated by
of wind that blew through the lobby. Strangers hur
with their bags and nobody gave me a second look
hunched forward to hide my face, like I'd come down
a bad case of invisibility. I hadn't felt this way since Eli
though it was a different sort of desolation.

My voice sounded thick as I left a message. "Like I sa
I'm really sorry. Please call me when you get this. I'm
the train station. I'll...be here until six. I'm going home."

The time ticked away while I ran my phone battery down,
listening to sad music. I left buying my ticket until the last
possible minute, but Max didn't call. He didn't come, either.
But I'd known he had a habit of taking off when he was
hurt, so this didn't come as a surprise, even if I felt pretty
battered. So I got up and silently ran my debit card through
the machine, buying a coach seat for Ann Arbor.

Last resort, okay.

I pulled up Evan's contact and called, below sea level in
every possible way. It wouldn't surprise me if he refused to
help out. Murphy's Law was all over me today.

He picked up on the second ring, obscenely cheerful.
"What's up, funny girl? Did you miss me?"

"Um. So. My plans fell through, and I'm in a bind. I'm
coming into Ann Arbor by train tonight, late, and I could
really use a ride. Is there any way—"

"I'll be there," he said. "What time?"

I checked my ticket. "Eleven-twenty, assuming we're on schedule."

"Meet me where the taxis line up, okay?"

"Yeah. Thanks. I'm sorry to put you out."

"It's not a problem. I didn't have plans."

"I'll give you gas money."

His voice came across gentle. "Don't worry about it right now, I can always dock your cut of our next gig for transportation fees. See you in a few hours."

My chest hurt as I hung up. My battery was down to 20 percent, so I put the phone away. No more music, unless the train had charging stations. Probably not in coach, I guessed. There was still no word from Max. He must have been home by then or nearly so, if he'd driven straight through. It was almost six, and the garbled announcer called for us to board over tinny speakers.

So this is happening, I thought.

And got on the train alone.

CHAPTER TWENTY-FIVE

Evan was waiting when I came out of the train station. He hopped out of the van and studied me for a few seconds. But all he said was, "Is that all you have?"

I nodded. "Thanks for coming."

"It's fine. You'd do the same for me."

"Except for the fact that I don't have a car."

"Details." His breath showed in a puff of smoke, and he exaggerated a shiver as he opened the door for me. "Come on, let's try to get you home before one."

"That'd be good."

But I was scared of going to the apartment, too, afraid of facing Max and how hurt he must be. It was worse because I had to acknowledge my own role in that. But it was too cold to make Evan stand around while I freaked out. So I climbed in, then he shut the door after me and rounded the van. The vehicle shifted as he got in, reminding me how solid he was.

My parents wouldn't approve of you either, I thought.

We drove for, like, five miles in complete silence before he said, "Do you want to talk? If not, I'm turning on the radio because this silence is kind of soul-killing."

"Sorry. I don't really *want* to but I probably owe you an explanation."

He shook his head. "If you'd rather listen to music, it's fine."

As he said that, I realized I wanted someone else's opinion, preferably a guy, because I hoped maybe Evan could tell me just how bad I'd fucked up on a scale of one to ten and what I should do to make it up to Max. So before he reached for the dial, I started talking. Since he'd noted that I must have money because I didn't flinch over dropping eighteen hundred on keyboard equipment, this probably wouldn't come as a complete shock. He listened in silence until I finished.

"Damn," he said finally, shaking his head. "Your mom is some piece of work, Courtney."

"She wasn't so bad before."

"Before?"

Before Eli died. Before I lost it. Before I woke up in a white room, her rocking and crying, "I can't lose you, you're my precious baby, my whole world." I suspected whenever she looked at me, she saw that same lifeless, broken girl, someone she had to make decisions for and protect at all costs. But knowing that didn't change how I felt about what had happened with Max.

"My boyfriend died when I was in high school," I said. "And I didn't handle it well. Ended up in rehab."

"Damn. So we got ourselves a real rock star on keyboards." He sliced a questioning look toward me when I didn't even crack a smile. "Too soon? Not funny?"

"It wasn't the joke. I just don't have a laugh in me right now."

"You want my opinion, then?"

"Please." That was why I'd told him, after all. Well, that, and a sense of obligation, since he had come out late at night to help me.

"If it was me, I'd feel like shit. I'd figure you were fucking around with me, slumming until graduation. If we were together and you didn't bother to give me a heads-up, I'd think you either didn't take us serious or didn't care about me taking one right in the face. Worse, maybe you thought it'd be funny to shove me in the deep end to see if I sink or swim."

"Shit. *None* of that's true."

"He doesn't know that. I hate to say it, but for a smart girl, you sure fucked up."

Letting out a heavy sigh, I bowed my head. "I know."

There was no point in explaining my motivations to Evan. I'd save the truth for Max and hope he had a smidgen of understanding tucked away. I couldn't stand it if this was the end for us. The drive back to Mount Albion went quicker than I wanted and slower than molasses. But an hour and ten minutes after I got in the van, he pulled up outside my apartment.

"You live together, right?"

I nodded.

"If things get too awkward, you can crash at my place for a while. I have a spare room and my uncle's not coming back until November."

While the idea that things might go that badly sent my stomach into a permanent spin, it was also comforting that Evan was willing to put me up, though he knew how I'd screwed up. I let out a slow breath, staring up at the building. From the front, it was impossible to tell if Max was home, but a glance around the parking lot and I located his bike, parked in the usual spot.

"I appreciate it. Well, I guess I better go up, huh?"

"It won't do any good to put it off," he agreed.

"See you next year. I hope." With that, I grabbed my backpack and went to face the damage.

Part of me hoped Max would be asleep, just so I had an excuse to put this off, but I knew he wouldn't be. When I unlocked the apartment door, he was on the couch bathed in the flickering light of the TV screen with a beer in his hand and two empties on the table next to him. He didn't speak as I closed the door behind me. In fact, he didn't even *look* at me.

"Max…"

"Go to bed," he said in a monotone.

"I'm not moving until you talk to me."

At that, his mouth compressed, a muscle jumping in his neck. "You're determined to have it out tonight, huh? Fine. Let's do it."

"I'm really sorry."

"For what? For blindsiding me with your two-million-dollar condo and your bitchy, diamond-studded mother? Or for letting me think we make sense together?"

My throat tightened. "That's not funny."

"Do I look like I'm laughing? I haven't kept any secrets

from you, Courtney. You know exactly where I'm from. But I knew jack shit about you, apparently."

"I messed up. I know that. But there's a reason I didn't say anything. I'm begging you to just listen, okay?" I dropped my backpack and sank onto the floor. It wasn't intentional but I ended up on my knees, leaning against the couch. It had been such a long fucking day that every part of me ached, but I just couldn't walk away until we hit some semblance of understanding.

"No, I think I'll talk instead." Max downed the rest of his beer and then crushed the can in one hand. "Let me guess, you wanted to be sure I wasn't just another broke asshole chasing you for your money."

"No, that's not it at all," I choked out.

"What, then?"

"I was afraid this would happen. That it would change everything and you wouldn't see me the same anymore."

"Well, you were right." He still hadn't looked directly at me. Instead, he was staring at the infomercial on TV like the kitchenware could unlock the secrets of the universe.

"Please don't say that."

"Unlike you, I'm not a liar, Courtney. Not even by omission."

"What do you want me to do?" The tears were choking me, a knot of sea salt about my neck. Between the pain and lack of oxygen, it felt like my chest was on fire.

"Be who I thought you were."

"I'm still me," I protested.

"You're a rich girl passing in my neighborhood. I hope it was a good time."

"Was?" My voice shook.

"I thought that was pretty clear by the way your mom treated me."

"What she thinks and what I do have never been remotely the same."

He ignored that, breaking my heart a little more. What had been a hairline fracture widened into a fissure. I could almost taste the blood, a coppery echo in the back of my throat. I clenched my hands into fists to stop myself from crawling over and clinging to his legs. That wouldn't soften his mood any, and I couldn't even blame him for what he was saying. Not when I'd hurt him so badly.

"Let me ask you this… What are you even doing here?"

"Where?"

"Mount Albion. With the money I saw in Chicago, your parents could've bought you a spot anywhere, just about. Why aren't you at an Ivy League school? That's where you belong."

That made me mad because he knew about Eli, about rehab. I hadn't kept that part of my life a secret from him at all. So I snapped, "My GPA was terrible, Max, and my SATs were worse. I mean, shit, I was wait-listed even here at Mount Albion. This was the best I could do."

He let out a sigh that was nearly a snarl and snapped out of his chair. For a few seconds, he towered over me, but I wasn't scared. Then he dropped to his knees, facing me with a sadness that I never, ever wanted to see in his beautiful brown eyes. Tears trembled in his lashes and he blinked them away without speaking.

Countless moments later, his voice came out gravel-rough, hoarse as if he'd spent that time crying. "See, that's exactly the problem, Courtney. You just proved my point."

"Huh?"

"You think I didn't hear your disdain just now? 'This was the best I could do.' To you, this place is a waste, and you're clocking time. But you got any idea how fucking proud I am that Mount Albion took me? I saved for two years, ate ramen, pored over grant application requirements in the library before my shifts. I begged strangers at the adult education center to help me figure this shit out. Some days, I ate nothing but pride. So Mount Albion is the best I could do, too, but…in a completely different way."

Oh, God. He's right. What did I just say? I couldn't breathe.

He went on, "You have everything, including parents who care enough to act crazy on your behalf, and you don't want it. I have nothing and I'm fighting for every inch."

"I'm really proud of you," I managed to say.

"Why? You think what I achieve is a reflection on you? 'Look at me, I'm so awesome supporting my hard-luck boyfriend.'" He sighed and closed his eyes. "*This* is why we don't make sense. You've never lived in the real world. I didn't understand the scope until meeting your mother, but things are crystal clear now."

"I'm definitely not as independent as you," I admitted. "But I'm working on it. I don't expect you to take care of me."

"If you talk him around, your daddy can find me a job somewhere, right? Probably buy our first house, too. Which would be *fucking awesome*, if I was for sale."

My nails bit into my palms so hard that I felt them slice through and a sting of blood seeping in red crescents. Too late, I understood how much I'd hurt him and how little I could do to change it. I didn't think it would matter if I told him that I never considered what my father earned to be mine—that I didn't come from a long line of trust funds. Talking about the 50K I had from my granddad would probably sound like a boast when I'd only mean that it was all I had that was mine, money he'd saved up over his whole life…and that was why I'd never touched it, why I was still thinking about whether I should use it to start my indie label. If I failed, it would be like pissing on my grandfather's legacy.

"I can see this is too big for an apology."

"Yeah," he said with awful finality.

"Just to be perfectly clear, we're breaking up now?"

He pushed up on his hands, returning to his chair. Except for the shine of his eyes, I could almost believe his indifference. "It was done when I left the condo, when I didn't answer your texts or calls. But you wanted to scrape it raw, so we have."

"Okay. Sorry." It was all I could do to get those two words out without crying.

I dragged myself upright, found my backpack; it was nearly enough weight to topple me over. Somehow I stumbled to my room and shut the door quietly behind me. My head was a mess when I fell on my bed, just a constant whirl of what-ifs and inchoate plans to get him back. The tears surprised me; I didn't even realize I was crying until I touched my cheeks and noticed how wet my pillow was. They were silent tears, thank God. I choked back all sounds, not wanting Max to hear me. I was still crying when I passed out, and when I woke early the next morning, my cheeks were still damp.

I have to go, I thought.

There was just no way I could stay, and Max had been

here first. So instead of making breakfast or taking a shower, I got out my suitcase and packed it. The boxes I'd used to move from the dorm were still in the closet; they only needed me to bust out the packing tape, so I could fill them with my belongings. I didn't even know where I was going but I kept collecting my stuff like a robot because if I thought too hard about why this was necessary, I'd end up in a ball on the floor.

I wished I'd told Max that I loved him. If I said it now, he'd take it for emotional manipulation. And he wouldn't be 100 percent wrong. Exhaling, I looked around to make sure I hadn't forgotten anything. But nope, all that was left was Kia's stuff. It was hard not to think this room was cursed, man. First Lauren had flunked out, then I had to move because of a messy breakup. But it could be argued that if she'd studied and I hadn't gotten involved with my room-mate, we both would've been fine. And Nadia had moved out for adorable reasons.

It took all my courage to open my bedroom door, but the apartment was deserted. Though Max's bedroom door was closed, I knew he wasn't in there just from the empty feeling. I didn't feel like eating, so instead of fixing food, I used the fridge magnets to leave him a final message. I Am Sorry. I Will Miss You. Not nearly enough, but it was all I could give him.

Then I called Evan, who picked up on the first ring, like he was expecting my call. "You okay, funny girl?"

"Not remotely. Is your offer still good?"

"Sure. But I expect you to pay rent. This isn't a free lunch, you know."

"Just let me know how much."

God only knew how I'd afford double rent payments since my parents had cut me off. If I called to tell them Max and I were done, they'd send me new cards and pay off my lease, glad to have me away from him. *But I'm not doing that. This is my problem, and I'll figure it out.*

"How soon do you need me there?" he asked.

"ASAP. My ex isn't here right now, and I kind of feel like he's making himself scarce until I clear out." Maybe I was wrong about that, but I couldn't feel good about Max sleeping at the garage or in his secret river spot, especially in this weather.

It was your *home first. I won't take it away from you. I guess that means I can't email Michael anymore.* And that hurt as much as if he were actually *my* brother, and I wasn't allowed talk to him. *No more Uncle Lou. I can't really hang out with Kia and Angus anymore, either. Since Nadia's outside the apartment, I can probably still hang out with her, as long as Max isn't around.* Every breakup ended in friendship casualties with people taking sides.

Every time I thought about calling or sending texts, the tears started fresh. In the end, I decided to postpone explanations until after break. No reason to ruin any else's holiday. Grief made it hard for me to haul stuff down. At one point, I sat on the bottom step and cried until I couldn't breathe. Outside, I swiped until my face was chapped and cold, probably dusty, as well. My eyes were so swollen, I could barely see. But half an hour later, I had all my stuff downstairs on the sidewalk.

Evan pulled up just as I sat down on the curb to wait. "Jesus Christ. You look like slow-roasted hell."

I couldn't deny it. "You have a way with words. You should write lyrics."

"We can work on that while we're rooming together. Get in the van and warm up. I'll load up for you."

"I can't let you do that."

"I'm not convinced you can stop me." He poked me with a fingertip and I wobbled.

Conceding the point, I stumbled over and got in, then closed my eyes, tilting my head against the back of the seat. Evan was good at manual labor, so within a few minutes he was in the driver's seat, briskly rubbing his hands against the cold. He checked the heat, then glanced over at me.

"Looks like I owe you again," I said.

"Don't worry, I'm keeping a tab. At this rate, you'll be my indentured keyboardist."

I was supposed to smile at that, but I couldn't. If I fell down another step, I'd be in the doctor's office, claiming I needed help sleeping. Pretty pills, pink and blue, one to take the pain away, another that let me pretend I was still alive.

"Okay." It was easier to agree to be his musical slave, echoes of how I used to be.

Evan cut me a worried look. "You sure this is your best move? Taking off to stay with another guy won't win you any reconciliation points."

"He thinks I'm a complete waste of space. At this point, the only thing I can do is get out of his way."

CHAPTER TWENTY-SIX

For two days after the breakup, I wallowed, and Evan let me. He made sure I ate one meal a day, but otherwise, he didn't pressure me to be productive. But on the twenty-third, he tapped on my bedroom door, and it took me a full five minutes to schlep over to open it. When I did, I noticed his worried look.

"I'm alive, don't worry."

"That's not why I'm here. I just wanted to tell you that I'm taking off."

"Oh?"

"Yeah. I promised my mom I'd come home for Christmas this year. So I'll be gone until the twenty-sixth. Will you be okay here? Without a car and everything."

I nodded. "It's fine. I have other friends."

From his expression, he was wondering why I wasn't staying with them, then, and why I hadn't called them for a midnight pickup at the Ann Arbor train station. But he was nice enough not to poke holes in my pride. Evan just nodded.

"Okay, well, there's food in the kitchen. No more than you've been eating, it should hold you until I get back." He hesitated, seeming torn.

"What's wrong?"

"I just feel shitty leaving you alone on Christmas."

That started a laugh out of me. "You know I'm Jewish, right? Mostly lapsed, but still."

"Shit, yeah, I forgot. That makes me feel better. I'll only be an hour and a half away, so if you need to talk, call me."

"I promise I'll be fine," I said.

Taking my word for it, Evan headed out. I spent the next three days trying to figure out what to do. Obviously I couldn't stay with Evan forever, and it wasn't particularly convenient to get to campus from here. If he still went to Mount Albion, I wouldn't mind giving him gas money like I used to Angus, and letting him drive me in, but as Evan put it, his college enrollment was "lapsed." No ready solutions came to me, though I did find out that there was a bus stop a mile and a half away, so, though it wouldn't be easy, I *could* get to school from here.

Mostly I glommed TV shows online and felt sorry for myself. But I wasn't on the verge of breaking; this wasn't like Eli, after all. Because while he was irrefutably gone, Max was across town, probably feeling as bad as I did. Which shouldn't have made me feel better, but if I couldn't be with him, it was sort of comforting to picture us sharing the same pain. It was hard to sleep, so I stared out the window a lot, watching as fat, white snowflakes sputtered down. We got at least two inches as I watched that night, and I didn't fall

asleep until 5:00 a.m. I had no tears left, only a burning regret over the way I broke something so beautiful.

I'm sorry I hurt you.

Because Evan would yell if I didn't, I made sure to eat.
When he came back, he was loaded down with presents
and bags of leftovers. He seemed worried, but I was still
alive and no worse off than when he'd left. I helped him
put stuff away while inspecting the delicacies his mom had
sent home: turkey, mashed potatoes, peas and carrots, fruit
salad, rolls, cherry pie.

"Wow, that's some haul."

"She's convinced I don't cook."

"Does she know you're out of school?"

He nodded, stacking containers in the fridge, which was
down to eggs, ketchup and a few bottles of beer. "Yeah, I
thought a music degree would be a waste of time."

"Are you thinking about going back?"

"Maybe. If I can figure out what to do with myself. It
pisses me off to waste money."

"That makes sense." I took a breath. "I was wondering…
Would it be a huge problem if I stayed until graduation?"

"Not for me. It's nice having a roommate. But are you
moving in June? We haven't really talked about it." He had
to be asking because of the band.

"Maybe. I don't have my shit together as much as most
seniors."

"No life plan?"

I laughed wryly. "I don't even have a day plan."

"Well, as soon as you know, give us a heads-up, okay?
Since Dana and Ji Hoo both have another year, if you go,

we'll need to audition keyboardists again." Evan sounded like he'd rather pull out a few teeth with needle-nose pliers.

"You'll be the first to know."

"Thanks. You want me to fix you a plate?"

"Nah, I ate already. I'll have some tomorrow."

He looked like he wanted to lecture me, but instead he got out some sheet music and a battered notebook. "I wasn't kidding when I said I'd make you work on some songs. This is how far I've gotten."

For the rest of the break, we worked until we managed to finish one of his works in progress. Lyrics didn't come easy to me, but it was pretty satisfying when we finally produced something to play for Dana and Ji Hoo when they got back. Evan handled most of the melody, though I did come up with a nice bridge. On the downside, it was cold as hell working out in the garage. I was shivering when we finally came in.

"I'm making coffee," I said.

"Fine by me. Two sugars, no milk."

As I worked the machine, I wondered what Max was doing, if he had somebody with him. Angus and Kia should be home soon, but I had no idea when. I'd held off on texting them so as not to ruin their trips, though maybe I was giving myself too much credit. Me moving out might register as more of an inconvenience, especially when they heard Max's side of the story. In this scenario, I was definitely the black hat, though not from bad intentions.

Road to hell, good intentions. Check.

"What're you worried about?" Evan asked, as I brought the drinks to the living room.

"Just wondering how many friends I'll lose when the word gets out."

"Ah. Yeah, dividing up the social circle sucks."

In the end, it wasn't as bad as I feared. On January 4, I sent texts to Angus, Nadia and Kia, explaining the situation in brief. Angus replied at once: Seriously? Shit. You guys were so good together. I'll miss you, C. But we'll go out drinking next weekend, okay? I'm your DD.

I sent back, Sounds good. Thanks.

It took Nadia half an hour, but she was even more concerned. Are you okay? You want to come over for dinner some night this week? I promise my cooking is better now.

But I couldn't face the thought of running into Max. So I answered, I want to hang out, maybe we could go out instead?

Nadia's text pinged five minutes later. Sure, name the night. I'll make it work.

Aw. Angus and Nadia still love me.

Kia didn't reply until the next day, but her message made me smile. Girl, I've so been there. I'll buy coffee at the Pour House, okay? 2pm Tuesday.

Honestly, I'd thought it would hurt more or feel more real, once our friends all knew we weren't together anymore, but nothing could be worse than seeing Max's face that night. Everything else felt like baby steps away from ground zero, crawling up the sides of an emotional crater that all but leveled me. There was still no sun; outside—and in my head—it was always winter with skeletal trees and perpetually gray skies. But in fat, depressing Russian novels, they always kept moving, even with snow up to their chests.

So I did, too.

Monday I hiked to the bus stop and caught the first route to campus. Since I wasn't sure how long it would take, I ended up at my early class almost forty minutes before I needed to be there, but I took it as reassurance that I could plan my way around these problems. Breaking up with Max wasn't the end of everything; it only felt that way. Some days it hurt so bad, it felt like I couldn't breathe for missing him. But I still went to my classes.

I didn't break.

You thought Max was making me weak, Ma. But really, by loving me and by telling me about his life, he taught me to stand on my own.

Though I had to run from the business building, I met Kia for coffee the next day. Every time I saw her, it was a fresh surprise how gorgeous she was. Today, she had on jeans, boots and a red sweater, but on her lean frame, the outfit came across as expensive and elegant. If I wasn't so completely in love with Max, now that she and I weren't sharing a room, I'd totally flirt with her. Though she looked nothing like Amy, they shared the leggy build that rang my bell.

She'd managed to snag a table somehow, and as I approached, she skimmed me up and down, then gave an approving nod. "You don't look as bad as I thought. I know you're crazy about Max."

"How is he?" I had no shame, apparently.

"I don't see him much," she admitted. "Since I got back, he's working all hours."

"He doesn't come home at night?"

She raised a brow. "How the hell would I know? You want to check in, call him."

"Like he'd tell me."

"I hate to burst your bubble, but I didn't meet you to talk about boys."

A rueful smile worked its way out. "I suppose not. Let me guess, you're wondering about the apartment."

"Yep."

"I'll pay rent until I can find someone to take over my side of the room."

"No need," she said. "I have a friend from home transferring this semester and she was going to stay with her cousin, but the house is pretty crowded already. This would work out better for both of you. So I wanted to talk about your furniture."

"Wow, really? You don't know how bad I needed a silver lining right now. This has been the shittiest break ever."

Kia nodded, wearing a sympathetic expression, but she didn't let me digress. "Did you pay for January already?"

I nodded; I'd mailed the check on the thirty-first. Afterward, I'd fretted for hours because I had no money coming in. I'd given Evan three hundred, which left me pretty broke. I'd get paid if/when the band played its next gig, but we weren't doing shows regularly enough for me to feel comfortable with that as my sole support. Which meant I needed to find a job.

But first, the apartment.

"Okay. I'll get the rent money for you from Miranda. Since you left your bed and stuff, I figure you don't want it?"

"I bought everything from Lauren for two hundred."

"One fifty sound fair?" Kia asked.

I raised a brow. "Really?"

"You never heard of wear and tear?" She was grinning while she mercilessly negotiated the deal.

"You should be a cutthroat corporate attorney, not a doctor."

"Whatever. I'll meet you here, same time next week, with the money. Okay?"

"That would be great. I really appreciate this."

"It's good for me, too. Otherwise you'd probably give your half of the room to the first freak who asked, so you don't have to pay double."

I smirked. "Maybe."

"See how you are?" Kia took her coffee and stood. "Now I gotta go. Don't forget to come next Tuesday."

"As if. Your girl owes me money."

"True." With a wave, she hurried out of the coffee shop, her dark hair fanning out in the icy winter wind.

When I noticed all the dirty looks I was getting for hogging the table alone, I grabbed my latte and headed for the library. It seemed like I should get used to spending time there, as I couldn't leave campus until my classes were done for the day. On the plus side, I'd waste less time since it was forcing me to study and work on assignments.

But first, I had a favor to cash in. Taking a deep breath, I got out my phone, but I was completely puzzled when it said No Signal. I wandered around the quad for, like, half an hour, trying various spots. Nothing worked. And eventually, it occurred to me that my parents must've turned off my cell service. *They really weren't kidding about cutting me off.* I suspected they'd thought I'd cave before now, come crawling back begging for forgiveness, but hell would freeze before that happened when I hadn't done anything wrong.

Since I had time before my four o'clock, I walked to the pharmacy closest to campus, hoping they'd have a prepaid

SIM and cellular time cards. I spent thirty bucks between the two and then I hurried back and headed to the computer lab. Five minutes of searching on Google and I had basic instructions on how to unlock my phone. The internet warned me to be cautious about backing up my data, but everything was on the cloud anyway, so I went through the steps as instructed and couldn't resist a chair dance, prompting some looks from people nearby, when it worked exactly as described. Then I swapped my old SIM for the new one and went looking for a pay phone to activate my new number. I barely finished getting my phone back online before I had to run to class. Afterward, I texted everyone who might care that I had a new number.

Being okay on my own—that was my number-one priority. I had to prove to Max that I wasn't a princess who depended on her parents. Maybe if I did, he'd understand how little I cared about their approval. I wished my mother loved me in a less controlling way, but I'd long since made peace with the idea that I'd never meet her expectations, and I had no desire to live for my folks. One day, hopefully they'd accept me as I was.

If not… Well. I'm still me.

I was pretty damn tired, though, when I finished up for the day, and there was still the matter of the empty fridge to deal with. There was a small mom-and-pop grocery store adjacent to campus, which relied mostly on business from dorm dwellers, but it would work for me, too. Usually I went shopping with Angus or Max brought stuff home, and I just paid my portion of the grocery bill. Things were so easy before and I didn't appreciate how much it felt like a family until I started thinking about all the things I needed to take care of on my own. I filled a small shopping basket, which translated to four grocery sacks. They were heavy as I trudged down to the bus stop, and even more so for the mile and a half to Evan's house.

I felt good about what I'd accomplished when I let myself. Evan had given me a key, which meant I lived here. *The breakup's real.* Part of me kept hoping Max would show up on his bike and tell me he wanted to talk, that he understood or he missed me. But that was pointless wishing. I'd screwed up bad enough that he didn't trust me anymore. I had to start again and show that I was the kind of person who could be relied upon. That wouldn't happen overnight.

Dana, Ji Hoo and Evan were all in the living room when I struggled through the back door. They all stared at me strangely, then Evan sprang up to help me with the bags.

"Why didn't you tell me you were coming home? I went over to grab these two anyway, so I was around campus today."

"Oh. Well, I didn't know…and I didn't want to bother you." More, it was that I didn't want to rely on him; he'd done enough.

"So you're shacking up with Evan now, huh?" Dana teased.

"Yeah, what's that about?" Ji Hoo wanted to know. "I thought we had a strict no-dating-other-band-members policy?"

"Separate rooms, people. Get your minds out of the gutter." I knew they understood, but it seemed better to play along than to let them see how emotionally ransacked I was. My heart was like somebody had robbed the place, throwing shit everywhere with torn clothing and dishes broken on the floor.

"You got groceries?" Evan asked.

"Yep. I'm tired of living on white rice and beer."

"She has a point," Dana admitted.

"So, are we rehearsing tonight?" Monday wasn't a usual night for it, but maybe things would change now that I was living here.

Evan shook his head. "Nah, but I wanted to play them our song."

"Oh, right." Once I finished putting stuff away, I headed out to the garage with him.

We'd worked on this long enough that I remembered my part by heart, so I gave the sheet music to Dana and Ji Hoo. Evan and I sang it; it was a moody, bluesy song with lyrics chock-full of regret. Tentatively we were calling it "Might Have Been," and the other two closed their eyes as they listened.

"Wow," Dana said, once we finished the run through.

Ji Hoo nodded. "That's really tight. I might suggest…"

They offered some suggestions and we tweaked both melody and lyrics until we all thought it was pretty much perfect, then we played it as a group, but strangely, Dana and Ji Hoo didn't weigh in on vocals.

Afterward, I asked, "What was up with that?"

"It sounds better with just you and Evan," she said.

Ji Hoo seemed to agree. "Yeah, that's a duet if I ever heard one. You're basically telling a story about a dying relationship, so it's more powerful this way."

"I don't think I should be singing on my own," I protested.

Dana shrugged. "There's some edge, you're unpolished. But it works here. Makes it sound more...raw. Courtney Love doesn't exactly sound like angel."

"True," Evan put in. "But I'd compare our Courtney more to Johnette Napolitano."

My brows shot up. "Wow, really? She was awesome in Concrete Blonde but her solo work is good, too."

That night, we ended up doing an impromptu rehearsal and then Evan cooked for us, using the groceries I brought home. Ji Hoo and Dana stayed pretty late, long past the usual cutoff, and I was feeling almost...decent by the time they left. While Evan took them home, I put away the equipment in the garage. I'd seen him do it often enough.

Though it was late, I had one more phone call to make. I got my phone out, exhaling in a nervous rush. Amy was a night owl, so this shouldn't bother her. She might not answer, though, since I had a new number. It rang four times before she picked up.

"Yeah?"

"It's me," I said.

"Oh, you got a new number. I'm surprised you're calling me with it."

I ignored that. "Were you serious about wanting to make it right between us?"

"Definitely."

"Then I need a favor. And then we can call it square."

CHAPTER TWENTY-SEVEN

As agreed, Amy recommended me to her manager; he called me in for an interview a few days later, but I got the job myself. Pretty good for someone with zero work experience. I started the next night, and by the end of my first shift, I had an all-new respect for people who worked in hospitality. It sucked taking orders from drunk college students and the tips weren't that great, either. But it was money coming in.

My work schedule meant that rehearsals changed according to my work requirements, though, and I felt bad about keeping Dana, Ji Hoo and Evan waiting while I figured out what nights I could do it. There was no alternative, though, since I wasn't a princess anymore. On the bright side, I'd saved myself from the tower and was now frolicking in the village on my own.

My friendships weren't totally devastated, as I'd feared. I had dinner with Nadia and I'd met Kia for coffee to collect my money, which helped me survive until my first paycheck. In time, I started hanging out with Amy and her girlfriend, Elena, too, who was a pretty woman of Mexican descent with a compact, curvy figure and big brown eyes. The best thing about her, however, was her sense of humor. Angus was the only person I hadn't seen since I moved out, and his relative silence, compared to how it used to be, made me think he was cutting ties in solidarity with Max. That hurt but it was relatively low collateral damage, socially speaking.

A month after the breakup, I was drinking with Amy and Elena at the bar where we worked. Since the bartender liked us, he was prone to giving us beer on the cheap. Considering it was Tuesday night, the bar was pretty full, though two-dollar drafts might have been the reason. I had the weird feeling someone was watching me, but I swept the room and didn't see anyone leering.

The front door swung open; Max and Angus came in, distracting me from the odd prickle. I froze, pretending I didn't see them, but Amy didn't seem to register my reluctance. She leaned forward, eyes wide, as she tracked their movements through the bar. The place was packed enough that he didn't spot me right off.

"Isn't that your ex?" she whispered.

Elena smirked. "The irony of you asking her that."

I wished I could hide behind the pitcher. Instead I nodded silently, watching him with hungry eyes. It was possible to pretend everything was okay when I couldn't see him, but with him here, it took all my willpower not to run over and beg for forgiveness again. If I thought it would help, I'd get on my knees. But he'd made everything pretty clear before.

I hadn't given up on us, exactly, but I wanted concrete

changes to show him first. Then I could say, *You said I don't live in the real world, but I do. I've done this on my own. I'm someone you can count on. Really.* There were no guarantees, even then. We might really be done. And if so, well. I didn't regret the changes I was making.

From this distance, it didn't seem like he'd regained the weight he'd lost working doubles so he could take time off to meet my parents. His jeans hung off his hips and when he shrugged out of his leather jacket, his shoulderblades jabbed the back of his shirt in like bony wings. I also noticed that he'd cut his hair, no more long, shaggy waves. In fact, it looked like he'd let somebody at his head with a pair of clippers, since he just had dark stubble left, and the new look made him look more ferocious, since he was all hard angles and sinewy muscle. His face no longer seemed sweet and handsome; there was an edge to him that hadn't been present before, like he'd become a razor blade, capable of making people bleed. With dark ink twining around his arms, he looked...dangerous. Belatedly it occurred to me that he might be trying to live up to my parents' bad expectations.

Heart aching, I watched him take a draft beer from the bartender. His forearms were bare, showing prominent wrist bones, and his hands were chapped from working in the cold. Even at this distance, I could see the redness of his knuckles, the raw spots where his skin had cracked. And there was nobody to make him take care of himself. My eyes stung.

"Are you going to talk to him?" Elena asked.

I shook my head. "Not now. He doesn't look...friendly."

As I glanced across the bar, I caught Angus's eye. For a few seconds, I thought he'd cut me out completely, but then he lifted his chin in a silent hello. But that drew Max's attention; when he spotted me with Amy, he froze. Even from here, I could see his teeth clench. With a faint sigh, I finished the beer in my glass and tossed down a few bucks to cover my share.

"I'm done for the night. I need to head out before the last bus."

"You sure?" Amy asked. "I can run you home."

She and Elena had hung out with us at Evan's house a few times, but I wasn't in the mood anymore. So I shook my head. "Don't worry about it. Have fun, you two."

Elena lifted Amy's hand from where she was holding it under the table and kissed the back of it. "That's a given."

It made me smile to see both of them so happy, so I wasn't feeling 100 percent horrible when I wove through the maze of tables toward the exit. I shouldered my backpack and pulled up my hood, as it was still fucking freezing. This winter, we were getting lake weather with damp, icy winds and I'd feel it down to my bones by the time I got back, between waiting for the bus and walking home from the stop. Evan would probably yell at me for not calling, but he wasn't responsible for me.

But before I could take off, someone grabbed my arm. I glanced over my shoulder, unable to believe it. "Max."

He dragged me to the bathroom hallway, the quietest place in here. Even so, it was still loud, between the music and drunk people laughing. "What the hell are you doing?"

"Leaving, until you stopped me."

"Why are you with Amy?"

I could've said I wasn't *with* her, but technically, it wasn't his business. "You broke up with me, remember? You don't get to have an opinion on my life choices."

His teeth ground together. "No common sense. None."

"Thanks for the input." But it hurt too much to look at him. Before, his eyes were all melted chocolate and caramel, but now they were more like slivers of marbled agate. "If you don't mind, I need to go."

I turned.

His voice came as I reached the arch leading back to the main bar area. "Are you okay? Do you... Where are you staying?"

I could've said something sharp, but I didn't want to hurt him. Really, I just wanted him to love me like he used to. But I understood that I'd wrecked it. Even if I spent hours on my knees, I couldn't put it back together with regret and glue. Maybe in a few months, I'd have enough of a track record on my own for him to believe in me.

"I'm at Evan's place."

His intake of breath made me realize that the truth might be worse. That one night, just before we got together, he was crazy jealous when Evan brought me home. I turned around slowly, not wanting to see Max's face, but I couldn't resist. If it bothered him, it could mean he wasn't really over me—that we weren't done, as he'd claimed—but on more of a hiatus while he worked through the shit I'd put him through. Other than Eli, I had little experience with relationships, so I was feeling my way through a minefield, trying my best not to make it worse, trying not to cause a catastrophic explosion.

"Is that right? I guess that tells me what I needed to know," he said roughly.

"What're you—"

"Took you how many years to move on from Eli? But a month later, you're already with someone else. That tells me a whole lot, Courtney."

"He's my *roommate*."

"So was I," Max said.

"Would it be better if I was staying with a girl? You can't trust me that way, either." That was painful because I'd heard people say it before, like it was funny. *Oh, you're more likely to cheat because you have twice as many potential partners.* And there was so much wrong with that logic that I could die of old age trying to articulate it.

"True." He let out a pained breath, rubbing his chest like it hurt. "Never mind. This was an excruciatingly bad idea, go about your business."

"For what it's worth, I truly am sorry. It was lack of forethought, not malice. And their money isn't mine. I wanted you to meet my folks, but I never—"

"Just stop." Max's shoulders slumped, and I fought the urge to wrap my arms around him, reminding myself that he wasn't mine to comfort anymore.

You're the one who hurt him.

"Okay, well. Take care."

Walking away from him hurt even more this time around. My boots felt like they weighed forty pounds each as I left Max standing between the pay phone and the men's room. I wanted nothing more than a clean getaway, but Angus pounced on me as soon as I got near the bar.

"What happened?" he demanded.

"When?"

"Just now. Did you make up?"

A bitter laugh escaped me. "Not hardly."

"Why not? I'm seriously fucking worried about him, Courtney. He barely eats. All he does is work and go to class. He doesn't even play video games. I mean, you *saw* him. Whatever he did, how bad could it be? Can't you forgive him?"

Stunned, I gaped for a few seconds. "I think you've misunderstood, dude. Under no circumstances did I break up with Max. He did the dumping, not me."

"Holy shit. No way. Then why's he like this, if it was what he wanted?" Then his mouth tightened. "Wait, was it like Josh and me? Did you cheat on him?" Angus looked like he was ready to slap the snot out of me.

I took a painful breath. "If Max didn't tell you what happened, then I'll respect that. But no, I didn't. Never, ever. I love him like crazy."

"I'd tell you to come home and fight the battle close-up, but that ship has sailed."

"How's Kia's friend?"

"Maddie seems nice. She's young, though. Only a sophomore."

"But she's not a pain in the ass to live with?" I felt guilty that I'd bailed so fast without any of the discussion that usually preceded a move out.

"Nah. Actually she's superreserved and studious. Rarely leaves the room. Most of the time, it's like she's not even there."

"For some reason, that makes me sad."

"Between her and Kia, who's always at the hospital or doing labs, it's way quieter at home. I've been spending a lot of time at Del's," he admitted.

ANN AGUIRRE

Leaving Max alone. My heart ached.

"I thought you were mad at me."

Angus patted my shoulder. "Sorry. Lately I'm slammed. It's all I can do to treat Del as well as he deserves and keep up in the program."

"It's okay. I'm busier lately, too, between school, the band and work."

"You got a job?" His brows shot up in astonishment.

"Yep. Here, actually. Come by some Friday night. I'll take good care of you." Maybe. Provided I wasn't overworked, handling too many tables.

"Give a heads-up for your next show, okay? I want to see you play if I can."

"Definitely. You can bring Del, call it a date night."

"Awesome."

"If you really want us back together, you could...help."

"How?"

"You know how we used to leave each other messages on the fridge?"

"You and Max? Yeah."

"Could I text you one, daily? You can put it up for me."

He hesitated. "You really think it'll help?"

"Maybe not. But what else can I do? Whenever we talk, it's...bad."

"Then I'll give it a shot." As Angus had always been perceptive, he could probably tell I was itching to get out of here before Max reappeared. "Be good, Courtney."

"Talk to you later."

Since I had regulars here and other employees might want to chat, too, I rushed toward the exit and darted out before anyone else could intercept me. Outside, I inhaled the frosty air, sharp as icicles in my lungs. Then I headed across the parking lot. A few seconds later, the door banged open again. Part of me wished it was Max, but I didn't dare hope as I turned and spotted the last person I ever wanted to see again—that asshole, Jared. This wouldn't be good, but I was too far from the door to get back in easily. Yet I'd have to be an idiot to head to the bus stop now. I stopped, trying to figure out the safest move in this scenario. The noise in the bar meant it was probably too loud for anyone to hear if I screamed.

Maybe you're overreacting. But it was hard to believe he had noble intentions in following me out here. "What do you want?"

"I told you this wasn't over. Come on, we need to have some private words." He took a step toward me and I backed off, suddenly aware how dark it was, away from the building.

Someone will leave soon. Or head into the bar from the parking lot. I just need to stay calm and keep away from him.

"I can hear you just fine from there."

There was an ugly cast to his expression. "I can't stand bitches like you."

"Feel free to tell me off. I'm listening."

Calculating the distance between the door and me, it seemed unlikely that I could dodge past him to go inside, but I had to try. Waiting hadn't yielded any help in the past minute. Surreptitiously I pulled my phone out of my pocket, trying to dial 911 behind my back. Later, if they decided I'd panicked pointlessly, so be it. *Better a live chicken than a dead duck.*

Taking a breath, I bolted for the entrance, giving Jared a wide berth. About ten feet away, he grabbed me from

ANN AGUIRRE

behind, and in trying to get me away from the doors, he twisted my arm until it felt like he might break it. *If I resist, he snaps my radius. But if I let him take me off somewhere, it gets worse.*

I opened my mouth to yell for help, but he clamped a palm across the bottom half of my face, smashing my nose and lips. His other arm around my neck meant he could kill me with one twist; I'd seen him grappling with Max. Fear spiked through me as he dragged me toward the back of the bar. *There won't be anyone around to help.* Before I could get lightheaded, I struggled with all my strength and aimed a furious kick at his shins. This wasn't his first time terrorizing a woman, apparently, because he shifted to avoid it. There wasn't room for me to bite him, though God knew I tried. I started feeling fuzzy.

In last-ditch desperation, I slammed my head backward. Maybe he wasn't expecting me to fight because my skull caught him square in the nose, and the crunch of cartilage made him stagger, weakening his hold enough for me to get free. *Fuck. I wish I had mace, pepper spray, anything.* If I was faster, I'd make a break for it, but he had a foot on me, and I'd never been quick. So I swung my backpack off my shoulder and moved slowly with it in front of me like a shield. If he came at me, I'd hit him with all my business books.

That'll hurt, right?

"You should let this go," I warned.

Jared's face was a mess, blood trickling from his nose. I could feel the stickiness on my hair, too. He shook a little as he came toward me, and belatedly I recognized the signs. He was high as hell, evident in the glassy shine of his eyes. That meant there was no reasoning with him. I backed away, swinging my bag with more determination than any real skill at self-defense. As he lunged, I'd never been more conscious of being short and female.

Terror went from zero to sixty when he dug into his jacket pocket and came out with a switchblade. The knife flicked open, then he edged closer. I tried to knock it out of his hand with my backpack, but he was jacked up and he sliced me on the hand. The sudden, stinging pain made me drop the bag. Twenty more feet, and there would be people to help, to hold him until the cops came. It was possible Jared wasn't crazy, but meth made him that way. I'd met guys like him in rehab, so now that I knew his deal, it was hard to hate him completely.

I was still scared shitless.

If I turned and ran, I'd end up with a knife in the back. Somehow I knew it without a shadow of a doubt. But I didn't know what else to do. So I wheeled and bolted, knowing I couldn't possibly sprint fast enough. Jared's footsteps rang on the asphalt as I skidded, my lungs too tight to scream. And then, somehow, I was in Max's arms, as he spun me, slamming me against the exterior wall. I didn't see the knife go in, but I felt the blood, spilling hot over my splayed hands. The world went strange and sideways, echoes and neon, people running, other hands, mouths, voices. None of it changed the red trickling into the dirty snow.

And I screamed like I'd never, ever stop.

CHAPTER TWENTY-EIGHT

Another inch, and he would've died before we got to the hospital.

I sat in the waiting room with Angus holding my hand, too frozen to cry. Amy and Elena stayed for a while, and Nadia came in just past midnight. She sat down on my other side and put an arm around me, but I didn't look at her. It was all I could do to breathe. *This…this is my worst nightmare.* Max wasn't sick before he got together with me, but now he was in surgery. *I'm toxic to the people who love me.*

"It's not your fault," Nadia said. "That guy has a history of substance abuse."

So do I.

The only thing that made me different from Jared was that I'd abused prescription meds, not illegal drugs, and my parents had the money to put me in an expensive rehab program. Otherwise, maybe I'd be cooking shit on a spoon by now and selling my ass to buy more. *I'm not stronger or better than Jared. I just got lucky.*

Unlike Max.

It was past two when the doctor finally came to talk to us. Nadia was asleep on my shoulder and Angus was whispering to someone on the phone. Del, I supposed, though it might be Kia. He hung up as soon as he saw the tired-looking surgeon head toward us.

"Are you here for Max Cooper?"

We approached as a group, and I nodded. "Is he okay?"

"He should be. He's in recovery now." She said some more stuff, more technical, but my ears were ringing and I couldn't focus. This was a small hospital, only a few floors, and they seemed friendlier than the one I'd visited so often for Eli. At first the staff had been really rigid but toward the end, they'd let me come in and out of Eli's room as much as I wanted. Tears burned at the back of my eyes.

"When can we see him?" That was really all I cared about.

"When he's transferred to a regular room, you can check on him." The doctor was young, enough to worry me, and she looked exhausted. In a few years, this would be Kia. "The nurses will let you know when he's out of Recovery."

"Thank you," I said softly.

The doc gave us some directions so we could wait closer to Recovery and I led the way. Nadia walked me up, and then she said, "God, I'm glad Max is all right. I hate to do this, but I have to work tomorrow. I'll stop in afterward, okay?"

"Sure." I let her hug me.

With a final squeeze, she hurried off, leaving me with Angus. We sat for over an hour before a nurse came to tell

us Max's room number. "He's groggy but awake and asking for someone named Courtney."

"That's me."

Angus put a hand on my shoulder. "Want me to go with
you?"

"No, it's okay. I should hear whatever he has to say."

No matter how bad it is.

My hands trembled as I followed the man down the hall.
He opened the door for me and I went in quietly, waiting
for my eyes to adjust to the dim light. The wound on my
hand had four stitches; I'd had it treated in the ER after they
took Max, before the police interviewed me. It had been a
really long night. I sat down in the vinyl chair, staring at his
pale, thin face. So many echoes, I couldn't stop the shaking.
Losing him this way... Just, no.

You're better off without me, I thought.

His eyes opened, fuzzy, but scanning for something.
"Courtney?"

"I'm here."

"Are you okay?'

Seriously? What the hell. I made a weird sound, unable to
decide if I was about to laugh or cry. "You're confused about
who's actually hurt here."

"He hurt you, I saw the blood."

"Just a gash on my hand, you idiot. What were you *thinking*? Why didn't you hit him?"

Max turned his head away, showing me his chiseled profile, the stark contrast of dark stubble against white hospital
linens. "I wasn't."

"What?"

"Thinking." His voice was so rough that I got up to find some ice chips.

"I'll be right back."

Even when Eli couldn't have anything, they usually allowed him that. I checked with the nurse to be sure, and she hooked me up. When I came in, Max was watching the door, white-knuckled on the sheets. He let out a slow breath as I sat down again.

"Don't leave like that again." He was blurred and fuzzy-sounding, so I wasn't sure we should engage about anything serious because it might be leftover anesthesia, yet I couldn't shut him down.

So I only nodded, offering him some ice. He opened his mouth and let me put it between his lips, just like Eli. I half shook my head against the comparison. *Max is not Eli. He'll be fine.*

"Go ahead," I said.

"I come from a long line of violent assholes, told you that from the start. But my first instinct wasn't to hit him. It was to save *you*."

It hurt to breathe. "It would've been better if you'd let him—"

"Couldn't. Seems like I'm the only one who's allowed to hurt you." His eyelashes fluttered, telling me he didn't have a lot more focus left in him.

Before I could answer, he winked out. Shaken, I tiptoed out of the room to find Angus. I had no idea where we stood, but I wouldn't be leaving. Angus pushed out of his chair, green eyes shadowed by deep circles. He rubbed tired eyes and came toward me.

"How's he doing?"

"He's out again. We only talked a little before the pain meds kicked in. You can probably look in on Max if you want. The nurses don't seem to mind."

He nodded. "They're more rigid at the bigger hospitals. And sure, I'd like to see him."

Max didn't stir when we came back in. Angus stood for a few seconds at the foot of the bed, then he beckoned me out of the room. "Is there any point in offering to stay?"

I shook my head. "I'm not leaving until he gets out. I can spare the time more than you, too. In the morning, I'll notify his professors, call his boss and get in touch with his family."

Angus raised a brow. "Wish all my exes were as devoted."

"You know I was against that in the first place."

"So instead of fridge magnet messages, you're going to smother him with your infinite, nurturing love?"

"Shut up." I gave him a gentle shove. "Go home and leave me alone."

Before he did, Angus hugged me for a really long time. "I'm glad you're both okay. Please take care of him, he's one of my best friends."

"Mine, too," I whispered.

The hospital was quiet when I slipped back into Max's room. He hadn't stirred and I collapsed into the chair next to the bed, physically exhausted but also emotionally wrecked. I swallowed hard and tried not to cry. With every fiber of my being, I rejected the girl who sat in the glow of medical equipment and wept beside a boy. For strength I took his hand and bent my head over it, touching my brow to the back.

I must've fallen asleep because I woke with a sore spine

when the nurse came in to perform her morning ritual and note all the information on his chart. Max was awake and staring at me when I sat up. Most likely I looked like buttered death, but it wasn't like he hadn't seen me this way before.

"Are you hurting a lot?" I asked.

He shrugged. To preserve his dignity, I went to get some food from the vending machine, as it was too early for the cafeteria to be open. Drinking a Coke and eating some crackers kept me out long enough for the nurse to do her job.

"You're still here," Max said when I stepped in.

"It's the least I can do to stay with you."

"If you're only here because you feel like you owe me, then take off. I'll be fine."

"That's not why."

He looked away as I took up my place at his side again. "I feel like I said some crazy shit last night, but—"

"You don't remember?"

"Not completely. Why did you stay, Courtney?"

This was a half-truth. "You asked me not to go."

"And that's the reason?"

"I'm sure you know I love you," I said. "So where else would I be?"

But when I glanced over at Max, he was kind of...frozen, dark eyes locked on mine. "You say that like it's nothing. But nobody ever said that to me before. Not even you."

"I know, and I'm sorry." I took a shaky breath, staring at him as much as I could, trying to create a mental picture, though this wasn't how I wanted to remember him. "Once you're recovered, we have to go back to making a clean break." Otherwise this might kill me.

"Why?" he asked.

"Because you don't want me around. I ruined what we had, and I hate myself for it. But what more can I do?" It was really hard to talk for the tightness in my throat. His ice chips had long since melted into lukewarm water at the bottom of the cup, so there was no remedy for it.

The silence lasted long enough for me to die in my head a hundred times.

"What if I want a do-over?"

"Huh?"

"I want to turn back the clock, make it so that trip to your parents' place never happened. I never got blindsided, never broke up with you."

"But...it happened. We can't pretend it didn't."

"Then can we pretend I accepted your apology?"

"No pretending. But...you can do that now if you want. If you're sure."

"Being with you is the only thing in the world that makes sense," Max whispered. "I said it didn't...because I was scared. Finding out where you come from, damn. That was a rude awakening. I don't know a coffee spoon from a dessert spoon. I won't ever impress the kind of people your parents respect. But...I'm dying without you. You took all the music when you left, Courtney. I can't tell you how many times I almost called. And one time, I did...but you changed your number. I thought—"

"Oh, my God. No. I wasn't avoiding you. No, no, no." Hastily I explained how my parents had cut me off and canceled my cell service. "I have a new number. Nadia, Angus and Kia have it. You didn't ask them?"

He shook his head. "After what I said? I couldn't stand for one of them to answer, 'Dude, she hates you. Take a hint.'"

"I didn't fall in love with you in a few weeks. It was so slow and deep that I'll never stop feeling it. You think I could move on this fast?"

"I was afraid you had. Especially when you said you're staying with Evan."

Yeah, he'd seemed pretty jealous last night. "Are you kidding? I've been working on a master plan to win you back."

"Seriously?"

With a half smile, I outlined all the steps I'd taken to prove my independence, including the job I'd gotten at the bar. He listened with an expression that was half troubled, half astonished. And when I finished, Max hissed in pain as he sat forward, reaching for my hand. Snapping to the edge of my seat, I gave it to him, hardly daring to believe this was real.

"I hate that I'm the reason you cut ties with your folks," he said soberly.

"You're not. They're being judgmental assholes. In time they'll get over it and we'll patch things up as best we can. Or they won't. In the end, they're the ones missing out. After all, we've got Michael and Uncle Lou, Aunt Carol and Uncle Jim..." I paused long enough for what I was saying to sink in. *Yes, your family is mine, too.* "Plus we have some incredible friends. And more important...we have each other. We'll never be alone, Max."

He studied my face with layered, curious intensity. "Are you *sure* you won't regret giving up so much to be with me?"

"Are you sure you don't want someone prettier, who looks like she belongs at your side?" Yeah, I went there.

Rage flared, before he understood what I was getting at.
A slow smile formed at the edges of his wonderful mouth.
Even pale and thin with eyes like he'd been to war, he was
still the most beautiful person I'd ever seen. I carried both
his hands to my lips and kissed the palms one by one. He
shivered a little.

"Don't make my heart race," he complained. "They're
monitoring that shit."

I grinned. "Sorry."

"No, you aren't. Not remotely."

"Guilty."

"So tell me about this master plan of yours."

Compulsively, I stroked his fingers, reveling in the warm
roughness of his skin. "You want to hear what you missed
out on by getting stabbed?"

"Duh."

"Well, step one—enlisting Angus to spell out messages
of love on the fridge."

"Like what?"

"Lines from poems. Song lyrics. Simple groveling for
Wednesdays. It'd depend on the day, naturally."

"Naturally," Max agreed with a faint smile.

"Would it have worked?"

"Probably. Though if you make this sound too awesome,
I might change my mind and let you make this up to me
Courtney-style. What else was in the works?"

"Well, nothing was solid, but…I was going to see if Nadia
could get you to go to one of our shows. I talked to the guys
in the band, and we've added a new song to our set list. I
was going to sing 'Amazing' to you. See how well I had it
planned out?"

"I don't know that one."

"It's by Johnette Napolitano. From Concrete Blonde," I added, thinking that might connect for him better.

He tilted his head back, seeming pensive. "Yeah?"

"What's that look about?"

"I was just picturing what it would've been like. If you'd gotten Nadia to drag me out to a club somewhere to see a show I didn't want to watch and then suddenly, you're on-stage, dedicating a song to me."

"Max likes this, check yes or no."

With two fingers, he etched a check mark in the air. "Yes."

"I still can, just not as part of the big reconciliation effort. This way, it'd be because I'm crazy about you."

"That's even better. Would you…sing it now?"

I had the song in my phone, actually. If I played it on low, I could sing along quietly without bothering the other pa-tients. Since the nurse just came in on rounds, we wouldn't see anyone until they brought his breakfast in an hour or two. So I nodded.

"At this point, you can have whatever you want. Choose wisely."

"Just the song for starters."

Incredibly embarrassed but also pleased, I found "Amaz-ing" in my music player, knowing it probably wasn't the romantic ballad he expected, but I didn't have the voice to carry one off. The song was dark and raw, but the chorus was absolutely spot-on. Closing my eyes, I hit Play and gave it everything I had. A cappella singing was tough, and sing-ing along with my phone probably didn't help a whole lot, either. But hopefully he wouldn't laugh.

When I finished, it took me forever to open my eyes. He wasn't even smiling, and my stomach dropped. "Was it that bad?"

His voice came out husky. "Thank you for feeling that way about me. Until I met you, it never even occurred to me that I could be sunshine to somebody else, like you are to me."

I felt a goofy smile forming. "You haven't said it back, you know."

"What?"

"That you love me."

"That's only four letters, how can it be big enough to describe how I feel about you? I don't love you, I worship you. I want to carry you on my back for five hundred miles, build a bridge and then name it after you."

A soft, giddy laugh burbled out. "The Courtney Kaufman Bridge does have quite a ring. But can't I have a highway instead?"

"Maybe Courtney Kaufman-Cooper?" Max suggested.

Both my brows shot up. "Are you proposing?"

"More like telling your fortune. You will marry a dark-haired stranger."

"I will *not*."

"Sure, you will. Who's stranger than me? I broke up with you for being rich."

"No, that was because you trusted me, and I hurt you. I'm so sorry."

"I'm over it. Your priorities realign at light speed when you get shanked."

"Since when do mechanical engineers build bridges?" I wondered aloud.

Max grinned. "I didn't say it was a realistic goal."

Breakfast arrived then, the usual post-op diet, so it took me half an hour to get Max to eat anything. In the end, I had to feed him while his eyes twinkled devilishly. It wasn't like I minded, plus he was so cute pretending his side hurt too much to move his arms.

"I'd kiss you," he said. "I really want to. But I taste like not-brushing-my-teeth and hospital food. Honestly, we should've planned this whole thing better."

"Agreed, F+ at perfect reunions, but as long as we're together, it's good by me."

"True. Do you know what I've been doing?"

"Taking meds?"

"No, since you've been gone."

I shook my head.

"Class, projects, the odd shift at the garage. But mostly I've been working on your car. I can't wait to show it to you. I was kind of obsessive, actually."

"Are you kidding? I figured you went at it with a hammer."

"I was planning to put a stupid red stuffed heart in the driver's seat when I got it in drivable condition. Then I was going to make a speech about how this car is like me, we're both kind of fucked up and you can't see the shape of my heart—my heart was a metaphor for the car engine—just by looking, but we'll always get you where you need to go, no matter what." He let out a long breath. "Man, I'm glad I didn't do that. No wonder Angus laughed when I told him."

"The moment would've only been complete if you'd played 'Shape of My Heart' on the stereo while you were talking."

ANN AGUIRRE

"Would it have worked?" he asked.

"Max. All you ever needed to say to me was, 'Courtney, come home,' and I'd have walked through a blizzard to you, even if it meant freezing to death on the way."

"I'd much rather you live with me than die for me."

"That goes double for me, idiot!"

"Is that a new endearment? I don't hate it. Just...stay. Please."

"I will," I promised. "I won't leave you alone here."

"That's not what I mean. The hospital doesn't scare me. Being without you? Yeah. That's a hell I don't want to see ever again. I love you so damn much."

I melted. "Me, too."

Then I kissed him. Not deeply, since he was right about the breath and the taste, but I felt like I'd die if I didn't. Afterward, he held me as best he could, and the pleasure was indescribable. I thought I'd never be with Max like this again.

"I hear they're letting me out tomorrow, barring any complications."

"Never drop the *C* word in a hospital."

"Are you positive you're okay? With Eli and everything." His lean face was soft with concern. That expression choked me up; I didn't think I'd ever see it from Max again.

"Yeah. I held up. I'm stronger than I used to be." There were all kinds of things to talk about later. After all, we had a future to plan. But for now, I was with the guy I loved.

Max moved his hands slowly down my back, and I felt his breath on my neck. He seemed to be smelling my hair, which sent a shiver through me. "No matter what happens, we'll be fine."

And we were.

EPILOGUE

Providence, RI
Six years later

As I walked past the front desk, the phone rang. "Gone Elijah Records, Margo speaking. How can I help you?"

Hearing that never failed to give me a thrill because it meant I'd actually done it—made my dream come true. I'd talked the name over with Max because I was worried it might bother him, but he understood that it was a gesture for the boy I'd lost, not meant to take anything away from the man I loved.

When I mentioned it, he'd said, "I'd have to be a dick to mind. I mean, I'm here with you. I get to be with you because he's not."

Yeah. Still crazy about Max.

Hard to believe sometimes, but the company was doing well. In the beginning, it was a shoestring affair, and I didn't have half the equipment I needed. I worked out of a basement for a while. After I left the band, Racing Sorrow found a better keyboardist and they were the first group I signed... and last week, their second album was certified gold. Critics compared them to Imagine Dragons and they were on the cover of *Billboard* last month.

I didn't waste your money, Granddad.

The receptionist listened for a few seconds and then asked with a silent lift of her brows if I was in. I shook my head. She tucked the phone into the crook of her neck and got a pen to take a message. It was late on Friday afternoon, and I was heading out for a rare weekend off. Usually I'd be in the studio even on Saturday, plus I had a box full of demos to listen to, but Max and I hadn't taken a vacation in over a year. I was missing the hell out of him, actually, because his job required him to travel sometimes, and he'd been in Phoenix for the past week checking prototypes at a satellite facility.

But he was due home tonight. I was meeting him at the airport, and then we were flying to Myrtle Beach together. Excitement made me skip out of the office and to the parking lot. My gorgeous, cherry-red Opel GT was waiting, exquisitely restored. Max gave it to me instead of a ring the day he proposed. I got the ring later, but the car? I would never, ever part with it.

My phone rang as I was heading for the airport so I put in my earpiece. "This is Courtney, talk to me."

Max came across the line, a smile evident in his voice. "You know how sexy it is when you're in shot-caller mode?"

"You could tell me."

"If I get you too excited, you might end up in a ditch. Are you almost here? We're boarding in fifteen minutes."

"I'm at long-term parking. Just let me get my bag...and I'm getting on the shuttle bus right now."

"Liar, you're locking the car."

"You know me too well. I'll be there soon."

I found him waiting near the second set of doors, slightly rumpled from the first flight, but also incredibly handsome. None of the travelers passing by knew about the ink hidden beneath his jacket or the scars he'd gotten early in life—or the one he'd taken protecting me.

His lean build hadn't changed much since college, and he wore suits beautifully. Today, he had on a dark blue pin-stripe with a purple tie and charcoal-gray shirt. Very few men could pull off a vest, but he was so damn hot spinning in impatient circles, looking for me, that I couldn't resist running at him like a defensive tackle. He caught me in his arms and spun me around, then lowered his head for a long, long kiss.

"Mmm. I missed you." Smiling up at him, I dragged him toward security.

"You have our boarding passes?"

"Of course. Margo's very efficient."

"Work going okay?"

"You know it. Indie labels now account for forty percent of the market." I teased him by producing the same statistic I always quoted when he asked.

"Yeah, yeah. Come on." He took my hand.

It was a bit of a scramble, and we were among the last to board, but soon we were settled in the first-class cabin, waiting to take off. I asked for champagne while Max got

ANN AGUIRRE

orange juice. With his free hand, he laced our fingers together and gave a tired sigh.

"I wouldn't do this for anyone but you," he mumbled.
"I'm tired and I want to sleep with you in my own bed."

"Please. You know you're dying to see everyone. It's been,
what, two years?"

He thought about it and nodded. "Sounds about right.
We got together in Vegas last time."

These days, Angus had a clinic in Hollywood while Del
worked as a corporate attorney in LA. Kia was a trauma surgeon at a hospital in Baltimore while Lauren ran a security
company in Toronto; she'd married Nadia's brother, Rob,
who had a syndicated TV show. Of our old crowd, so far
Nadia and Ty were the only ones with kids; they had a little
girl three years ago and were still in Michigan, though she
taught in Ann Arbor, and he'd become an architect.

My parents were starting to make noises that it was time
for us to get started on grandchildren, but as ever, I was
ignoring them. Though it took a full year of silence, they
eventually apologized to both Max and me. Last time I saw
them, it was at Uncle Lou's house. Ma liked him a lot, and
once they'd talked about Max's past, she couldn't mother
her son-in-law enough. He still wasn't used to her brand of
devotion, though. Sometimes I caught him staring at her
with quiet terror like she might strangle-hug him to death.

"I hope the house is big enough."

I grinned. "If not, we'll have people crashed out on the
floor, just like the old days."

"Hopefully they'll be wearing pants."

"You can dream. Nadia said Lauren might be inviting

other people, too." I kissed his cheek as the flight attendant announced cross-check.

"Who?"

"Friends from their hometown, I think. Is Michael coming?"

"Not sure. I invited him. He said he'd try but he just started a new job and he might not be able to get the time off."

"He's still dating Maddie?" I was asking about Kia's friend from home, younger than us, three years older than Michael. Now *that* was a story.

"As far as I know. He gets grumpy when I bug him about his love life."

"Understandable. You were pretty snappish when he was pestering you to propose to me already, remember? He was *so* worried you'd let me get away."

He smiled at me with his eyes. "No way. Am I crazy?"

Preening a little, I admired the white-gold princess-cut ring on my finger, along with the elegant band beneath it. Max's ring was pretty scarred up from the work he did. Maybe I'd buy him a new one for our anniversary. Just then, the plane jolted into motion, backing away from the terminal. I'd always hated takeoffs and landings, though I didn't mind flying once we were in the air. Max tightened his hand around mine because he understood that about me. At this point, I couldn't think of much he didn't know.

"You ready for this?" he asked softly.

"Yep." The rest of our life was waiting, along with our best and dearest friends. "Let the adventure begin."

★ ★ ★ ★ ★

AUTHOR'S NOTE

THANK YOU!

I'm so glad you read *The Shape of My Heart*. I hope you enjoyed it.

Would you like to know when my next book will be available or keep up with my news? Visit my website at http://www.annaguirre.com/contact and sign up for my newsletter. You can also follow me on Twitter at https://twitter.com/msannaguirre, or "like" my Facebook fan page at http://www.facebook.com/ann.aguirre for excerpts and contests.

Reviews help other readers, so please consider writing one. I appreciate your time and your support.

The Shape of My Heart is the third book in my new adult romance series. The first was *I Want It That Way* and the second was *As Long As You Love Me*.

Again, thanks for your readership; it means the world to me.